THE WRONG WAY
TO CATCH A RAKE

Lara Temple

MILLS & BOON

First published in Great Britain 2022
by Mills & Boon, an imprint of HarperCollins*Publishers* Ltd,
1 London Bridge Street, London, SE1 9GF

www.harpercollins.co.uk

HarperCollins*Publishers*
1st Floor, Watermarque Building,
Ringsend Road, Dublin 4, Ireland

The Wrong Way to Catch a Rake © 2022 Ilana Treston

ISBN: 978-0-263-30207-3

12/22

MIX
Paper | Supporting
responsible forestry
FSC™ C007454

This book is produced from independently certified FSC™ paper
to ensure responsible forest management.
For more information visit: www.harpercollins.co.uk/green.

Printed and Bound in Spain using 100% Renewable Electricity
at CPI Black Print, Barcelona

Lara Temple was three years old when she begged her mother to take the dictation of her first adventure story. Since then she has led a double life—by day she is a high-tech investment professional, who has lived and worked on three continents, but when darkness falls she loses herself in history and romance...at least on the page. Luckily her husband and her two beautiful and very energetic children help her weave it all together.

Chapter One

Palazzo Gioconda, Venice, September 1822

'I disagree.' Lord Wrexham's deep voice was slightly slurred, but it still carried easily across the main salon of the Hotel Gioconda. 'Not all love songs are about fornication. One of the best was written about a tree, but I doubt King Xerxes wanted to penetrate it with anything but his axe.'

The silence that followed his pronouncement was broken only by the warbling song of a gondolier passing in the canal below. Phoebe Brimford suppressed a sigh and tried to concentrate on her book. After a fortnight at the hotel, she was no longer surprised by Lord Wrexham's wine-soaked mischief.

The responses of the other residents of the hotel were just as typical. Mr George Clapton, son of the British Consul in Venice, was watching Lord Wrexham as if a slug had crawled out of his soup, and poor Mr Arthur Hibbert, Lord

Wrexham's only ally at the hotel, was tugging at his cravat, a bad habit that intensified the more his friend drank. Since Lord Wrexham drank often and a lot, Mr Hibbert's cravats were rarely in good order.

Other than Phoebe and her aunt, the only other residents were Mrs Banister and Mr Rupert Banister, a wealthy widow and her shy son. Poor Rupert's ears had turned an interesting shade of pink at Lord Wrexham's pronouncement, but Phoebe very much hoped Mrs Banister's poor hearing meant she'd missed this latest provocation. That faint hope went up in smoke as Mrs Banister prodded Phoebe's knee with her fan, demanding loudly, 'What was that about a tree?'

Phoebe set down her book and smiled politely. 'Lord Wrexham mentioned an aria by Handel, Mrs Banister. *Ombra mai fu*. Where King Xerxes sings of his admiration of the plane tree. It is a lovely song.'

'A song to a tree? What will those foreigners think of next?'

'*Mama!*' Rupert Banister whispered, now flushed to the roots of his flaxen hair.

Phoebe considered pointing out that, as an Englishwoman in Venice, Mrs Banister was herself firmly in that scorned category. However, her position as companion to Lady Grafton made such directness inadvisable. If she'd had any thought about crossing that line, it was chased away by her employer, who was eyeing her with a glint of amused warning in her dark brown eyes from the sofa opposite. Instead she said, 'To be fair, Handel did spend most of his life in London.'

'That's right,' said Lord Wrexham, sauntering over to their corner of the salon. 'He was just as English as our dear first King George, and far nicer if the stories are true. *He* didn't beget a pack of bastards with his pack of mistresses. Oh, don't fuss, Hib. I'm only two sheets to the wind. It will take at least two more bottles to make it three.'

'We shall retire to our rooms, Rupert,' Mrs Banister announced, casting an awful glare at Lord Wrexham. 'I find the air in the salon rather close.'

'Yes, Mama.' Mr Banister directed an apologetic glance at Phoebe and her aunt and hurried to help his mother out of the room.

'Poor pup.' Lord Wrexham leaned on the back of Phoebe's chair as he watched Mrs Banister's majestic exit. His coat smelled of cinnamon and whisky, a not unpleasant combination. 'Not likely he'll ever get out from under until she's dead and buried.'

Phoebe couldn't in truth argue with his assessment, so instead she replied, 'He's a very pleasant young man.'

'He might be, but don't pin your hopes on him, tiger eyes. That dragon won't release him easily.'

'Dom!' Hibbert's voice was sharper than usual,

both his brow and cravat now creased. 'It is bad enough saying all that about Handel and King George, but now you go too far.'

'What did I say?' Lord Wrexham said mulishly. 'Why shouldn't Handel write a love song to a tree? *They* don't nag or ask for baubles.'

'Neither do they drink themselves into insensibility, Lord Wrexham,' Phoebe stated more tartly than she usually allowed herself. She was more upset by his comment about her eyes than the implication that she was trying to ensnare Mr Banister. She didn't mind being plain, but she'd always thought her eyes unfortunately distinctive and even unsettling. Not even wearing spectacles prevented people from noticing their yellow-amber hue, encircled in a ring of dark brown.

Lord Wrexham's own dark blue eyes focused on her, half hooded by his long lashes. His grin was lop-sided and his dark hair was a tumbled mess, but he was still the handsomest man in the room by a mile and he knew it, and was only too willing to employ his looks to smooth the feathers he ruffled.

'Quite right, sweetheart. But men are damn unreliable beasts. Much better to give your heart to a tree or a lump of peat, no?'

'Much better not to give it to anyone, my lord. I am certain I can make better use of my own heart than anyone else.'

'That's a dashed good point, isn't it, Hib?' he

replied, clapping his friend on the shoulder and weaving a little. Mr Hibbert clasped his arm and sighed.

'Come along, Dom. Maybe you should rest a little before you…'

But Lord Wrexham merely slipped away, not even noticing as he knocked over a small table on his way out to the back courtyard. Poor Mr Hibbert righted the table with a resigned sigh and Mr Clapton sniggered, clearly enjoying the show.

'He's probably off to cast up his accounts.'

Phoebe ignored Clapton's comment, but thought it would be best if that was indeed what Lord Wrexham had wandered out for. The less spirits he held down, the better.

Not that it would make much difference. She'd watched her beloved uncle Jack drink himself to death and there had been so many times she'd allowed herself to hope he would stop. Until she had finally come to accept he could not. That there was nothing she could do to save the man who had saved her from a cursed life and given her and her aunt purpose and pride. Most of life lay beyond her control, which was why she was all the more determined to control what parts of it she could.

In the end the drink would likely take Lord Wrexham, too. One way or another. The previous night it had only been Mr Hibbert's swift action that ensured his friend hadn't ended up feeding the fish in the Grand Canal when he'd nearly taken a stroll off the hotel jetty.

Mr Clapton had been quite titillated with that as well, pointing out to Hibbert that a good dunking might at least have sobered his friend. Phoebe didn't share Clapton's optimism. Habitual drunkards were far more likely to drown than be sobered by finding themselves in the canal.

Not that many other than the kindly Mr Hibbert and some of the town's gamblers and women would mourn the passing from the world of Dominic Allerton, Marquess of Wrexham, and heir to the Duke of Rutherford. Not even his own father apparently. Perhaps especially not his own father. George Clapton had told Lady Grafton and Phoebe it was no secret the Duke would not in the least regret if his eldest son met with an untimely end and made way for his younger half-brother, a model of ducal rectitude.

Poor Mr Hibbert did his best to protect his friend, but Lord Wrexham, like many tipplers, was convinced he knew best and headed down his path to ruin with all the conviction and enthusiasm of a religious pilgrim. And all the while the ladies flirted and sighed at the waste and the men looked on with smirking superiority.

Phoebe looked on and puzzled and said nothing.

'I do apologise for Dom,' Hibbert said into the silence. 'He can be a capital fellow, but...'

'Pray don't bother apologising, Mr Hibbert,' Lady Grafton intervened in her languid drawl. 'You're a dear to care, but I don't think you are having the slightest effect on that beautiful young man.'

'Not so young any more.' Mr Clapton had joined them as well and he cast a less than pleasant look at the now empty doorway. 'He must be well north of thirty.'

'My dear Mr Clapton.' Lady Grafton's tones were slightly less warm. 'He and you are both young men to me. Let us leave it at that, shall we? Now, do run along with your friends. All this fracas is bad for my complexion.'

George Clapton flushed at the rebuke and stalked off. Mr Hibbert sighed once more and followed him. Phoebe waited until they were out of earshot before smiling at her aunt.

'Talk about dragons, Milly.'

'I can be one when I wish, Phoebe. Such a pity about poor Lord Wrexham. He might be a penniless drunkard, but he is by far the best-looking Englishman in Venice. They say that was why Byron decided to remove to Ravenna, you know. Couldn't bear to be outshone.'

Phoebe picked up her book. 'Nonsense.'

'Well, that is what they say. Or was it that Byron fell head over heels in love with that Adonis, only to have Dominic prefer the attentions of the Contessa Morosini? I cannot keep the tales straight.'

'Since our arrival I've noticed *they* have said a great many conflicting and mostly fictitious things about Lord Wrexham. No doubt Lord Byron left because he was in debt, again. Or bored, again. And if he *was* in love with Lord Wrexham, which I admit wouldn't surprise me in the least as he appears to have loved dozens of men and women in his short life, I don't doubt his monstrous vanity allowed him to recover post haste. Pretty boys are impressively shallow and resilient. I doubt either of those men know what love is.'

'And you do, darling Phoebe?' Lady Grafton smiled and yawned.

'A hit, a very palpable hit, Milly,' Phoebe acknowledged with an answering smile. Milly's façade slipped a little.

'It's a strange and motley group we find ourselves among. I'm accustomed to standing out, but Venice outshines me by several suns. Don't you find it strange that Lord Wrexham and Mr Hibbert have taken up lodgings here? It strikes me this is a rather tame arrangement for someone of Dominic's nature.'

Phoebe nodded. The same had occurred to her. 'It does appear that the Palazzo Gioconda attracts the drifting English, for better and for worse. Clapton is a nasty sort, but at least he and the dreaded Agatha Banister are excellent sources of gossip, so we should cultivate them.'

Milly made a sound very like that of a large and satisfied cat. 'I cultivate everyone, love. Even lechers and martinets. Now, do be a dear and close the door. That poor boy has left it open and there's a dreadful draught. I'm practically a block of ice.'

Phoebe ignored the exaggeration and crossed the salon towards the courtyard door. The marble floor was cracked and scuffed by years of impoverishment, but the gloom hid the wear and tear as well as the layers of tallow smoke grime adhering to the gilt-embossed moulding. The enormous chandelier above was quaintly decorated with cobwebs, and Phoebe doubted it had been used that century. Mrs Banister had complained, but Phoebe didn't mind this shabbiness in the least. She and Milly had seen better and worse lodgings during their travels. And Venice was, after all, Venice.

The courtyard was dark and heavily silent, and instead of closing the door as commanded she descended the wide stone steps and stood for a moment enveloped in the cool darkness of the Venetian night. The courtyard was mostly an empty expanse with some large old urns along the edges that might have once held flowering bushes but now served merely to catch rainwater for the washing. In the dark they looked like a knot of skulking figures plotting sedition.

At the far end there was an arched wooden door that led to San Stefano Square. Lord Wrexham had probably wandered off that way in search of more wine, women, and song. Or rather wine, women, and cards. At least she presumed that part of his activities involved women. Both women and men seemed to buzz around him like fruit flies about an overripe melon. There was little doubt that the bedrooms of many of both sexes in Venice were open to the handsome Englishman if he chose to grace them.

Phoebe was not as judgmental on this front as some of the other English guests. Both she and her aunt had had enough of preachers and righteousness after being raised in a brutally zealous community in Northumberland. 'To each his, or her, own' was Phoebe's motto. It was perhaps not very proper from a moral standpoint, but it felt right.

'Come to see if I'd kee…keeled over?'

The voice, slurred and quite near, jerked her out of her idle thoughts and she turned with a start. In the darkness she hadn't noticed him seated on a stone bench alongside the building, his elbows on his knees, a silver flask clutched in one hand.

'No, Lord Wrexham,' she replied matter-of-factly, 'I came to close the door. You left it open and Lady Grafton doesn't care for draughts.'

'There're always draughts in these mausoleums. Might as well be living in a tent.'

'I don't think it is quite that bad.'

'Never lived in a tent, though, have you?' he challenged.

'Not yet. Have you?'

'I did. When we had them. Under the sky when we didn't.'

She remembered now. Hadn't Mr Hibbert mentioned they'd been in the same regiment during the war? Perhaps that explained this poor man's drinking. Enough men had returned from the wars as cracked vessels, never quite holding themselves together as they once had. She inspected the faint outline of his profile. It was a lovely profile.

It really *was* a waste. But then, being handsome was no guarantee of merit. Often quite the opposite. Even as damaged as he was, he was still endlessly indulged and sighed over. All that adoration clearly wasn't doing him a lick of good. She settled her shoulder against the door jamb.

'Well, if one must live in a draughty tent or mausoleum, then Venice in autumn is an excellent location.'

'God help me; don't tell me you are one of those incurable optimists.'

'God help me; don't tell me you are one of those privileged moaners.'

He turned his head and his eyes caught the shiver of light from one of the curtained windows, two slashes of silver like the eyes of a wolf materialising from the woods.

'You think I'm a…a moaner?' There was a peculiar tone in his voice. She could not tell whether he was outraged or amused.

'I think...' Phoebe drew herself up short. 'I think you very much don't wish to know what I think, Lord Wrexham. Since you now appear sober enough to be left to your own devices, I shall bid you goodnight.'

'Wait a bit. What if I *do* want to know?' He leaned back against the peeling wall, arms crossed, the flask tucked to his heart.

'I think I pity your valet. Your coat is going to be covered in plaster dust. But I dare say that is better than if you'd ended up in the canal.'

'Don't have a valet. Can't afford one lately. Or much else for that matter. Which is why Hib and I are reduced to contaminating this would-be hotel with my presence. And that wasn't what you were thinking.'

'You have no idea what I was thinking.'

'No, but it was a sight more damning than worrying about my coat. I've seen you giving me pitying looks.'

She was grateful for the dark. She supposed she had, which was foolish of her.

'I doubt it. I certainly don't think you deserve pity, Lord Wrexham.'

'Sorry, *censuring* looks, then. You and Clapton and Mrs Banister and Hibbert and the others.'

'Paranoia is a worrying sign of mental deterioration, Lord Wrexham. And as for Mr Hibbert, you are not only being unfair, but also unkind. He has been nothing but good and generous towards you, often to a degree I find baffling. And not once has he indicated he considers himself above you because of your weakness. If you cannot see that, then you are truly further along your path of self-destruction than I had reckoned. And, since you have sobered enough to begin feeling sorry for yourself, why don't you set a precedent and brew yourself some tea and go to bed early?'

She'd said far more than she'd intended and she waited for his outrage, but he merely gave a short laugh. Contrarily, his surliness was fading as he sobered. No doubt he would soon be in need of more spirits, but in these strange moments between rising from and sinking back into whisky-soaked oblivion, she could catch a glimpse of what he had once been. These were moments when she did indeed pity him. Not that she would tell him so.

'That's quite a speech for someone usually so quiet,' he said. 'You're right about Hib. He's a good fellow. Can't seem to convince him I'm a lost cause. He thinks I saved his life once. Didn't, of course. Pure chance my bullet took out the soldier aiming for him. Makes him sentimental. Why don't you give *him* a speech about wasting his time on fribble like me?'

'Because unlike him I don't waste my breath on lost causes.'

'Ow. That hurt. You go for the jugular, don't you, Little Miss Primrose?'

'Primrose?' she asked, confused.

'Prim but rosy with your fox-red hair, like one of Veronese's models all wrapped up in stays and neck-high fichus. You dress and act like a governess, but behind those spectacles you've eyes of a cat high on a wall looking down on the dogs gathering below. You know you can't overpower them but you're damned convinced you can outsmart them.'

She was feeling quite red at the moment, her cheeks flushed with both annoyance and alarm. Thank goodness it was dark out here. She really ought to return to the salon, but, since this was the first interesting conversation she'd had in the past few days, she stayed where she was.

'Interesting. I've always noted that some people are much nicer when drunk. It appears you are in that group, sir.'

He laughed again and patted the bench beside him.

'Then all you have to do is stick around a half-hour or so. As soon as I get my strength back, I'm off to refill my flask. Then I'll be sure to shower you with compliments if that's what you wish.'

She shook her head. 'No. It isn't.'

'Are you certain? Everyone likes a good word now and again. For example, I could tell you your mouth is looking quite tantalisingly both prim and rosy at the moment. That's a hard combination to manage. Your upper lip is a little on the thin side, though it has a lovely line to it, but your lower lip is an invitation for sin. Are you certain you don't share your mistress's taste for late-night trysts, Rosie?'

Her flush had spread to her chest but she did her best to keep her tone flat. He was clearly trying to unsettle her and she was damned if she'd show him he'd succeeded. It was becoming a matter of pride not to stand down first.

'If I did, I'm certainly not likely to tell you, Lord Wrexham. And I would most certainly not choose a man so far gone he is unlikely to remember my name come morning.' A moment's silence fell after that rather blunt blow and her embarrassment was joined by a thrust of shame at her meanness. 'I shouldn't have said that. That was cruel.'

His laugh was soft. 'Honesty often is. It's a miracle you've survived ten minutes as a lady's companion if this is how you usually speak your mind.'

'It isn't.'

'Well, I don't know if I'm flattered to be singled out for such candour. Or is this a roundabout way of flirting?'

'It isn't,' she said again.

'No. Not your style. Pity. Best run along, then, before those clods in there start wondering whether I'm having my evil way with you.'

For a moment he sounded quite sober. No doubt he was impatient to find his next flask of wine.

She was tempted to tell him again not to… To at least try… She shook her head at herself. There was no point in that. She'd tried for years to stop her uncle from sinking to the bottom of a bottle, but sink he did. If she could not save the most important person in her life, the likelihood of deflecting a stranger from his chosen path of destruction approached nil.

'Good night, Lord Wrexham. Do watch your step when crossing the bridges. It would be a pity if you didn't make it through the night.'

Chapter Two

Watch your step.

Dominic very much doubted anyone at Palazzo Gioconda would feel any degree of regret if he were to breathe his last that night. Well, Hib would, but Hib didn't count.

To be fair, after that tongue-lashing he rather thought Miss Rosie Prim might feel some degree of guilt. A conscience is a damnable thing.

He smiled at the nickname he'd bestowed upon her. She clearly hadn't appreciated it, but it suited her. Her kind didn't care to feel undignified; they liked to lecture others about dignity, which was rather rich, given the shameless pleasure her aunt took in the carnal delights of Venice.

He had to give Miss Rosie Prim some credit, though—she never showed any disdain towards her aunt. Either she felt none, or she was an extraordinary actress with an acute sense of self-preservation. It was possible but unlikely. He rather thought she just didn't care. Numbed by life and circumstance. So long as her aunt supported her, she turned a blind eye.

He glanced at his pocket watch. He shouldn't have stopped to exchange barbs with Miss Rosie Prim; he was running late. He crossed dell'Accademia Bridge and glanced over his shoulder.

'Watch your step.'

Her cool words echoed in his mind. Across the canal, the Moorish façade of Palazzo Gioconda looked less decrepit in darkness. Candles flickered in some of the higher windows as the guests prepared for another night of delights. Soon they would join hundreds of revellers all around Venice in gambling and gluttony and fornication. It was a perfect city for men like him—cast out from their own worlds and hanging onto others'.

Perfect for schemers and thieves, high and low.

He turned his back on the sight and headed deeper into Dorsoduro, weaving a little as he crossed the stone bridge over a narrow canal that cut in from the sea. Venice had eyes, as he knew well. Eyes and knives poised to slip between one's ribs.

Moonlight scarred the inky water, watched by windows in the high walls on either side. Perhaps they'd witnessed men swallowed by these fingers of the sea, but they would never tell.

One day he might very well not make it through the night, but he doubted it would be due to a fall from a bridge.

* * *

'Did you enjoy yourself out there with the beautiful bad boy of Venice?' Lady Grafton set her tone even deeper than usual as she leaned back against the mountain of brocade pillows on her bed. With her claret-coloured dressing gown fanned out over the bed like a bloody wing, she looked the image of a decadent empress. The curling rags securing her dark hair spoiled the impression a little, as did the laughter in her eyes.

Phoebe sighed and sat on the small sofa by the windows overlooking the canal.

'Don't be silly, Milly. There is nothing enjoyable about watching a man destroy himself, even if he does it with a quip and a smile. I was merely curious.'

'About?'

'Many things. He did confirm he had a bad run in the casinos and is forced to economise, but that doesn't quite explain why he chose the Gioconda. It is too…tame.'

'In that case, what is George Clapton doing here? Tame is the very last thing I would call that unpleasant young man.'

'True, but he came to stay because of those horrid Farnsworthy twins. I was rather hoping he would leave now they've departed for Florence with their parents, but it appears he enjoys being out from under his papa's thumb.'

'Understandable. Sir Henry is a dry stick if ever I saw one.'

'Dry sticks catch fire quickly, Milly dear. And that still doesn't explain what Lord Wrexham is doing here.'

'You are overthinking things, Phoebe. The Gioconda has many advantages for someone of his ilk. It is close to all his beloved casinos, and, despite calling itself a hotel, there are so few servants that one can come and go at all hours without being noticed. May I remind you we chose it for precisely those reasons? I certainly don't wish for any busybody servants gossiping about *my* night-time activities.'

Milly's voice sank into a seductive coo and Phoebe threw her a quick distracted smile. It was all true, and yet…

Milly sighed. 'Something else is bothering you and that bodes ill for us. What is it?'

'I don't know. Everything is going well so far. The local nobility has taken a shine to you and we are invited everywhere. Even Mrs Banister has decided that your title and wealth offset your scandalous tendency to fall in love with foreigners and wander off with them into the night.'

'She is simply delighted we have arrived.' Milly laughed. 'Nothing pleases her type more than having someone to look down upon. The person I truly pity is that poor son of hers. I hope he finds the gumption to rebel.'

'I doubt it. And if he does, he might very well do so in a manner that will do him more harm than her.'

'Do you think that is what happened to Wrexham?' Milly mused. 'Agatha Banister said his mother died when he was a babe and apparently the Duke is extremely upright and proud.'

Phoebe wrinkled her nose at that. 'My least favourite kind. What other gossip did she offer?'

Milly rolled the stem of her wine glass between her fingers, casting shimmering shapes on her silk dressing gown.

'She said he was raised by the Dowager Duchess, who was shockingly scandalous and filled her house with artists and actors. Not a salubrious environment for a child.'

'I don't know about that. It sounds more salubrious than the very pious one we were raised in.'

'I would not call what afflicted our family piety, Phoebe. I never ascribed to the dictum that serving God should necessarily lead to cruelty.'

'Fair enough. Well, whatever accounts for his need to drink himself into oblivion, it is a pity. He was once a very intelligent person.'

Milly smoothed the silk of her gown against the coverlet. 'He still is, dear. Don't underestimate him merely because he is a drunkard and a gambler.'

'I am not. I've seen how well he plays the casino tables before spirits cloud his judgement. And

Uncle Jack survived for years as one of the best agents of the Crown before the drink dragged him under. Perhaps he reminds me of him.'

'My dear, I adored Jack, but he was as plain as old toast, while Dominic is one of the handsomest men I've ever laid eyes on and I've seen and sampled my fair share. That is the pity of it. Still, he may be in exile, penniless, and drinking himself to death, but believe me, the moment his pious papa kicks the bucket and Dominic becomes the next Duke of Rutherford, London's best families will line up their daughters to bid for the impoverished duchy. And what is more, those daughters won't put up a peep of protest. His looks and charm and the foolish fantasy that they shall be the one to Reform the Rake will have them climbing over each other to snag him.'

Phoebe watched her aunt's face. 'Do you fancy him?'

'Goodness, no. You know my taste runs to bears, not sleek, taut panthers, and Lord Wrexham is definitely in the latter camp. Give me a big, burly fellow any day over a work of art like Dominic.' She sighed blissfully and Phoebe couldn't help smiling.

'Like Alexei Razumov?'

Milly pantomimed fanning herself. 'For once our mission presents me with such outwardly promising material. It is only a pity he hasn't the intelligence or the heart to match his physique. Still, he shall do very well for our purposes here.'

'He certainly appears taken with you. Don't rush matters, though; not all the pieces are on the board yet.'

'I'm certainly in no hurry, Phoebe dear. For the moment we are only what we appear to be. A wealthy widow and her meek companion, here to enjoy the hedonistic pleasures of this beautiful city. That is all.'

Chapter Three

The sun shone merrily on Venice and cut through the dusty windowpanes of Signor Martelli's bookshop on a narrow alley in Dorsoduro. Having made it through, the rays settled on a plain straw bonnet and played gaily with its orange sash.

Dominic paused outside the window, watching the two people within.

The orange ribbon was a new addition, but he knew that bonnet and the prim woman attached to it. A woman who most definitely should not be a good half-hour's walk from the Palazzo Gioconda in a rather dubious part of Venice frequented by impecunious artists and hungry poets that insisted on believing Venice would spur them on to fame.

Watch your step.

Miss Rosie Prim's parting words to him the previous evening had echoed tauntingly in his mind all through the night, adding an edge to his night-time activities.

Clearly another case of someone preaching what they didn't practise.

Dominic gave in to temptation and entered the bookshop, all too happy to point out she should heed her own advice. The shopkeeper apparently agreed with him. He was holding a book to his chest, perspiring freely, and babbling helplessly in a mix of Italian and English.

'But, *signorina*, this book is not at all *per giovani donne innocenti*…it is…how do you say?…it is…*ah, mio*…'

'I think he's trying to say the book is too warm for gently reared young women, Miss Prim. Allow me, Signor Martelli.' Dominic leaned on the counter and held out his hand for the book. Signor Martelli surrendered it with a sigh of relief.

Miss Brimford's already rigid back had snapped to attention at the sound of his voice, but her posture now would do a Swiss mercenary proud. She turned and fixed him with her distinctive tawny eyes that despite their colour always managed to look frosty.

'Kindly *do* explain, Lord Wrexham. I'm afraid my Italian is not sufficiently proficient to discuss such mature matters. I shall depend upon your excellent good sense to make clear precisely why this book poses such a threat to my gently reared self.'

Since this speech was delivered in Italian, he

had to scrub his hand over his bristly chin to hide his smile.

'Very well. Far be it from me to come between a woman and…' He opened the rather battered cover of the book. 'Good Gad… *Fanny Hill*?'

'Heavens, he can read,' said Miss Brimford, and twitched the book out of his momentarily un-nerved hands. She laid some coins on the counter and walked out. Signor Martelli shrugged and took the coins.

'I tried,' he said, 'but even the *innocenti*, they must learn somewhere.'

'Excellent philosophy, Martelli. But one would think they'd start on a rather lower rung of the ladder and work their way up.'

Dominic left the shop just in time to catch her shadow disappearing into a narrow alley-way leading east. She walked without hesitation in the maze of alleys and over bridges, ignoring the occasional suggestive cries from gondoliers and tradesmen with the imperiousness of a queen.

Dominic closed the distance between them a little. She stopped.

'Did you want something, Lord Wrexham? The directions to the nearest wine cellar, perhaps?'

'No need, I know them all. I was trying to be chivalrous and ensure you weren't lost. I'm still not clear on that.'

'The dell'Accademia bridge is precisely five turns from here. Left, right, left, right, and left

again. Along the way is the store of Signora Cavalli. I shall stop there for a purchase. Perhaps
five minutes. If you wish you may wait and carry
my packages back to the palazzo. I myself shall
continue to the basilica for a further half-hour.'

By the time his outrage made way for a response she was off again.

In the fortnight since he'd taken lodgings at the
Palazzo Gioconda and until the previous evening
Miss Brimford had rarely addressed ten words at
a time to him, though her cool, watchful looks
had been more than expressive.

She was making up for it with a vengeance.

He ought to tell her precisely what she could
do with her packages. He might yet, just to see
those tawny eyes fire up again. He was quite certain he'd noticed flecks of jade-green tucked into
the gold.

He grinned and set off in pursuit. He could do
with some entertainment after his rough night.

Blast.

Phoebe had remained longer than usual inside
Signora Cavalli's paper shop, hoping Lord Wrexham would grow bored and leave, but the damn
man was still lounging against the wall outside,
arms crossed and chin sunk into his crumpled
cravat.

Usually choosing a treat from the Cavallis'
beautifully crafted collection of writing paper

succeeded in distracting her mind from everything, but today a certain cocksure drunk had ruined what had begun as a lovely morning. There was no reason to feel embarrassed in her purchase of John Cleland's book, but embarrassed she was. She'd even been tempted to tell him she was not purchasing it for herself, but that would be cowardly.

'Don't tell me you too are planning to put pen to paper and create an epistolary masterpiece,' the brute said the moment she stepped out of the shop. 'That seems to be the ambition of almost every Englishwoman in Venice, second only to capturing the perfect sunset over St Mark's Cathedral in watercolours.'

'The wine has addled your sense of direction along with your wits, Lord Wrexham. The cathedral faces west. If the sun ever sets over it, David Hume will pop out of his grave and say: "I told you so."'

She walked past him. She was tempted to shove her package at him like a footman, but he would probably drop it in the first canal he crossed.

He followed her with a husky laugh. '*Fanny Hill* and David Hume's *Enquiry*. I'd give something to see your bookshelves, Miss Brimford.'

She sighed. She'd been correct. Somewhere in that spirit-fogged mind were the remnants of a decent education. What a waste. If she'd been at all like her mama and papa, she would have taken it as her mission to reform the wastrel and turn him to the Path of Light.

Luckily she wasn't like them in the least. She had no illusions about the inherent virtue of man. Or the inherent evil of woman.

'Well, *I'd* give something to see the back of you,' she muttered as she ascended the steps of a bridge over one of the small canals.

'Hmm… I *am* said to have a rather fine posterior.'

The book slipped from her hands and skidded towards the openings between the wooden railings. In her mind she already saw *Fanny Hill* sinking into the murky water of the canal, but Lord Wrexham lunged, catching it just as it teetered on the edge. It was so fast it seemed for a moment he too might go over by sheer force of momentum. She grabbed his coat, fisting her hands in the sun-warmed fabric. He straightened with a grunt, tucking the book under his arm, and plucked the wrapped package of Cavalli's papers from under her arm.

'I think I *will* carry your purchases for you, Miss Brimford. It is safer for both of us.' He secured them both under his arm and then added, with less of a bite, 'You may let go of my coat now, I think I've found my balance.'

She dropped his coat and pressed her hands together. 'Can you swim?'

His dark brows rose. 'I can. Why?'

'It seems inevitable you will one day end up in a canal. It would be nice to know you have a fighting chance when you do.'

He smiled, his eyes echoing the colours of the water behind him. 'Such consideration. I am touched. Can you?'

'Can I what?'

'Swim?'

'Yes.'

'Of course.'

'Why of course?'

'Because it is the less likely answer. Unexpected. Like you.'

It was not a compliment, but it felt like one. Damn the man, she would not blush. She set off eastwards once more.

'Where are we going?' he asked.

'*I* am going to the basilica. *You* are not. Our ways will part by the dell'Accademia bridge.'

He strolled on, oblivious to her hints. 'Why the basilica? Off to commune with God? I seem to remember someone mention you were raised by missionaries.'

'*Begat* by missionaries, but that is it. I was raised by my uncle and he was as much a man of God as you are a teetotaller.'

'Goodness, do they do everything in extremes in your family? So how did you end up as Lady Grafton's companion? I must have been asleep when they were gossiping about you two.'

He was impossible. It was easier to just give him the bare minimum of her story than continue to sidestep his intrusive questions.

'She is my aunt and a widow and wished to travel and for that she needed a companion.'

'I see. How long have you been a companion?'

'Six years.'

'And before that?'

'I told you. I was raised by my uncle.'

'An economic story.'

'An economic life.'

It sounded so dry and proper like that. Women in her position didn't even need a name. She was Lady Grafton's companion. Companions were destined to be someone's apostrophe until they became obsolete or died.

She shuddered. Thank goodness she had escaped such a fate.

'Cold?' he asked, and she shook her head and looked up at the strip of bright blue sky visible above them. In the narrow little alleys, with the blank earth-coloured buildings tight around them, it was pleasantly cool, and she loved how when they passed over a bridge or through a square the sun caught them, like a child or a dog pouncing on them in play: *Aha! Caught you!*

'It isn't truly a hard life, being Lady Grafton's companion,' she said. 'We have been to France and Belgium and Austria and now Italy. Perhaps I am luckier than some of my old school friends who married well and are now surrounded by six children and a philandering husband who beats them when he's drunk or loses at cards.'

'There are other options between those two extremes,' he replied softly.

She could feel his gaze on her profile, as if trying to force her to look at him and reveal some secret. She didn't look. She preferred him as a disembodied voice. The conversation had become far too…intimate. As if he had entered her mind, explored the landscape, and was now comfortably ensconced in an armchair in her favourite corner, stubbornly refusing to move on.

'Are there?' she challenged his assertion. 'All too often there aren't. Not for most women and even less for women like me.' She gave a sigh of relief as the basilica came into glorious view. 'Now, if you will excuse me…'

He ignored her pointed dismissal. 'I'm coming in.'

She almost laughed at his determined tones, as if he was contemplating jumping into the Thames in January.

The silence that fell on them as they entered was as heavy and fluffy as an angora muff. She stood for a moment soaking it up, wishing this infuriating man would leave so she could enjoy it. Well, he would soon grow bored. She went to a bench by one of the great pillars where the light from the high windows around the cupola was stronger, and took out her book.

'You are planning to read *that*. In *here*.' His shock was evident and she couldn't help laughing.

'Why not?'

'Why not?'

'Careful, Lord Wrexham, your respectable up-bringing is showing. Is there a better place to read the *"stark naked truth"* than a church?'

She opened the book and began reading. The rim of her bonnet shut him off from view but she knew he was still standing there staring at her. There was some pleasure to be had in shocking people, particularly people who appeared quite unshockable.

Well, this was a turn-up for the books.

Dominic had always been good at probabilities, which was why he was a fair gambler, but this was a combination he could not have predicted: standing in the Basilica di Santa Maria della Salute watching the daughter of missionaries read a book about the happy life of a prostitute.

Not that anyone could tell. Miss Phoebe Brimford sat as stiff and still as if she held a book of sermons. Only the tip of her nose and a tendril of reddish-brown hair were visible past the rim of her plain straw bonnet with its jaunty ribbon.

He glanced down at the page, his gaze catching on a familiar phrase.

'All my foundation in virtue was no other than a total ignorance of vice…'

Only yesterday he'd have presumed that statement was true of Miss Rosie Prim, but he rather suspected he'd misjudged her. She didn't appear ignorant of vice, if only by exposure through her aunt's hedonistic life. He'd watched Lady Grafton flirt outrageously with many of the foreign dignitaries currently populating the city, flaunting her wealth and her voluptuous curves. As far as he could tell she had a penchant for large, stocky men and had quickly become a firm favourite among the Russian diplomats and in particular a rather loud member of their lines, Prince Alexei Razumov. Dominic wondered if Lady Grafton knew that Razumov was far more interested in her jewels than in her. Or if she cared. Probably not.

He wondered if Rosie Prim cared. Probably. She was a cool little thing but her loyalty towards her aunt was unmistakable and he'd never detected any resentment on her part. Twice already he'd seen her aunt wander off with her new flirt and leave her companion to find her own way back to the palazzo, and both times Phoebe Brimford had done so with the resigned calm of many years' experience.

Initially he'd assumed her calm was the result of being beaten down by years of neglect. But today had made it amply clear that, far from being beaten down, Phoebe Brimford was a force to be reckoned with. She was also a study in contradictions: the trappings of a governess wrapped around a sharp-witted spitfire.

He went to settle on a bench where he could watch her.

She'd mocked her plain looks but he couldn't see it. It was true she wasn't pretty like Lady Grafton, who was blessed with the looks of a black-haired china doll with a childlike mouth and large, dark eyes. But he'd never found mere prettiness interesting. He liked something with an edge to it. Something worth watching.

That was one reason he liked Venice. It wasn't pretty. It was abrupt and demanding and alive with the tension between man and nature. Its beauty came in bursts of the unusual—a sudden garden blooming with pink and white oleanders, a bridge reflecting in the canal, the sleek line of a gondola cutting through murky jade water... Those moments would always make his heart expand.

This strange, anomalous woman was a surprising extension of Venice—layers of contradictions and raw contrasts and surprising twists and turns.

Alluring...

Her mouth was a case in point. He'd thought her thin-lipped but last night as he'd taunted her he'd noticed her lower lip was a lovely, pillowy curve above a very definite chin. He liked the line of her jaw, too—a lovely sweep from the ear peeping out from the unruly waves shoved under the bonnet.

And then there was her scent. He'd noticed that last night, too—faint at first but growing more definite as she stood in the cool stillness of the courtyard, like a flower blooming as darkness fell. It reminded him of the garden at Palazzo di Benedetti, where the old Contessa had brought bushes of jasmine and orange and lemon trees from Amalfi, complete with a boatload of earth. The orange blossoms had already fallen and the green pips were swelling into winter fruit, but the jasmine was in full bloom now, the tiny pink-white flowers unfurling into fragrant stars.

Was it a perfume she used? A secret vanity? Whatever it was, he liked it. The scent would likely be strongest just there, at that shadowed triangle beneath her ear, in the silky waves of her hair that she usually pulled back so brutally.

She hadn't bothered this morning because he could see the waves peeping out from under her bonnet and about her face. He had a rather mad notion of slipping that ribbon loose and the bonnet off and watching that tawny-brown mass tumble over her shoulders…

Not thoughts for a church.

Not thoughts for anywhere. Certainly not for him, he realised with a twinge of surprise. It was merely that she was a puzzle and he had a penchant for puzzles.

He leaned back to stare at the cupola with its windows dulled with the grime of hundreds of years of incense and candle smoke. It might be quiet, but she really should be reading somewhere with more light, and a breeze, perhaps a chaise longue with some cushions under a pergola in a lush garden somewhere. A setting suited for reading erotic literature, caressed by light and air and the honeyed scent of oleanders.

He had yet to see her hair in anything but a schoolmistress's bun or tucked away beneath a bonnet, but his active imagination was equal to the task and unravelled long tresses over her now bare shoulders. He smiled at the image, enjoying the perverseness of placing Miss Rosie Prim in that sybaritic setting. She would likely hurl that book at his head if she knew what he was thinking.

He spent a moment assessing her figure. It was neither slim nor voluptuous. Her dress was doing its best to mask her form, but he rather thought she had a pleasant figure, certainly one that would do well on the damask chaise longue with nothing but her hair and her spectacles between her and the Venetian breezes. After all, she wouldn't need much in the warm privacy afforded by his imagined garden; she might as well be comfortable.

She glanced up, her eyes a shimmering golden-brown, like sunshine cutting through amber. He frowned a little as he realised she wasn't wearing her spectacles now.

The image of her in his garden popped and fizzled. Pity.

'What is so amusing, Lord Wrexham?'

'Oh, life.'

'I am impressed you still think so. You must have drunk more this morning than is apparent.'

Out of long practice he held his smile through the flash of resentment, but she must have seen something because she looked down and closed her book.

'That was uncalled for. And mean. I apologise.' She stood abruptly and made a strange gesture with her hand. He stood as well, disarmed by her evident regret. Besides, he told himself, it was facetious of him to resent it when people believed the fiction he'd toiled so hard to create.

'Don't waste your apologies on me, sweetheart. I won't remember them any more than I will the insults.'

Her eyes narrowed, regret replaced by the intent look he'd seen her wear often—weighing his words. Weighing him. Not with the condemnation or the covetousness he was accustomed to, but with…interest. Curiosity. As if *he* was a puzzle to be unlocked. Then her gaze fell and the silence of the church became filled with all the sounds that had been there before yet hadn't. The echoing of footsteps, the creaking of the chains holding the incense lanterns, the cooing of doves high up in the cupola.

'I shall be returning to the palazzo now, so you may give me my packages, Lord Wrexham.'

'You are done here?'

She shrugged. 'I might as well be. I find it hard to concentrate when I am being inspected like a weevil by a naturalist.'

So do I, he almost said, but remembered his role and smiled. 'Not a weevil, sweetheart. My images were far more…pleasing.'

She gave a snort. 'Pray don't strain yourself. I'm not a fool, Lord Wrexham. And you have nothing to gain by charming me.'

She stalked out and he followed, pricked by a twinge of remorse. Which was foolish. She was right, he had nothing to gain by charming her. If she'd been an heiress or the bored wife of one of the local potentates, then perhaps. But impoverished companions to lesser members of the English nobility definitely didn't justify expending his personal resources.

Still, she managed to do something few people had done in the four years since he'd left London for Venice. She amused him. That was something, wasn't it?

At the entrance to the alleyway to the palazzo she stopped. 'Thank you. I shall carry the package from here. Good day.'

He handed her the package without a word and watched until the courtyard door shut behind her.

Chapter Four

'Did you hear? The carnival thief has struck again. A fabulous pearl and amethyst necklace was stolen from a palazzo in Cannaregio.'

Phoebe kept her eyes on her book, but her attention swivelled towards where George Clapton and Rupert Banister were playing cards and gossiping.

'Where did you hear that?' Clapton demanded.

'My valet heard it from the maids. He said the servants think it might be one of the Italian rebels. The Austrian empire might be firmly in control here, but they are especially unpopular after they came down so hard on the uprisings in Piedmont and Naples last year.'

Rupert's voice rose with his enthusiasm for the topic. He'd confessed to Phoebe that if he had his way he would join the Foreign Office and travel the world. Unfortunately, Phoebe suspected he was unlikely to have his way until his mother was removed from it, which was a pity.

'Did the thief leave a card again?' she asked.

'He did, the prince of hearts.' Rupert's voice was dreamy, which didn't surprise Phoebe in the least. No doubt the thought of a dashing corsair appealed to someone of his romantic disposition.

'Prince of knaves more like,' Clapton sneered. 'Those Carbonari rebels are nothing more than a nuisance. They haven't a chance against the might of the Austrians. If he is a rebel, my father says they'll hang him twice when they catch him.'

'*If* they catch him,' Mr Hibbert interjected, joining the two men. 'He's been rather lucky thus far.'

'Of course they'll catch him,' Clapton dismissed. 'It's a matter of pride for Herr von Haas. Especially now so many dignitaries have descended upon Venice ahead of the Congress in Verona next month. Von Haas isn't the kind of man to stand idly by while his rule is undermined.'

'Since when has the prince of pomposity von Haas been made Viceroy?' interjected Lord Wrexham. 'I thought d'Inzaghi was the Emperor's top local puppet.' They had none of them noticed his entrance. Occasionally he moved with a degree of stealth that would have been impressive for a man of greater sobriety and lesser inches.

'D'Inzaghi is the governor of the whole region of Veneto,' Banister clarified with earnest patience, quite as if Lord Wrexham were half his age. 'But everyone knows it is von Haas who controls Venice. They say he reports directly to Chancellor Metternich.'

'Poor d'Inzaghi, then,' Lord Wrexham said as he sprawled on the chaise longue Phoebe's aunt had recently occupied. 'Can't be easy having to cede the Queen of the Adriatic to that stuffed shirt von Haas.'

He hung his leg over the low arm rest and plumped a pillow under his head, settling back with a sigh of pleasure. It was a pose hardly suited for a men's club, let alone for a drawing room presently occupied by two gentlewomen.

He looked as if he'd slept in his clothes, yet it wasn't his disarray that caught their attention, but the wink of blood-red fire from a new ruby earring he sported. Mrs Banister gave a loud sniff and turned her back on him.

Phoebe placed her finger in her book. 'I found Mr von Haas to be a very intelligent and cultured man.'

The three men turned to her in surprise, as if they had forgotten her presence. Which was possible.

'Are you in the habit of consorting with the local uniforms, then, Miss...uh... Miss Grimforth?' Lord Wrexham enquired, turning his head towards her with a grin.

Rupert Banister cleared his throat and even Mr Clapton looked rather red at Lord Wrexham's mix of vulgarity and rudeness in mangling her name. Phoebe raised a brow.

'I had the felicity of conversing with him after the performance of *Don Giovanni* at La Fenice,' Phoebe said calmly. 'And, to answer your question, I am in the habit of consorting with anyone who can hold a decent conversation, Lord *Wrexit*.'

He blinked, a fugitive smile flashing in his blue eyes at her retaliatory name-mangling. 'Well, that rules me out. I don't think I've had a *decent* conversation in years. It sounds…uninspiring.'

Phoebe wanted to whack the fool on the head with her book. After yesterday she found his smug mannerisms even more annoying. 'Well, perhaps you ought to make a study of Herr von Haas. He is not only clever and handsome, but is also well versed in Venetian history and a most amiable conversationalist.'

'Amiable? Von Haas? Last time our paths crossed he was so amiable he almost made me a guest of Venice's dungeons. Damn damp things, those. I'd rather make a study of you, Miss Primworth.'

'Miss *Brimford*,' Rupert Banister hissed.

'No.' Lord Wrexham shook his head. 'Doesn't suit her. Miss Prim is much better. Except for the eyes. Bold as brass. *Audentes Deus Ipse Iuvat.*'

'Boldness might have helped Hippomenes win

Atalanta's hand in marriage,' Phoebe responded, primly, 'but as a rule I don't think God rewards boldness as much as he does calm calculation.'

'Oh, boring. Well, I never liked Ovid anyway. He wrote far too much.'

She widened her eyes. 'Oh. Was that a quote from Ovid?'

His own eyes narrowed at her blatant assumption of false ignorance, but he could hardly call her out on it when he himself enjoyed playing the dunce so much.

'Bold as brass,' he repeated, his voice velvet rubbing against polished wood as he extracted himself from the sofa. He was a tall man, with a body that reminded her of a painting she'd seen on the wall of the small church near La Fenice. It was of David preening after slaying Goliath, his sandalled foot resting upon the giant, his body long and lithe, the muscles clearly defined but far more elegant than the bulky protuberances on the fallen form of the giant he'd slain.

'The eyes never lie, do they, Miss Fire and Brimstone?' Lord Wrexham prompted, his voice sinking into those husky registers that thrilled his admirers so.

'Anything and anyone can lie, Lord Wrexham. It is the truth that requires effort.'

'My, my, we have a philosopher amongst us,' he murmured, plopping himself back down, but this time on the sofa beside her. Rupert Banister made a strange sound, rather like a chair taking the weight of a particularly well-endowed matron.

'By my tally she's ahead, Wrexham!' Clapton exclaimed with a quick, sharp laugh, watching the exchange with the same avid attention as he might a cock fight. 'I say give up before she tears more strips off you.'

Lord Wrexham gave him a sweet, almost innocent smile, but his voice was anything but innocent when he replied. 'Miss Prim can tear anything off me she likes, Clapton.'

He turned back to Phoebe, his long lashes casting shadows over eyes so deeply blue they seemed almost violet, his sharply sculpted mouth softening into a blatant invitation. Phoebe's mouth watered. Her skin felt as thin as a cobweb, bared to the elements. He might be a drunkard on his way to perdition, but he was still an expert seducer.

She repeated those words in her mind. *This is how this man survives.* This is the *only* way this man survives. It has nothing to do with you. You are nothing more than a witness to his skill and his impending tragedy. That is all.

It didn't feel like that was all. It wasn't smart, but for the first time in many, many years she ignored caution and patted the space on the sofa between them. 'Let he who dares, approach, Lord Wrexham.'

His lips parted. Surprise, unease. Good.

Rupert Banister made the same sound as before—between a muffled squeak and a squawk. George Clapton sniggered, but his breathing accelerated.

Lord Wrexham did approach, sliding closer on the sofa, though not as close as she had expected. She leaned forward and tugged off his clasp earring and tucked it into his waistcoat pocket.

'Rubies don't suit your complexion, Lord Wrexham. A simple gold loop would do.'

Dominic's ear tingled, and not just because of Clapton's delighted guffaw. He had to resist the urge to reach up and rub his now bare earlobe. It hadn't hurt—the clasp had come off easily—but her touch had surprised him, her fingers warm against the sensitive skin there.

He'd not expected her move. In fact, he'd not expected anything. That was part of the pleasure he was coming to expect in crossing swords with Miss Rosie Prim. It was a foolish occupation he'd fallen into recently. Taunting her and sparring with her definitely enlivened the time he was forced to spend at the Gioconda as he went about his business. The temptation to succumb to this new pastime once more had assailed him the moment he'd entered the salon and seen her seated stiff as a governess, her gold-rimmed spectacles glistening around her tiger's eyes as she read one of her probably improper books. He was a glutton for punishment apparently, because Clapton was right—she'd won all the rounds so far.

He ought to be annoyed. Instead he was… strangely hot. And bothered.

Very peculiar. He found himself wishing she *would* tear some more strips off him, preferably in private this time.

No, Dominic, he admonished himself. This is neither the time, nor the place, and most certainly not the right kind of woman even if he was inclined to indulge, which he wasn't. It was merely the novelty. The surprise. A pleasant surprise for once.

He sighed and patted the pocket now holding the ruby earring.

'Perhaps I shall follow your suggestion. After all, "*Gold gives to the ugliest thing a certain charming air, for that without it were else a miserable affair.*"'

She frowned. He could almost see that quick, clever mind leap from shelf to shelf in search of the origin of his quotation. Finally, a hit. He smiled down at her.

'And now this "*miserable affair*" must depart in search of something far more valuable than gold.'

'*Is* there anything more valuable than gold?' Clapton asked with his usual urbane sneer. He must practise that every morning in his shaving mirror.

'Of course there is,' Dominic replied. 'The blessed oblivion to be found at the bottom of a wine bottle. I bid you all *adieu*.'

Chapter Five

A frisson of warning tingled up Phoebe's nape a moment before the squeak of the bookshop door. She didn't turn, but something in the shadow that obscured the sunshine or the scent of warm wood and cinnamon warned her of the new entrant's identity even before Signor Martelli smiled and called out a greeting.

'Signor Domenico!'

'Morning, Martelli. What banned books are you peddling to respectable young ladies this fine morning?'

Signor Martelli grinned. 'No, no, not today.' He held up the copy of a volume of Dante's *Inferno* she had purchased.

'For me?' Lord Wrexham asked with delight, leaning his elbow on the counter.

Phoebe tried very hard to quell her smile. It took quite some effort. 'No, Lord Wrexham. Though you might wish to purchase a copy of your own. It shall provide a good travel guide for your future destinations.'

He laughed. 'You think I'm going to hell?'

She sighed. 'I don't believe in hell.'

'Goodness. An optimist. We are all to crowd into heaven, then?'

'I don't believe in heaven either, or purgatory, or in any form of afterlife. When we die, we feed the worms and that is that.'

Signor Martelli looked far more scandalised by her words than by her previous purchase, and she wished she hadn't been goaded into answering. When she stepped outside into the Venetian sunshine she was no longer surprised her new nemesis fell into step beside her. Resentful, but not surprised.

'Apparently we have the same meandering schedule, Miss Brimstone,' Lord Wrexham said, chirpily oblivious to her thoughts. 'And the same route. I was just on my way back to the palazzo.'

Phoebe wondered whether he'd spent the night at a casino or in someone's bed. Despite his stubbly chin and rumpled evening clothes, he didn't look as worn as he ought to be by a night of dissipation. Perhaps he'd been lucky enough to fall asleep at the tables before he did too much damage to his purse and health.

'From where?' she asked, curiosity overcoming prudence. After all, he asked her all manner of intrusive questions. Why not turn the tables?

His mouth picked up at the corners, transforming the sharp lines that bracketed his mouth into smiles.

'From a friend's house.' He paused and added, 'A male friend.'

She shrugged. 'The ladies shall be very disappointed to hear that.'

He laughed out loud. 'He's only a friend. We were in the army together.'

'Is he also a gambler?'

'Of course. The worst kind. He wins. It's very annoying.'

'So I dare say your pockets are empty if you spent the night playing cards with him.'

He shoved his hands into said pockets, but he was still smiling. 'I'm not that dense. He runs a gaming hell here and he knows all the best tricks. We play for peas.'

'Peas?'

'Peas. He grew tired of having to lend me money only to win it back from me. So now we play for peas. I shell them, though.'

It was too absurd and she laughed. At least he had a sense of humour about his weaknesses. If he was going to the devil, he'd have a good laugh with Charon as he sailed across the River Styx.

'Where are you heading? The basilica again?' he asked as he fell into step beside her. 'I wouldn't recommend it. It's one of the local saints' birthdays today. It will be full to bursting.'

'Oh, I had no idea.' She looked around the narrow streets, disappointed. She's been looking forward to her little reading corner. As if to commiserate, her stomach grumbled loudly. 'I'd best return to the palazzo,' she said, embarrassed.

'You'd best have something to eat first. It's almost noon and I'd wager you haven't eaten anything today. Do you ever eat before you escape in the morning?'

'I always carry some walnuts with me.'

'Walnuts! You're not a squirrel. And that's an insult to Venice. We'll stop along the way so you can refresh yourself with something a little more substantial. I know just the place.'

'Lord Wrexham…'

'Yes, yes, I know. But it is on the way back and I dare you to say no once you see what's on offer.'

What was on offer was a little trattoria overseen by a couple that looked as if they'd stepped straight out of a painting by Breughel. Giulia and Matteo Schiavanti were both large and round and greeted Lord Wrexham with cries of pleasure and an explosion of Italian mixed with a Venetian dialect so idiomatic Phoebe's hungry mind struggled to untangle it.

She did notice, however, that, like Signor Martelli, they also called him Domenico, which was rather sweet. Clearly he'd charmed this nice couple as well as quite a few others in his adopted town. He seemed to have the knack of having people take him under their wing.

And then he probably took full advantage of them.

She concentrated on the restaurant. It was a simple affair, with solid wooden tables and chairs and an open door leading out into a small, trellised garden with more tables. The most distinctive thing about the place was the smell flowing in from the kitchen. Here was garlic and bay leaves and butter and the lemony scent of the pickled artichoke hearts that stood in an enormous jar on a wooden counter.

Before she could even realise what was happening, a cool glass was pressed into her hand by Signora Schiavanti, her rough palm closing around Phoebe's with an exhortation to, 'Drink! Drink!'

The wine was from her son's vineyard near Garda, she added, her bright brown eyes both expectant and confident.

Phoebe drank a careful sip and a new world filled her like smoke—a world of sunsets turning mountains orange and purple, the soft earth letting go of the last heat of day...

'Oh...' She let her breath out and smiled at the woman. '*È meraviglioso*. Sunset in a glass,' she said in Italian and the woman clasped her hands to her bosom.

'*È vero! È vero!* That is exactly true. Did you

hear, Matteo? Sunset in a glass. That is what Giacomo should call it. Come, come. You are too thin. You shall eat. Today is Tuesday. *Risotto al nero di seppia*. No one can resist it!'

Phoebe hadn't intended to stay or eat anything, but somehow she was seated at one of several empty tables, a bottle of ambrosia between her and Lord Wrexham and two large plates of the strangest thing she'd ever seen.

'It's black.'

'It's delicious. Try it.'

'That's your answer to everything, isn't it?' she said crossly.

'Close enough. Just a little taste. Giulia will be devastated if you don't.'

'Oh, damn you to hell.'

'Yes, undoubtedly, but try it anyway.'

She picked up some of the dish on the tip of her fork. Food should really not be black. It reminded her of the peat bogs near her childhood home. It smelled of the sea and garlic.

'What is it made of?'

'Just one bite. It's not poisonous, I promise.'

'You promise all manner of things, Lord Wrexham.'

'I haven't broken any of those promises yet, have I?'

'The day is young.' She closed her eyes and took a bite, her knees pressing hard together, her shoulders tense.

Damn the man for being right again.

It was divine. Sea and garlic and butter and the earthiness of the rice all moulded into something as comfortingly warm as a hearth on a winter's day and yet as exotic as this whole floating city.

She opened her eyes. He had his fork halfway to his mouth, but he was watching her with that intent yet warm curiosity that was so unsettling.

'So you were right. Don't gloat,' she said tartly, and he laughed.

'I won't. I'm happy you like it. It is one of Giulia's specialities. Once they open in an hour this place will be utterly overrun and it will all be gone by mid-afternoon.'

She took another bite; it was even better than the first. She sighed with pleasure. 'How do you know all these people?'

'I get around. When I'm not drunk, I enjoy exploring.'

There was a tinge of bitterness there and she felt a surge of pity and regret again. 'Can you not stop?'

His smile had gone. 'It's harder than it looks. Stopping something like that.'

'I know.'

'You know?'

'I watched my uncle drink himself to death. It took him ten years, but he finally succeeded. He kept saying he would stop. He did try, really, but each time... He was a brilliant man. He said sometimes his mind was so…noisy, he needed to quiet it and the only way was brandy.'

'Let's talk of something else,' Lord Wrexham said, his gaze on his plate as he traced lines in his Stygian rice.

She nodded. 'Yes, let's. Now that I have admitted this is delicious, could you tell me why it is black?'

'Are you certain you wish to know?' He looked up, his grin curving up the corner of his mouth. He had an amazing capacity to push bad things away, for a while at least. She smiled against her will and took a sip of her sunset wine.

'Yes.'

'Ink.'

Her jaw sagged. 'Ink? As in…*ink*?'

'No, as in squid ink. They squirt a dark ink in the water when they are being chased by predators. Very clever tactic.'

Phoebe stared down at her plate. Squid ink. She giggled and shoved her fork back into the delicious slitheriness.

'And these little pieces…'

'Squid.'

'Squid and squid ink.'

'And garlic.'

'Of course.'

'Do you require smelling salts, Miss Brimford?'

'I require the recipe. Or the address. I shall

have to return here once more before we leave Venice. Can women come alone?'

'Probably not advisable. I'll accompany you.'

She shook her head. It was an empty wish anyway. 'This was enough of a gift. You are very annoying, but you are also very nice. Thank you for being kind. Especially after I have been so…'

His eyes were more hooded now, more like he'd been when he'd followed her that day after the bookshop. The shields rising.

'Disapproving? Tetchy? Ill-humoured?'

'Impolite. Ungracious.'

'No, no. You were gracious even when impolite. It's quite a gift.'

Phoebe smiled. 'Thank you, Lord Wrexham.'

'You're welcome. And enough with the Lord Wrexham nonsense. My name is Dominic.'

'I am aware, however…'

'Try it. It's a bit hard about the edges, but very soft in the middle.'

It took her a moment to realise he meant his name and not a dish. Or himself. She couldn't resist trying it out.

'Dominic.'

It was quite strange, but she *felt* it. A rich creaminess in the middle, bracketed by a firm yet flaky crust. She tried it again. 'Dominic… It feels like freshly baked bread.'

His eyes narrowed, his lips parting as if she was offering a piece of that imaginary loaf. He had a beautiful mouth; his lips were sharply drawn and she liked the little lines on either side. They told her a lot about him that she didn't think he would want people to know. They revealed the difference between the smile he showed people and the real smile he couldn't hide. And they told her when her arrows hit home.

She blinked and looked away. The wine was more powerful than she'd realised.

They sat for a moment in silence, then he pointed his fork at her plate.

'Eat. There's another treat after this.'

'I don't know if I can handle any more treats.'

'It is a very light treat. And inkless.' He motioned to Matteo, who had come to stand in the doorway, wiping his hands on his apron. At Dominic's request he grinned and nodded, and when he returned he was carrying a tray with two glasses with spoons sticking out of them. The smell of lemons preceded him.

'Ices?' Phoebe asked in delight.

'Limoncello,' Matteo said, slowly, as if she was hard of hearing.

She raised the small spoon and tasted carefully, still unsure of all these new flavours. The ice shavings bit into her tongue and the tart lemon burst in her mouth and both sensations were immediately overcome by a great wave of warmth.

If the wine had been sunset, this was sunrise,

and not the slow kind, but a great bursting of yellow light over the horizon, happy and hopeful.

She moaned as it melted down her throat, a confusing mix of fire and ice.

Dominic pressed a hand to his mouth as if to stifle a laugh, but she didn't care if she was making a fool of herself. The wine or the food or the company or everything had stripped away her defences, leaving her…happy. The kind of happy that had come in rare but precious bursts during her hardest years.

It was a long-forgotten sensation, but so real and so true her heart literally ached with it. Her eyes burned and she closed them for a moment, gathering the feeling to her like a dream about to fade upon waking.

She was grateful he didn't speak. She was far too close to saying something regrettable.

They finished their food and ices in silence and then Matteo and Giulia came out and Phoebe gushed her pleasure and was somehow pressed into giving her word to return on Thursday, when another treat would be prepared.

It must have been the effect of the lemon liqueur and the company and her own sad little heart, but if any of them had asked her to go for a swim in the canal right now she probably would have said yes.

She watched Dominic-Domenico say his goodbyes to the lovely proprietors. She wasn't one to find a man attractive merely because he was handsome, even extraordinarily handsome as this man undoubtedly was, but there was something about him that went beyond his looks.

Perhaps it was how he'd managed to make her do things against her will again and again. No, she corrected, *not* against her will. Against her better judgement, perhaps, but absolutely and utterly aligned with her will.

Dangerous, that.

She pressed aside the fumes of wine and liqueur and squid ink and admitted to herself, slowly and very reluctantly, that this man was dangerous to her in a manner she had never previously encountered. She'd let him tag along without any real resistance and she'd said yes to visiting restaurants and eating oddly coloured food, and if he asked her for something else entirely... Well, she would say no, but she had to admit she would be very tempted to say yes to that as well.

But when he joined her outside all he did was hail a passing gondolier and they slipped back into the rhythm of the city and suddenly she was on the palazzo's jetty, her parcel held to her chest, this strange man watching her from the gondola.

'It seems I shall see you Thursday, then, if not before. Yes?'

She swallowed and nodded and then said, 'You needn't—'

'Go on,' he interrupted. 'I want to see you safe

inside before I leave. I dare say you're not used to spirits before noon.'

'It was already noon when we—'

'Are you planning to argue with me about that as well?'

She shook her head and did as she was told, walking carefully along the uneven jetty, the sun warm on her head. When she turned at the door the gondola was already pulling away, Dominic's profile a series of hard lines against the choppy water.

Chapter Six

'Do you know, we have been in Venice over a fortnight and I am not yet bored?'

'I am very pleased to hear that, Milly,' Phoebe responded. 'Though I presume it isn't the beauty of St Mark's Square that is holding you enthralled at the moment.'

'I don't know. His name *might* be Mark. Or rather Marco. Isn't he divine?'

Phoebe inspected the young man leaning against the Loggetta del Sansovino below the Campanile tower.

'He is handsome, but then Venice seems rather blessed with handsome young men. He is a trifle young even for you, Milly.'

'Oh, pooh. Until I need a cane to walk, youth is a matter of the mind, Phoebe dear. Thus, for example, *you* are at least twice my age. *At least*.'

'I definitely feel so some days.'

'Then take a page from my book and let your

hair down a little. You shall shrivel into a prune if you continue at this pace. There is nothing wrong with interspersing duty with the pleasures of life. Otherwise what thoughts will you have to sustain you through suffering?'

'I have a good life, Milly. I enjoy what we do.'

'Well, so do I. But I enjoy other things as well. One day I shall retire from being one of Oswald's spies and I do not wish to regret not having tasted life. I don't mean that you must pursue physical relations with men as I do, but I would like to see you…explore yourself a little. Not merely through books. What we do for Crown and Country does not preclude that, you know.'

Phoebe sighed. 'I have not the faintest idea what you are speaking of, Milly. And right now we ought to be wholly concentrated on why we are here.'

'You are perfectly capable of holding two thoughts in your mind at once. I've seen you keep ten balls up in the air and not drop one. We have been at this for many years now. Half your life.'

Phoebe smiled. 'Not quite. We didn't know what Uncle Jack was about when he first took us with him on his missions. We were too awestruck to be in Vienna or Hamburg or Rome to notice anything untoward. I'm always surprised Oswald allowed him to take us with him.'

'You know Jack; he probably didn't ask him. And we *were* useful. No one suspects a man trailing behind a surly girl and a pretty widow of being a spy.'

Phoebe laughed. 'I was surly, wasn't I?'

'Well, you had every right to feel wary and unsettled after we escaped from God's Flock. But Jack knew from the start how sharp you were. Remember how he used to test your memory? *"What was on the east wall under the candle sconce in the ambassador's drawing room, Phoebe?" "What colour were the curtains in the hotel we stayed in outside Salzburg last week?"'* Milly mimicked Jack's deep voice and Phoebe's heart squeezed sharply around the pain.

'I miss him.'

'So do I, Phoebe. Sometimes I think I want to stop this life, do something else, but every other option feels…flat.'

Phoebe nodded and they stood in silence for a moment until their attention was caught by a patrol of Austrian soldiers crossing the square, resplendent in blue jackets, the sun bright on their pale hair and gilded medals. They bowed gallantly and moved on, and Milly sighed.

'How pleased I am we had to come to Venice. Such wealth and riches fill this city. Such… stallions.'

'Those fellows were naught next to these beauties,' Phoebe murmured, pausing below the four bronze horses mounted on the entrance to St Mark's Basilica. 'Did you know they stood here for six hundred years until Napoleon looted them and placed them on the *Arc de Triomphe*? And before that they stood for over a thousand years in the hippodrome in Constantinople before the Venetians looted them?'

'What a great deal of looting men engage in. How did they make their way back here, then? More looting?'

'You could say that. The Austrians demanded their return after Napoleon was beaten at Waterloo.'

'I wonder who will loot them next. Someone will, you know.'

'Probably.'

'Men.' Milly gave a gusty sigh.

'Come. We are here to find a way to break into von Haas's private offices at the Procuratie, not ogle the menfolk of Venice.'

'I am perfectly capable of doing both. But I admit our prospects don't look good. The entrances on the square are too exposed and well-guarded and the only entrance behind is through the bridge from the royal gardens, which are fenced and gated.'

'But they will be empty at night, which the square most certainly won't be. I shall have to find a way to explore them.'

Milly turned to her. 'Didn't Mrs Banister mention that von Haas fellow will be holding a ball?

Perhaps we could request a tour of the Procuratie while we're there.'

'The ball will take place at von Haas's palazzo along the western side of the piazza, not here. Have you received an invitation?'

'Not yet,' Milly replied without much concern, then smiled wickedly at Phoebe. 'If you wish for an invitation, I suggest you be nicer to George Clapton. As the British Consul's son, he is certain to be invited.'

'I am nice to everyone.'

'I said nicer. He's ripe for the picking, you know. All that bravado covers very thin skin. And I've seen him watching you when you read.'

Phoebe shuddered. 'Have you discovered when he shall return to the Consul's house?'

'Not for a while, I'm afraid. Apparently since he has moved into the Gioconda he and Sir Henry are on far better terms.'

'Hmm. Distance makes the heart grow fonder. Even of George Clapton. Still, I wonder.'

'You are always wondering. I recommend less wondering and more enjoying. Life is short and brutish.'

Phoebe sighed and turned away from the gate. Perhaps Milly was right. Those short hours at the Schiavantis' trattoria, the delicious food… The company of a beautiful, amusing, sad man… Those short hours had expanded well beyond the minutes counted out by any mechanical clock. It had become a memory—vivid and full of life. When she closed her eyes she could recreate the sights and tastes and textures. She would likely carry that memory for a long, long time.

Or, according to Milly, it might carry her.

'We had best turn back,' Milly said, her tone unusually sombre. 'It might be a long night, as I want to see how difficult this place is to approach in the small hours. It really is absurdly exposed.'

'Yes. I don't know whether it would be best to come through the northern alley or by gondola. Probably on foot. Too much traffic on the canal at all hours. Perhaps we should consider a plan other than breaking into the seat of Austrian power in Venice.'

Milly glared at the building. 'We've managed worse. All we need is some more information. And an opening.'

Phoebe smiled at her aunt's determination. 'Then let us secure both.'

They made their way back to St Mark's Square.

'Oh, look. Do you think they mean to arrest your friend?' Milly asked, and nudged Phoebe. In the middle of the square the four Austrian soldiers they had seen earlier stood in earnest conversation with Lord Wrexham. Amid the flaxen heads, his dark hair with its auburn lights looked even more devilish. Then the soldiers burst into laughter and one of them clapped Wrexham on the shoulder, and Milly gave a sigh of relief. 'Not today at least.'

'He would probably be safer in gaol than loose upon the town,' Phoebe muttered.

'Oh, I doubt he would stay inside long enough to make a difference. Some romantic or besotted soul would secure his release. Besides, we know that unless men like him wish to change, no outside force can set them down a safer path.'

As they watched, Wrexham slipped his silver flask and drank from it before offering it to the soldiers. There was more laughing and some discreet shrugging in the direction of the long building along the south side of the piazza where von Haas and his Austrian government held sway over the city.

The soldiers continued northwards and Wrexham remained where he was, but his gaze transferred to watch Milly and her, as if he'd known all along they were there. As he stood directly in their path to the Palazzo Gioconda they would have to greet him, and, though it hardly mattered, Phoebe felt an inner resistance, a sensation that usually beset her when something ahead was amiss. But Milly had already looped her arm through Phoebe's and there was nothing for it but to proceed.

They had hardly gone three steps when another small group of men exited the imperial headquarters. Phoebe immediately recognised von Haas and wondered if he would acknowledge them.

After her impassioned defence of his intelligence at the Gioconda only a couple days earlier it would be a tad embarrassing if Wrexham saw von Haas pass her by without even a nod. She could see the calculation enter Wrexham's gaze, a faint, malicious smile as the Austrians approached. Phoebe steeled herself for embarrassment. Von Haas's gaze slipped over them, moved on, and back. He stopped.

'Lady Grafton, Miss Brimford.'

They stopped as well. Wholly disproportionate relief flowed through Phoebe and she smiled. 'Good morning, Herr von Haas.'

'What a pleasure to meet you again, Herr von Haas,' Milly crooned and he nodded to her, but directed his rather stiff smile at Phoebe. 'You are exploring, yes? Did you indeed visit San Trovaso as we discussed?'

'I did and I am very grateful for your advice,' Phoebe replied with unfeigned enthusiasm. 'I don't believe I would have found that wonderful Tintoretto tucked away in the chapel otherwise.'

He bowed and managed another smile, a little wider this time. 'You have been visiting St Mark's just now?'

'No, we have just been to peek through the gate of the Giardini Reali. I was reading about Signor Santi's fine work there and was curious.'

His smile faded. 'The gardens are not open to the public.'

'Oh, we know. It was pure curiosity. And seeing Acerboni's gate was reward enough.'

Milly sighed. 'My dear Phoebe, I am certain Herr von Haas is not as interested in *gates* as you are.'

'But I am, Lady Grafton,' von Haas interpolated with a short bow that was as stern as his words. 'Boundaries are power. Fortifications, gates, laws. These comprise the skeleton and skin of any nation. They are a statement more than any of the medals those fellows wear.' He jerked his chin in the direction of the soldiers who had exited the building with him and were now speaking with Lord Wrexham further along the square. There was almost disdain in von Haas's voice, as if their medals were no more than child's playthings, disconnected from the valour they implied. Perhaps they were. They did seem to be wearing a great many for men so young.

'I never thought of it in those terms, Herr von Haas,' Phoebe said diffidently. 'But I quite see what you mean. Borders and their manifestations may define nations even more than they protect them. A gate is never merely a gate.'

His smile returned but was promptly tucked away as he answered her in all seriousness. 'Precisely, Miss Brimford. Signor Acerboni is the finest ironsmith in Veneto. The gate, his gift to the empire, created directly after our defeat of Bonaparte, was not a trivial matter.'

'Indeed not. I shall admire it with renewed interest next I see it. Thank you again for your insight on this wondrous city, Herr von Haas.'

'It is my pleasure to discuss it, Miss Brimford. Lady Grafton.' He bowed once more, and just as Phoebe expected him to continue on his way he turned back.

'I might perhaps be able to arrange a visit. To the gardens. If it interests you.'

His clipped words might have sounded discouraging, but Phoebe held gently onto the rope.

'It would interest me very much, Herr von Haas, but I am well aware that your duties here in Venice are many and heavy. I would not presume to add to them.'

'I would not consider it a duty, Miss Brimford. Not in the least. Good day.' With another curt bow he strode off.

Milly stood fanning herself gently, her gaze following the tall, well-built form.

'My, my,' she murmured. 'I have underestimated the potent seductive powers of meekness when laced with politics and art. Clever little Phoebe.'

'Hush,' Phoebe said as they moved forward. The soldiers around Wrexham nodded, a couple of them eyeing Milly with the hungry eyes Phoebe had seen so often. Milly smiled and hummed, but did not stop, trailing promise behind her like scent. Wrexham detached himself from the group and, to Phoebe's surprise, fell into step with them.

Milly smiled at him. 'You seem friendly with half the Austrian garrison, Lord Wrexham.'

'They are friendly with my poor purse. That short fellow with the cowlick won a hundred guineas from me last night.'

'Oh, dear, I do hope your pockets are not completely to let.'

'They are considering taking in tenants.'

'I do not doubt the list of hopeful lodgers shall be prodigious and varied.'

Phoebe saw his smile and eyes turn predatory as they often did before he let loose one of his particularly poisonous arrows. She knew Milly could more than meet his thrusts, but she didn't want the two of them at war.

'I thought I heard Mr Hibbert mention you served with some of the local soldiers during the war,' she said and his gaze shifted to her, the rapier focus tucked away even as she watched.

'Did he?'

'I am quite certain he did. In Waterloo.'

'Hibbert's grasp of geography is no stronger than his grasp of recent history. Those fellows are Bavarian. They were nowhere near Waterloo.'

'But they did fight the French, did they not?' she asked, widening her eyes as Milly did when she wanted to show she was interested. His own eyes narrowed.

'Eventually. They switched sides just before Napoleon was walloped at Leipzig. Clever fellows. Why the interest, Rosie Prim?'

'Why not? I find all manner of things interesting.'

'So you do. What a valuable companion you have acquired, Lady Grafton.'

'I am quite aware of Phoebe's value, Lord Wrexham,' Milly replied with more hauteur than usual. He transferred his smile to her, clearly aware she was feeling snubbed, and just like that Milly's coolness melted. Phoebe wanted to pinch her aunt for being so easy to appease.

They passed San Moisè Church and he held out his arm to Milly as they came to the bridge, standing aside to allow Phoebe to cross first. She hurried ahead, stopping on the other side. For a moment the couple stood silhouetted against the backdrop of the grand Baroque church, two dark-haired beauties against the ornate, pale marble structure. It would have made a delightful painting, but it filled Phoebe with foreboding.

She was not worried Milly would become involved with someone like Lord Wrexham; her aunt had far too great a sense of self-preservation. But still, something made the world darken, as if a mist had come between them and the sunny skies of Venice.

She turned away and tried to put her foolish fancies aside. Premonitions were all well and good, but she dealt in facts, not fiction, and the facts were far more mundane. A handsome man on his way to ruin was no true threat to Milly or to her. He was merely another of the many, many casualties of life. Some had died and some were dying, slowly. In the end they would all feed the worms.

She listened idly to them talk as they wove through the narrow passages towards San Stefano Square. Lord Wrexham fed Milly's hunger for gossip, amusing her without the malice Phoebe had been so concerned about.

When they reached the Duodo o Barbarigo bridge a high nasal voice hailed them from an approaching gondola.

'Stop this boat, young man,' Mrs Banister commanded the gondolier. 'Rupert, tell this fellow to pull alongside here. We shall take Lady Grafton and her niece with us back to the palazzo. It is far too hot to be out walking in these noxious alleyways.'

Rupert conveyed this command in his far more pleasant voice and the gondolier pulled alongside the steps leading down to the water by the bridge, all the while protesting in Italian that his gondola was not large enough to bear more than one additional passenger.

'Surely there is no need,' Phoebe said. 'It is no more than ten minutes…'

'Ten minutes?' Milly moaned. 'Every time

you say ten minutes, Phoebe dear, it somehow becomes an hour. Would you mind handing me down, Rupert dear? We have been walking simply for *ages*.'

The gondolier threw up his hands and Rupert eyed him dubiously.

'Perhaps I had best walk back so the ladies—'

'And leave Lady Grafton and me to the mercies of this scurrilous fellow?' demanded his mother. 'And who shall help me onto the jetty at the palazzo? Have you no thought to my welfare, you wicked boy?'

Rupert had been holding out his hand to Phoebe to help her down, but she smiled at him.

'You see to your mama and Lady Grafton. I know the way and it is not far. I shall likely be there before you.' She crossed the bridge before a new drama could take hold. The gondolier's exhortations that he had his gondola and his reputation to look to continued as he and his passengers glided towards the Grand Canal.

Chapter Seven

Somehow Phoebe was not surprised to hear Wrexham's now familiar footfall behind her.

'I do know my way, you know,' she said without turning.

'Yes, yes. The master navigator. That was very prettily handled. Poor Banister. That is what he is, no? A Banister for her to lean on. A few more years of that and there won't be much of him left. With any luck the gondola will sink and he'll be spared more of that nonsense. Why don't you rescue the poor fellow?'

'I don't rescue people.'

'No? You rescued Lady Grafton from the arrow I was just tipping in poison. Who were you saving? Her or me?'

'Neither of you need saving.'

'Then why bother?'

'You are imagining things, Lord Wrexham. Not all the world revolves about you.'

'But of course it does. As your world revolves about you and your aunt's world about her. We are each the only fixed point in our little dramas and the only person we can never escape, more's the pity.'

'Except in death.'

'Ah, yes. I forgot you believe in the finality of death. Practical even about the hereafter.'

'At least I am practical about what can or cannot be and I do not indulge in sulking or dipping arrows in poison when I am thwarted or upset.'

'I beg to differ. You have slung some rather impressive poison-tipped arrows at me when you are upset. And I am eminently practical. I've managed to survive this long on my wits and a few winnings at the tables. I choose my path, Miss Prim. It doesn't choose me.'

She snorted. 'So you think. You are just like Spinoza's stone.'

'Like who's what?'

'Spinoza's stone. You have heard of Spinoza, have you not? The philosopher?'

'I know who Spinoza is. In principle. I didn't know he had a stone. What did he do with it? Toss it at other annoying philosophers?'

She turned to face him. She knew that glimmer in his eyes—he was toying with her. Well, she would toy with him.

'It was a parable about free will. He said: imagine a stone that was thrown with great force and suddenly while racing through the air it gains the capacity for thought but has no way of knowing that it was thrown. It would attribute its motion to its own desire to be in motion while in truth it would be ignorant of the true causes. Shall I explain the parable in your context, Lord Wrexham? Or have you caught the gist of it?'

He rubbed his cheek. 'If you happen to find yourself thrown with great force, Rosie, I don't think *you* need wonder at the cause. You are annoying as all hell.'

'Ditto.'

'I wish you would stop trying to reform me.'

'I am not trying to reform you. But so long as you continue following me about I shall continue to share my opinion that you are an idiot as freely as I wish. You can of course remove both our objections by leaving me alone.'

He had a magnificent glare. She folded her arms. She had dealt with much, much worse than the glare of a spoilt pretty boy…man. Very much a man. And pretty was an insult to the power of his face and physique. It was very annoying he could have such an effect without even trying.

She tightened her arms. It was time to put an end to this strange…what? Friendship? Connection? If they'd been sixteen, she might even have thought it flirting, just as a boy tweaked a girl's braid. Except someone like him had no need to flirt with someone like her.

Pique. That was what it was. On both their parts. Perhaps a little more than that on hers. All the more reason to chase him away, like a stray dog one had mistakenly petted a little too long and to whom one was in danger of becoming attached.

She set herself in motion again, turning into the narrow passage that led to the last bridge before San Stefano. Halfway down the shadowed alley two men stood arguing with an old man brandishing a broom.

'Damn,' Wrexham muttered. 'Let's go another way.'

'There is no other way. Not without adding a good mile.'

'Sometimes it is safer to walk a mile rather than rub up against the Luzzattis.'

She slowed. Despite Austrian rule, the Luzzatti family controlled several of the parishes in Venice and not even the likes of von Haas cared to cross them. Perhaps it *was* best…

Too late. The smaller of the two men had glanced over and spotted them. He smiled and beckoned them forward. 'Domenico. *Fratello.*'

Wrexham made a small sound between a snort and a laugh, but he took her arm and moved her towards them, addressing the man in his perfect Italian.

'Did I lose anything valuable to you last night, Donatello? I'm afraid my memory is fuzzy.'

'I'm tempted to say you did, Domenico *mio.*

But there were too many witnesses that you paid your debt. This time.'

The old man with the broom took advantage to scurry away. The large Luzzatti, who had the face of a crushed gargoyle, looked as if he would give chase, but Donatello Luzzatti patted his arm and the latter grunted and went to lean on the wall, his gaze watchful as the smaller man addressed Dominic.

'I merely wished to remind you of your promise to Pietro. Since your memory is notoriously fuzzy.'

'Then you wrong me, Donatello. If there is one thing I would never forget, it is a promise to play *calcio* with your son's team. I value my hide too much.'

Donatello Luzzatti's smile widened. 'Good man. Don't make me come looking for you. I am happy when Pietro is happy. You like it when I am happy, yes?'

'I certainly prefer it to the other option. But I come for Pietro, not for you. He is a good boy.'

Donatello sighed and spread his hands, the cocky bravado slipping off him for a moment. 'He is too much like his mother. He wants to go to Bologna, to university.'

'Then let him go.'

'Perhaps. At least the boy plays good *calcio* like me. Don't fall off any bridges before the game. After that you may do as you wish.'

They stood aside and Wrexham took her arm and led her past. Once over the bridge and out of sight he gave a small laugh.

'There in a nutshell you have Venice. You and Donatello have something in common, you know.'

'We do?'

'Yes, a tendency to mention falling off bridges in a manner that makes me deeply uncomfortable.'

'*I* wasn't threatening you. Do you often play *calcio* for the Luzzattis?'

'When they ask. Aside from the tendency to lead to broken bones it is a healthy pastime. You should approve.'

'What happens if you lose?'

'Not quite as healthy. But they won't toss me off a bridge. Merely break something the game hasn't.'

'Really?'

He laughed at her expression. 'No. Then I won't be able to play in the next game. I've helped them win more than I've made them lose. *They* are also practical, Miss Prim.'

'I have read in the old travel books on Florence that it is a brutal pastime. I did not know they still play it, and in Venice.'

'They don't, not in the old Fiorentine sense. This is a local, informal version, rather like the one we played at school in England. The Luzzattis are rather a vain lot and they don't want their precious scions covered in scars and sporting broken noses. And since there is not enough sand here in Venice to soften the impact of being thrown to the stony San Polo piazza floor, the rules about how much damage you can wreak on your opponents are a little more stringent. It is mostly for enjoyment. *Calcio* is no longer in its heyday in Italy, but the people enjoy it, especially since bullfights were outlawed some years back.'

'So, no bets are made?'

'This *is* Venice. They would bet on the direction a horse's tail will twitch; it's in their blood. Why? Are you looking to bet against me?'

The sun fell on them with the suddenness of a swooping eagle as the alley opened onto Santo Stefano Square. She squinted and smiled up at him.

'Would that spur you on to win?'

'It might. On the other hand, I would hate to deprive you of what little wages Lady Grafton deigns to provide you.'

'She is not ungenerous.'

'Given your devotion and loyalty, unless she pays you a thousand pounds a year, I would say she is ungenerous.' He sounded offended on her behalf, so she didn't take offence. The sympathy of one purse-pinched person to another.

'Well, I shan't bet against you, then. Thank you for your escort, Lord Wrexham.'

'Wait a moment. We haven't arranged where we shall meet tomorrow.'

'I… What?'

'Tomorrow is Thursday. You promised to return to Matteo and Giulia's. The trattoria.'

'I don't think that is a good idea.' She shook her head. Not a good idea at all,

'You promised, Rosie. You would disappoint them?'

'They won't remember.'

'There you go, underestimating yourself again. They will. You do realise your cowardice will have grave repercussions? They will wonder whether you were merely being polite when you sighed over their *squid* and their son's wine and that will likely have them crying into their limoncello. Not to mention that it will reflect badly on me.'

She laughed at his nonsense, her strange fear unravelling a little. She was being foolish. He wasn't a threat. And he *was* proving to be useful.

'Come, you won't leave me to dine alone, will you?'

'I am certain you could convince half the noble ladies in Venice to dine with you.'

'Not at Matteo and Giulia's. They would be more shocked at the suggestion than if I asked them to undress in public. Much more.'

She noted he hadn't denied her assertion, only the location. Well, it was true. And not merely because he was so damnably handsome. She'd focused so much on his drinking and profligacy during their first weeks in Venice and she'd not adequately valued his charm. In fact, she'd been prejudiced against him *because* of it. That had been her first mistake. She'd made quite a few since and was about to make another.

'Oh, very well. When shall I meet you there?'

He raised a brow. 'I shall meet you at noon on the other side of Ponte dell'Accademia. You might become lost otherwise.'

She shook her head. 'I am almost never lost.'

'Stop arguing about everything. I shall meet you on the south side of the bridge at noon.'

He strode off before she could answer, swallowed up in the darkness of the passage.

Chapter Eight

Dominic settled against the wall of the church, squeezing into the slim strip of shade it provided. The bridge was crowded with Venetians, as loud in the noontime heat as they had been in the midnight cool.

He glanced at his pocket watch. There were some moments yet to spare before noon. He sighed. He would likely regret this.

When he'd first made the suggestion, his mind still steeped in Matteo's limoncello, it had seemed like a very good idea. He hadn't liked the way Phoebe had put herself down and he'd wanted to please her. The vestiges of a long forgotten chivalrous sliver pricking what was left of his soul.

That was a fine excuse for his first invitation, not so much for the second. She certainly hadn't expected it. If he'd just let her disappear back into the palazzo, she would likely never have thought twice about it. Like everyone else she had few expectations of him. Unlike everyone else, who often delighted in watching his self-destruction, she truly seemed sorry for him.

It stung, but it also made him do foolish things. Such as invite her to Matteo and Giulia's. Carry her parcels. Escort her and her aunt back to the palazzo. Be useful.

But *she* is useful, too, he pointed out to his cynical side. She might appear quiet and meek, but by some strange alchemy she put people at ease. Made them like her. Lady Grafton was a hedonistic cynic, but she was clearly extremely fond of Phoebe, not merely dependent upon her. And there was Phoebe's ability to engage difficult people without the slightest sign of effort. Like Mrs Banister and von Haas. The last person Dominic would expect to hold someone like von Haas in an extended and clearly mutually fascinating conversation was an English spinster with no consequence and more countenance than looks.

Strange, that.

And then there were Rupert Banister and George Clapton and even Hib. Perhaps it wasn't very surprising that the young men at the palazzo were so comfortable with her. Banister appeared torn between regarding her as a favoured older sister and something less innocent. As for Clapton... There was nothing innocent about the way Clapton regarded women. Perhaps he ought to warn her... No, it was none of his business.

Besides, he had little doubt she'd already noticed. She had a knack for noticing things others missed. People who had to survive on the favours of others often did. She'd certainly noticed some of his slips, like rescuing her book from its close encounter with a canal. She might not understand the strings pulling the puppets, but she noticed the anomalies. That could be useful.

He would make it useful; that would lessen this guilt and discomfort.

He glanced at his pocket watch once more. Still shy of noon. There was no call to be impatient.

'The bells have not yet rung, so I cannot be late.'

Her voice, both cool and warm, made him turn in something like alarm.

'Where did you come from? I didn't see you come over the bridge.'

'I didn't. I was out walking.'

She was fidgeting with her reticule, her gaze on the paving. She looked distracted. And tired.

'Did something happen? Did your aunt leave you in limbo all night?'

She shook her head. 'No. What is the surprise today?'

He pulled back on the reins at her evident rebuff. It was none of his concern.

'It won't be a surprise if I tell you.'

'Worse than squid ink?' She finally looked up and smiled. In the sunlight her eyes were old gold with tiny flecks of jade. Like the sun melting into the canal.

'Not as challenging. It is actually a very simple dish, but a local speciality. You might find it less exciting than squid ink.'

'But you like it.'

He smiled as well. 'I do. Come.'

She placed her hand on his arm, as if they were strolling through Hyde Park. Not that he'd been in the habit of strolling through Hyde Park with respectable young women. Or any women at all. His life in England seemed even further away suddenly, but not in a bad way. He felt…content. Venice was a fair place to be exiled to.

At the restaurant they were greeted with an enthusiasm that immediately negated her assertion she would not be missed. She had the grace to blush a little as he held her chair, and she laughed as he leaned in and whispered, 'I told you so.'

Once again they were the only inhabitants in the narrow yard, and Matteo had already set out the wine and glasses. Dominic placed one before her and took the other.

'Do you think you ought to?' she asked, and he paused with his glass midway to his mouth.

'Ought to what?'

'Drink wine. I noticed you have been drinking less these last days at the Gioconda. I can imagine it must be difficult, but perhaps…' She waved her hand. 'I apologise; I did not mean to interfere in matters that are none of my concern.'

He almost set down the glass, but didn't. He was right about her noticing things. Good and bad. Dangerous.

'It *isn't* your concern, but, given your uncle's history, I shan't take offence. I'm on a winning streak in the casinos at the moment and I usually drink less when I do. That's all. It doesn't hold. Now, you drink up or Giulia will think you have gone off her son's precious wine.'

She drank, but without the almost childish pleasure of two days ago. The tension lasted until Matteo came out with small plates of *baccalà mantecato*. She bit into the tangy, crusty cod and olive-oil mousse on slices of toasted bread, her eyelids flittering closed.

Matteo grinned down at her, clearly content with her wordless appreciation. 'A woman who can eat with such joy is a treasure. Just like my Giulia,' he said and gave a long sigh and ducked under the low lintel into the kitchen, where the sound of Giulia singing melded with the clatter of pots.

Phoebe licked her fingers and laughed. 'That was marvellous. I never thought to enjoy fish so much.'

'I'm afraid the main dish isn't fish today.'

'That wasn't the surprise?'

'That was merely to whet your appetite. Did

you know that once long ago the Duke of Venice insisted that all new peas of the season in Veneto be sent to his palace?'

'How selfish! Why?'

'His jaded palate fell in love with a peasant's dish he'd come across when a storm forced his noble retinue to stop in a small town near Trieste.'

'And so he decided his noble appreciation was more important than the peasants' hunger. Charming. Is that what we shall be eating?'

'Yes. I'm lowering your expectations, you see.'

'Not necessarily. One of my finest memories of food is of a plate of fresh bread and cheese in a small *albergo*.'

'Not your aunt's, I dare say. She has a taste for luxury.'

'That happens to some people who were raised without any.'

'Ah.'

'Don't be harsh with her.' There was a faint plea in her voice and it pinched at his chest.

'I'm the last person to pass judgement on others. My life is no testament to virtue.'

She was about to speak and he didn't know whether to be relieved or not when Matteo came out with two heaped dishes.

'*Rixi e bixi,*' their host announced, setting them down with a flourish, enveloping them in the scent of pancetta and *parmigiano*.

'*Rixi e bixi...*' she echoed, studying the creamy

risotto studded with plump green peas and pink pancetta.

'Rice and peas,' he translated, watching her teeth press into her lower lip. His own lip tingled. He looked down at his plate. 'Eat up.'

Dominic tried to keep his eyes on his food, he really did, but watching her eat was a revelation. She might have schooled herself into the little bites expected of properly raised young women, but she gave up all other pretences of polite eating. On the first bite she gave a little moan of pure pleasure that would have done a practised courtesan proud. Her lashes dipped, shielding him from the golden fire in her eyes, but that only made it easier to watch her.

Her cheeks were flushed with sunshine and wine, and, without her bonnet, tendrils of her tawny brown hair slipped free, brushing rhythmically against her cheeks and throat with the breeze that sneaked over the wall. Occasionally she would tuck them behind her ear or wrap a tendril around her finger, letting it slip free and bounce like a spring as she laughed at his nonsense. His fingers twitched with the urge to tuck them behind her ears for her, gather the varied textures of her skin—the different degrees of heat and...

'You are not eating, Domenico!' Giulia's voice exhorted and he snapped out of his reverie and applied himself to his own food. It *was* moan-worthy. The *Vialone Nano* rice was cooked into soft creaminess in pea-shell broth and butter. The peas burst sweetly in his mouth and the pancetta was both earthy and divine.

His mind and body relaxed as he ate and it appeared to have the same effect on Phoebe. Her tension fled and they were soon talking as if they were long-standing friends who had met by chance in a foreign town, sharing their delight in their discoveries.

He made her laugh with his tale how Jacopo the elephant, brought to the Riva degli Schiavoni to entertain the Austrian emperor, had graced His Grace by taking an impromptu dump on the feet of one of his exalted advisors. The Venetians, still smarting from being handed over to the Austrians as a prize in a war they had had no part in, commemorated this event by calling one of their favourite dishes *risotto al cazzata di Jacopo*.

She wrinkled her nose fastidiously at his story, but laughed none the less. 'I'm glad you did not tell me that before we ate, but I wish I could have seen that. In fact, I feel as if I have. You're a natural storyteller, you know.'

It was a mild compliment compared to some he had received, but heat caught him hard in the chest, as if he'd swallowed whisky too fast. He felt it crawl up his neck and cheeks and tried to laugh it away. 'I'm always ready to provide cheap entertainment, sweetheart. Ask anyone.'

He felt like a fool the moment the words were out. He wanted to take them back, but had no idea how. He waited for her to withdraw as well but she merely watched him over the rim of her glass, her eyes spearing him as they all too often did. Against his will his own dropped.

It was ridiculous that she kept winning these staring matches. He was accustomed to being stared at. His looks had ensured that from a young age. It had mostly been unwelcome, an intrusion, as if he didn't quite own himself, was little more than a statue in a museum to be gawped at and pawed at like a hunk of marble. He'd grown indifferent to it over time. He might not like it, but it was manageable. Often useful.

Except she didn't look at him like that. He could have stared that down any day. It was her curiosity and compassion that he was struggling with. It stripped away years and walls from him and he didn't like it. He didn't like being...seen. He might have hated people not seeing beyond his shell when he was younger, but now he enjoyed the freedom it gave him. The control.

The protection.

Seeing over his ornate walls might reveal the truth—that there was nothing *to* see even if she did manage to make it past the smoke he blew in the world's eyes. Nothing of value anyway beyond the work he did for Marcus and the Crown. No secret garden with rose-lined walks, but an arid landscape of rock and dirt and a few struggling weeds. It was easy for him to portray the jaded, foolish wastrel because it wasn't very far from the shallow emptiness that lurked beneath his own image of himself.

What bothered him most was that he felt her mind's gaze shaping outlines of things inside him that were not there. Or at least he had not thought were there until he felt them lurching clumsily inside him like ogres stumbling in the subterranean dark. It was unsettling.

More than that, it was frightening.

He forced himself to look up but she had already turned away, the two lines between her dark brows etched deep. A face accustomed to worry and thought and…kindness. She didn't like to admit it, he thought, but it was there, even in her unjudgmental tolerance of her aunt's foibles. And of his.

She shifted, her lips parting, as if there wasn't enough air in the Schiavantis' trellised garden…

And suddenly there wasn't.

The flush of heat that struck him was as overwhelming as the opening of a great oven—it pressed back at him, inside and out—sudden and brutal. The garden ceased to exist, the plain wooden chair beneath him, the warm scent of food and wine, the chatter and clatter from the kitchen, the creaking of the stunted cypress tree catching the wind from the sea. Everything beyond the two of them was swallowed into mist.

His only thought, if it was even a thought, was, *I want her.*

It was pure, carnal, harsh, ripping through him like a serrated knife gutting a fish. It let loose a cascade of need—to touch her flushed skin, press his mouth to the warmth of her neck, breathe her in, feel her heat against him, take...

His very skin seemed to crackle, split, as if some new being was clawing its way out of him. It was focused on Phoebe like a hungry wolf on a stray lamb, absorbing everything about her— the curve of her cheek, the swell of her lower lip, the scent of jasmine that drew him closer, that made him want to fill his lungs with her, fill her body with his...

The heat was clashing with waves of cold, like an illness, and with shock he felt a wholly unfamiliar shudder of lust rise through him.

And panic.

What the hell is wrong with you? Have you gone mad?

Not mad, snarled the beast. *I want her.*

The words of this foreign epiphany were so loud in his head they finally woke him. He drew a deep breath and shoved it all down as he would a green soldier raising his head above the battlements.

Still, it took him a little longer to think of

something sensible to say. 'I think I need some of Matteo's limoncello. Then I shall see you home.'

Matteo came out on cue with the two glasses frosting with moisture from the noon heat. She took her glass and gave Matteo and Giulia her warm, encompassing smile and they basked in her evident pleasure as she told them how much she loved the *rixi e bixi*. And all the while Dominic sat and stewed in the tightening agony of the strange pit he'd tripped into.

All his life he'd thought he was immune to this sort of nonsense. Watching men succumb to the idiocy of lust and love had been as perplexing as it looked ridiculous. He'd come to regard his own lack of passion as a badge of honour and a relief. Life was much easier without your cock sounding its opinion of people at every turn.

He had a friend who was tone deaf, who couldn't understand music and couldn't carry a tune to save his life. In his own case it wasn't music, but physical passion he could not fully comprehend. While his friends seemed to experience the full range of the pianoforte, he was limited to a single octave and that was one he usually played solo.

He'd learned how to pleasure women as everyone seemed to expect it of him. With time he'd come to enjoy pleasuring them—it made him feel good to see them happy even if he didn't derive much personal physical enjoyment from the act beyond the most basic physical reaction. He rather thought it was easier to do if one wasn't focused on attaining one's own pleasure. Certainly the women seemed to concur and as a result he'd developed quite a reputation that had been fulfilling in itself. It was always nice to have one's skills appreciated. And if sometimes he'd been envious of the stories his friends had shared of the pleasure they took in their sexual exploits, he'd compensated by patting himself on the back for not succumbing to mindless idiocy like most mortals.

Hubris.

There had to be a penance for the smug sense of superiority he'd indulged in all these years. For him penance had finally arrived in the surprising form of Phoebe Brimford.

He ought to be happy the gods were only demanding he pay in an example of precisely how and why lust led to mindless idiocy. He'd underestimated it. Being dropped into a vat of boiling oil might be more comfortable than that raking, twisting heat that closed down his mental faculties more effectively than laudanum. He very much hoped what had just struck him was an aberration. He wasn't at all certain he wanted to experience that sensation again.

He drank his limoncello, the ice shavings numbing his tongue and throat. They weren't quite as effective at cooling the rest of him. The impact of the beast was still thudding expectantly in his chest and loins.

How long did this nonsense last?

'The limoncello is still as delicious as I remember,' she murmured. 'I was afraid I had been dreaming.'

He beat back the flames and did his best to smile at her.

'You shall have to return here for more.'

She didn't look up. 'I admit I would like to taste their inky squid again.'

Say absolutely nothing, Dominic. Not a word.

'We can return next week if you wish, Rosie.'

She tugged her lower lip with her teeth, and his stomach curled in on itself.

'Perhaps. Though we might be leaving for Verona soon.'

He ignored the twinge. It was probably a good idea. No, it was an *excellent* idea.

'Verona. Lady Grafton has friends there?'

'No. She is keen to visit Romeo's home. It is her favourite play.'

'Not yours?'

'Not in the least. Two silly children making awful mistakes because their families are also fools. The writing is sublime, of course, but the story is pure foolishness.'

'You are not a romantic, evidently.'

'Not about people. I think I could become quite romantic about food if it is as delicious as this.'

'Then you had certainly best come one more time before you leave. Third time lucky.'

Her eyes flickered to his and fell and she set down her empty glass and rose. 'I must return to the palazzo.'

He stood as well and realised his body ached as if he'd just played ten rounds of *calcio*.

Chapter Nine

⟨ornamental divider⟩

They walked in silence along one of the narrow canals. A breeze ruffled the water, carrying the cool scent of autumn tucked among the usual scents of sea and spice and crumbling brick and rotting wood. It would be four years now since he'd left England. It felt shorter and longer, a great chasm filled mostly with echoes. Even with all he'd achieved, it felt as insubstantial as the rest of him.

When they reached the Ponte dell'Accademia he stopped in a pocket of shade and they watched a little knot of gondoliers that had slowed to gossip, laughing and insulting each other. One called out a particularly rude description of another's mother as he rowed away, followed by his opponent's laughing roar and shaking fist.

Phoebe laughed as well, turning to Dominic. Her bonnet still hung from her hand and her hair glinted with the same old-gold lights as her extraordinary eyes.

'Sometimes I don't understand men. In other circumstances that might have begun a brawl.'

He smiled, trying to centre himself, but she was having the same effect on him as trying to stand in a gondola. He felt the need to shift, find his balance. It was there, but it kept evading him.

'The key is not to think too deeply. They were in a good mood. On another day the same remark might yet spark a nice little vendetta. We're simple creatures, sweetheart.'

It was only when he saw her flush that he noticed the endearment. He'd thrown that word at her before but somehow this time it felt...true. She *was* sweet under that cool-as-a-cucumber façade. And her heart was far too big, and soft. And by some strange twist she'd come to like him.

As she might like a stray dog in need of shelter.

'I'd best go now. Thank you for that lovely treat, Lord... Dominic.'

His name sounded foreign, like the wind rubbing over the mouth of a bottle.

He shivered and moved into the sun and she followed, pausing when they reached the centre of the bridge. The sun was full on her hair now, warming it to the earthy colours of the palazzos on either side, complete with glints of gold and brass, the wind flicking strands about her cheeks. She looked as if she belonged here. Above the jade waters with the cupolas of the Basilica di Santa Maria della Salute behind her.

That day he'd followed her there seemed a long, long time ago.

'That's a tautology, isn't it?' she said. 'Your name already means lord.'

He searched for something to say. 'I was named for my grandmother, Domenica. And she was named for some long-ago relative. But by chance both she and I were born on Sundays, so perhaps that played a part.'

'She was the Italian side of your family?'

'She was sold to my grandfather when she was fifteen. Her family was very wealthy and she had fallen in love with someone wholly unsuitable, and my grandfather, who was in Italy at the time escaping his creditors, was convinced by her father to marry her and save her family from disgrace and himself from poverty.'

'Fifteen. The poor girl. That is horrid.'

Pain flickered in her eyes. A soft-hearted sweetheart.

'*Life* is horrid. It was that or a convent. I don't know what she would have preferred, in truth. It saved the ducal fortunes for a while, but my grandfather quickly went through her dowry as well.'

'Was she very miserable?'

'Not really. Her own father had been very strict and she loved London. She was beautiful and vivacious and she very quickly discovered her husband did not in the least mind if she took lovers since he had plenty of his own. Dommy—that was what I called her—was full of fun.'

'You knew her well?'

'Very well. She raised me after my mother died in childbirth when I was two years old. Dommy's house was always lively. She loved music and made friends among musicians and artists and there was always noise and…activity in her house. She even turned one of the drawing rooms into a studio for artists and she would model for them in the nude. She was considered very scandalous, but because she was Italian and a duchess it was almost expected of her.'

'And you grew up amidst all this?'

'It seemed perfectly normal to me. She enjoyed being the centre of attention and she was proud of her body and her wit and wanted me to be the same. I was painted more times than I can recall. I suppose quite a few cherubs and young Davids are modelled after me. Artists enjoy free models.'

'Did *you* enjoy it?' Her words were tentative, but they demanded an answer. Long lost memories popped up above the surface. Standing on the raised dais, the wood hard beneath his bare feet, his muscles aching from the pose and a wreath of leaves scratchy against his forehead. Someone turning him, touching him, someone telling him to raise his arm, bend his leg, everyone watching, eyes wide, like owls perched on their stools, their paintbrushes like evil wizards' wands…

He remembered the cold.

'No.'

'Did she know that?'

'No. She loved that people lined up to paint me. It made her happy. So I didn't mind.'

'But you did mind. You weren't like her.'

I wanted to be.

He was still sensible enough not to say that. He smiled and shrugged.

'It was long ago. I dare say there were plenty of things you did for your parents that you didn't wish to do.'

The compassion in her eyes slipped behind her barriers as he'd hoped, but the intelligence was there.

'That is true. But when I was seven I realised they were wrong about the world.'

'Seven? That is precocious. What did they do?'

'Told me that God hated people who read the books I wanted to read. I told them I would choose a god who didn't read over other people's shoulders and turn up his nose at them like a censorious old biddy.'

'Good for you, Rosie. Though I suppose they weren't too pleased with your answer.'

She smiled. 'No. I learned to keep my opinions to myself after that.'

He straightened, as alert as if a knife had just

been pressed to his throat. 'What did they do to you?'

She hesitated, looking out towards the basilica. 'Nothing dramatic. I was given a week of solitude to consider my blasphemy.'

He moved closer, oblivious to the flow of humanity around them. 'They locked you in your room for a week?'

'Not in my room. That was my first visit to the redemption closet where *"the rebellious dwell in a parched land"*, subsisting on a daily cup of water, dry bread, and plenty of prayer. When I pointed out the next verse was all about God knowing what we really need in our heart, which in my case was my books, they added two more days. So you can see why I enjoy reading Cleland's book in church.'

There was laughter in her tigerish eyes, but he felt only a vicious outrage for that girl. He wanted to reach through time and crush her parents' bones, one by one.

She smiled, canting her head to one side. 'You look very fierce. There's no need. As you can see, I am quite in one piece and perhaps all the better for having my illusions starved out of me. A world without gods makes a great deal more sense to me. Very freeing. I enjoy my life.'

'Yes,' he said slowly. There was definitely an air of contentment about her; a sense of peace that made no demands on anyone but herself. Perhaps that was why he felt so comfortable with her. Unjudged.

'But it was different for you,' she continued with that disconcertingly direct gaze. 'You loved your grandmother. I don't know that I ever loved my parents. Milly was always more my parent than they were.'

'Milly?'

'Lady Grafton. I suppose she was to me what your grandmother was to you. What happened to your Dommy?'

'She fell afoul of one of her lovers and he strangled her and then threw himself into the Thames.'

Her mouth rounded into a shocked O. 'Oh, no, that is terrible! How old were you?'

'Eight, I think. Perhaps nine.'

'I'm so sorry, Dominic.'

'You needn't sound so agonised. That was aeons ago, swee—Phoebe. Old history.'

'Losing the woman who was a mother to you is never old history.'

He sighed and continued down the bridge. 'I shouldn't have told you any of this. Now you'll put it in the box of reasons why I'm the feckless fool I am. I don't want your pity, Phoebe.'

'Sympathy isn't pity.'

'It is still annoying.'

'Says the expert at annoying people.'

'I am rather good at it, aren't I?'

'As good as you are at evasion.'

'Not as good as you on that front. You're the master, or mistress, of making yourself invisible. Down to the spectacles that you don't need to read.'

'I *do* need them.'

'You didn't wear them in the basilica.'

She drew a short, sharp breath. 'You...you unsettled me.'

He had?

'I thought I annoyed you.'

'That, too. I forgot them in my room, but I was determined not to give you the satisfaction of thinking that you'd made me give up my reading. I *can* read without them, but the words are a little blurry and it gives me a headache.'

'So I annoyed you, unsettled you, and gave you a headache.'

She cast him a quick sideways smile. 'That sums it up nicely.'

He almost told her she had the same effect on him, but self-preservation finally intervened. They'd reached Campo San Stefano and children were playing with a stuffed leather ball by the statue in its centre, watched by a group of old men. A strong kick sent the ball speeding their way and he kicked it back, angling it through the gap between the wooden chairs at the other end of the square. The boys and old men cheered with a great deal of hand waving.

'Nico! Vieni, vieni a giocare!'

'Non adesso,' he called back and turned her towards the narrow road behind the palazzo.

'They seem to know you well.'

'I told you, I like *calcio*. My grandmother taught me.'

'Your grandmother may have been imperfect, but she sounds like a most amazing woman. *Nico*.'

'She was.' He almost told her Dommy would have liked her, but they'd reached the door to the palazzo courtyard and good sense finally prevailed. 'Thank you for an enjoyable afternoon, Miss Brimford.'

'Likewise, Lord Wrexham. Aren't you coming in?'

He shook his head. 'I have business elsewhere.'

She nodded, her face turning serious again. There was no condemnation. Merely that flicker of worry. It was almost worse. Her stray dog straying.

'Good day, then.'

The door closed softly behind her.

Phoebe entered the coolness of the palazzo and stopped to absorb its echoing shabbiness. Was this how Cinderella felt at midnight? As lights and warmth and excitement shrivelled into rags and duty?

Foolish Phoebe, she admonished herself. You are certainly no Cinderella, and you knew it was a mistake to go with him today. You knew you would enjoy it. Him. Yet you went and you allowed yourself to be charmed enough to do something you've never, ever done—you shared yourself with him.

Except it wasn't his charm that had pushed her over that line—it was the pain he hadn't really tried to hide. She hadn't wanted him to stand there alone on that pedestal, bared, used, even betrayed by those who should have protected him. So she'd offered her own pain as solace.

She wished she could formulate some excuse for herself—sometimes she did employ empathy as a tool; it was amazingly effective in manipulating people. But she'd had no thought of that today. There had been no calculation to her revelations. She'd wanted him to share himself with her and she'd wanted him to see her.

Foolish, foolish, foolish.

This was how mistakes were made—and in her occupation mistakes could harm others beside herself. It was beyond foolish—it was dangerous.

Make your own memories, indeed. Well, she'd done a good job of that. She doubted she would ever forget her visits to the Schiavantis. She very much hoped people would not pay for her indulgence.

She made her way up the stairs to her room. In the lazy hours of midday most of the guests were resting in their rooms. Milly wouldn't need her until they prepared for their visit to the Montillio casino that evening, which meant she had several hours yet to stew in the juices of her own stupidity.

Now at least she understood better how this man survived and thrived. It was as if he'd found her secret list of wishes and ticked them off one by one. Clever, clever. She wondered if he'd set out to do it on purpose for the pure fun of proving his skill or because her barbs had piqued his pride and his curiosity.

Strangely enough she thought he was being honest, in a way. She'd felt he truly had enjoyed her company at the restaurant. There had been a moment when she'd glimpsed a sudden sensual intensity in his gaze, felt it reach out and grab her as if he'd touched his hands to her cheeks, his fingers to her mouth. Her whole body had lit with crackling heat, making her muscles contract, her pulse lurch forward. But then he'd looked away and she'd sat in silence, scalded inside and out. She had never considered it possible, but perhaps... perhaps someone like him wouldn't turn down the opportunity of bedding her. His kind could find pleasure in all manner of corners of this world. But he would as easily move on and make new friends and have new experiences. Until drink or illness overtook him.

She set down her bonnet carefully, rolling the ribbons into a neat spool. Then she sat on the side of her bed, her gaze taking in the sparsely

furnished room, her little pile of books, her plain
dresses neatly folded and hung. Despite her occupation, her life was a simple one. As agents of
the War Office she and Milly had no need for a
home or permanence. Today she was in Venice,
tomorrow Verona, the next day wherever that duty
called. She had not been labelled the Zephyr for
nothing. She was nothing more than a passing
breeze. Barely noticeable.

This strange…friendship—if it was even
that—with Lord Wrexham was an anomaly.

Remember who you are, Phoebe. *What* you are.
You may enjoy his jests and his unforeseen attentions, but that is all. In the end what matters is
what you and Milly have built on the ashes of your
old lives. And what you have built is prodigious.
You are an excellent agent. One of Sir Oswald's
most trusted, despite being a woman. Perhaps as
trusted as Jack had been in his heyday.

Her uncle's deterioration was a warning she'd
not fully comprehended until now. Sir Oswald
had cautioned her there would be times when she
would be tempted to relax her guard. When he'd
told her she'd be in the greatest danger if she ever
imagined herself in love, she'd shot back that she
doubted he warned his male agents of such even-
tualities. Rather than be annoyed, he'd laughed.

'I worry far less about you on this account than
most of my agents, Phoebe. Men are far more
likely to think with their cocks than you with

your cunny, to be vulgar. In that sense your aunt is far more like them than you are. But my role is not merely to train you to complete your tasks, but also to prepare you for all possible dangers and most especially those within each of us. This is one of them, and in all likelihood one day you will be in the unenviable position of finding your mind in conflict with your body. So when that day happens, as it will, I want you to consider how you will separate it from your duties. I would hate to lose my trusted Zephyr for something so ephemeral and transient as an infatuation.'

She shivered, as if she could shake off this foreign confusion as one could send a dress crumpling to the floor. Oswald and Uncle Jack had given her plenty of good advice over the years, but right now the most pertinent was the one decent piece of advice her father had given her before she'd escaped his shackles: 'Don't stare at the sun or you'll ruin your eyes.'

Well, that was applicable here. Don't stare at Dominic or he might ruin your good sense.

Chapter Ten

Phoebe wasn't fond of gambling, but she had to admit that some of the Venetian gambling halls were not only excellent places to observe people and gather valuable information, but also rather wonderful on their own account.

Many of the ones located around St Mark's were not attended by respectable women, not even women who trod the outskirts of society like her aunt. But their little English crowd often spent the evenings in grand old palazzos along the canal, many of which clung to the mantle of noble grandeur they had held before Napoleon's conquest ended eight hundred years of the Venetian Republic. Their salons and drawing rooms were now transformed into *ridotti*, resplendent with gambling tables, musical entertainment, and delicious food.

Phoebe had two favourites. One was Casino Venier with its elaborate frescoes and ornate fireplaces and Delft tiles, and the other was the Palazzo Montillio, a newer casino not far from Rialto bridge with an elaborate Moorish façade and now crowded to the gills with visiting dignitaries. Established by Count Giovanni Montillio and the infamous owner of one of London's most successful gaming hells, Sebastian Crawford, it had swiftly become a favourite among Venetian and Austrian nobility. It wasn't merely the sumptuous rooms, deep play, and excellent wine; Crawford had also introduced one of his trademarks—female croupiers and entertainers.

Whatever the secret of Montillio's success, Phoebe noted as she and Milly accepted glasses of cool champagne, the rooms were full to brimming with the cream of international nobility. She was glad to be concentrating on something other than her strange lapse earlier that day. She'd surprised herself by falling asleep that afternoon, lulled by the unaccustomed food and spirits. She'd woken a little groggy, but reassured she'd exaggerated her strange fancies. It was merely as Milly had said—she wasn't accustomed to indulging herself and it was rather pleasant to do so now and again.

She ought to take it more lightly, enjoy it only for what it was in the moment. That was the resolution she set before her and felt better for it—calmer and even cheerful. She was certainly capable of enjoying some of life's pleasures without misconstruing them, wasn't she?

'One would think next month's diplomatic Congress is taking place at Palazzo Montillio rather than in Verona,' Milly murmured, her feathered fan brushing her gently rouged cheek.

'Even dyed-in-the-wool statesmen need to let their hair down a little, Milly.'

Her aunt's grin turned predatory. 'I don't think it's their hair they'll be letting down by the end of the night, Phoebe, dear.'

Phoebe's laughter was cut short as she noticed a familiar figure descending upon them.

'Good evening, Herr von Haas.'

Von Haas gave a sharp bow and nodded at them. 'Lady Grafton, Miss Brimford. I am glad to see you here. I have made enquiries regarding the Giardini Reali.'

His words sounded almost accusatory and Phoebe proceeded cautiously. 'I had not meant to sound intrusive, Herr von Haas.'

'You did not. You sounded interested in earnest and you ignited my own curiosity. I have secured the company of the garden's caretaker for a viewing. I would be happy if you would accompany me. And Lady Grafton may come as well if she wishes.'

Phoebe did her best not to look at Milly. 'We would be delighted, Herr von Haas. It is very kind of you to think of us.'

'Good. I shall inform you when it is arranged.' He bowed once more, hesitated, smiled, and was off.

'Well,' Milly said after a moment.

'Well?' Phoebe asked, sipping her glass of wine.

'Perhaps he really does like them quiet.'

'Who likes what quiet?' enquired a familiar voice behind them before Phoebe could answer. She closed her eyes briefly and turned, inwardly reciting her good resolutions regarding this man.

'Good evening, Lord Wrexham.'

'So your championing of von Haas was not merely on academic grounds, I see, Miss Prim.'

'He invited us to view his gardens,' Milly crooned, her fan swinging lazily as she lingered on the last word.

'He invited us to see the Giardini Reali,' Phoebe corrected sharply. 'We discussed them when we met in St Mark's Square. As they are not open to the public, he very kindly offered to take us there.'

'A signal honour. He is a very busy man.' The drawl was back, but the eyes were still sharp.

'He is. Which makes his invitation all the kinder.'

'Von Haas hasn't a kind bone in his body. He certainly didn't get where he is today by being kind.'

'Perhaps he's lonely?' Milly twirled her fan,

the pink feathers dancing. 'Even the unkind and the uncouth can be human at times.'

Phoebe couldn't help smiling at Milly's fine thrust, but she watched Wrexham. Again she saw the flicker of something not quite nice in his blue eyes. They were a far darker blue than von Haas's and today they were the colour of the sea beyond the lido—a turbulent blue that mariners knew to navigate warily.

'Am I being uncouth?' he asked. 'It is probably as *someone* once told me: I am far nicer when drunk.'

'Goodness!' Milly's eyes widened. 'Who told you such an *uncouth* thing?'

Wrexham looked to Phoebe, his smile twisting a little. 'Someone with a disconcerting tendency to be honest at the worst possible moment. Watch yourself with von Haas, Rosie; he's not as blockish as he appears. Now I'm off to do something about making myself nicer.'

Phoebe wasn't foolish enough to respond to that, however much she wished to. He was soon swallowed in a group of Russians and Venetians, the Russians handing round flasks that she presumed were filled with their adored vodka. That would probably work even faster than his own flask of whisky. She wondered how much he would lose to the Montillio bank tonight.

'*Rosie?*' Milly asked, one dark brow arching. It was a very annoying skill her aunt had mastered.

Phoebe shrugged. 'He enjoys mangling my name. Brimford became Primrose and then somehow Miss Rosie Prim. He thinks he's clever.'

'He *is* clever. That's the problem. I'd give him the same advice he gave you about von Haas. Watch yourself with Wrexham; he's not as blockish as he appears. Whatever he is now, he was once a very clever young man.'

'I know. I don't trust him in the least.' It was only half a lie, she assured herself.

'Good. Now, since for some unfathomable reason von Haas is clearly not interested in *moi*, I shall have to settle for a Russian bear instead of the Austrian variety. Come along. The game's afoot.'

Dominic watched the two women cross the Faro room. Lady Grafton was clearly on the hunt after being overlooked by von Haas. The surprise on her face when von Haas had clearly preferred speaking with Phoebe had been almost comical.

Dominic wasn't as surprised as he would have been only a week ago. As he'd learned much to his dismay, Phoebe Brimford might be overlooked at first, but she most definitely had a way of making herself seen and heard. And felt.

'A frowning jester. The worst kind,' drawled a deep voice behind him.

Dominic didn't turn to greet Sebastian Crawford. 'History's best jesters are melancholic, Seb.'

'Perhaps, but it suits you ill. Have a drink.'

Dominic took the flask Crawford extended towards him and drank while Crawford surveyed his little kingdom.

'Do you realise, Dom, if the Palazzo Montillio were to sink into the sea, half the ruling houses in Europe would be sorely deprived.'

'Tempting, then.'

Sebastian threw him a cynical look. 'Dukes' heirs make poor anarchists.'

'I'd rather be a poor anarchist than this particular duke's son.'

Sebastian pressed his hand to his chest. 'I think… I think my heart is bleeding.'

'An achievement, since by all accounts your heart, if you possess one, is little more than a shrivelled old prune.'

'You're in a fine mood today, Wrexham. By the way, what did von Haas want with your little companion?'

'She's Lady Grafton's companion, not mine. He invited her to visit the Giardini Reali.'

'With *him*?'

'Yes.'

'Hmm. Very strange.'

'Apparently they share a passion for Venetian history and art.'

'So long as that's the only passion they share. He'll eat her alive.'

'Not Miss Prim. She's made of sterner stuff

than most,' Dominic replied, trying not to show how unpalatable he found the notion of Phoebe and von Haas sharing anything at all. 'Give me another pull on your flask and I'll go fleece your casino of some of its ill-gotten gains.'

Chapter Eleven

Phoebe inspected the female croupier presiding over the Faro tables of Casino Montillio. The woman was dressed in a black silk and lace dress, which was almost nun-like in its stark simplicity, yet succeeded in looking anything but innocent. She was called La Flamme, probably due to her flame-coloured hair which was cleverly echoed in Veronese's painting *Mary Magdalene in the Wilderness*, which hung on the wall behind her, as if Mary Magdalene herself had paused her discourse with her conscience and stepped out of the painting to fulfil the fantasies of the men crowded around the table.

Even von Haas seemed taken with her, watching her with a concentration that was clearly unsettling her because she evaded his gaze unless absolutely necessary. Phoebe could sympathise. Von Haas's stare was unnerving even if one did not know he held the reins of power in Venice.

He stood tall and stiff and yet compelling. Phoebe had to admit he was a handsome man, but unlike her aunt she did not find him attractive. He had no…vulnerability.

'Didn't they teach you in Companion School that it was impolite to stare, sweetheart?'

Phoebe's hand tightened on her wine glass at his sudden appearance. Again. The man must have velvet instead of leather on the soles of his shoes.

'No. They taught me it was impolite to sneak up on people, Lord Wrexham. And I wasn't staring.'

'Were, too. I wouldn't start getting ideas about von Haas based on a few gestures of politeness. He might look like an overgrown angel, but believe me, he is anything but.'

'I wasn't staring,' she repeated. 'I was watching the play.'

'Of course you were.'

She turned to him. 'If you must know, I was watching my aunt and her new beau. Do you know anything about him?'

It worked. He transferred his attention to Milly and Alexei Razumov, a stocky yet handsome Russian officer almost two heads taller than Milly, whose laughing gaze was currently fixed adoringly on Razumov as she hung on his arm. Razumov's gaze in turn was directed at Milly's bosom—or at the diamonds that pulsed and winked above it, it was hard to tell. His grin was wide and toothy and he looked as if he could eat her in one bite, and Milly actually looked as if she might enjoy it. Phoebe smiled inwardly. Milly's acting abilities never ceased to impress her.

She turned from Milly's practised exhibition to her new nemesis. Lord Wrexham was watching the players, giving Phoebe an opportunity to examine him. In the two hours that had passed since their earlier meeting, he had clearly been enjoying the liquid refreshments. His hair was tousled, his cravat loosened, and there was a warm, reckless edge to his smile. But she could tell he was still not as drunk as he was likely to be by the evening's end.

Again she had the urge to tell him to stop there, go home. Go back to England even.

Foolish Phoebe.

'Alexei Razumov,' he replied to her question. 'He's the son of a Russian prince and a pain in Count Nesselrode's behind.'

'Oh? Why is that?'

'Because Razumov's father supports Nesselrode's long-time rival for the ear of the Tsar, a very canny man named Kapodistrias. He lost his last tussle with Nesselrode and is currently in exile in Switzerland, but there are rumours Razumov is here to make friends with the Austrians and sway them into inviting his patron to the Congress next month as well.'

'Oh. And that would be bad for this Nessel-rode fellow?'

'Not just for him. Kapodistrias is all for convincing the continental powers to pick a war with the Turks.'

'Is there a chance of that?'

'It depends. Razumov has two advantages over Nesselrode. He knows how to make friends, and no matter how deep he plays he always finds people to frank him. Like your aunt.'

'Oh, dear.' Phoebe sighed looking back to the Faro table, where a male croupier had now taken over the bank. 'I do wish Milly would find someone less profligate.'

'Is that part of your duties? Chaperoning your aunt's funds if not her virtue?'

'Chaperoning her funds is *my* virtue. I must find her someone more stable. Who was the man who was remonstrating earlier with Razumov at the Faro table?'

'That was Nesselrode himself. The Russian foreign minister.'

'Oh. Is he married?'

'Good lord, woman, you aim high. Don't waste your aunt's time on him. Unlike many of these uniformed quacks, he is truly only here to promote the Russian cause ahead of the Congress. Find her someone more…doughy. They're safer.'

Despite herself, she burst into laughter. Two men who'd stood with their backs to them turned, brows raised. She flushed a little and directed an admonishing stare at them before turning back to Lord Wrexham. He was now watching her with the same narrow-eyed look she caught some-times—assessing, focused.

Not very drunk. She frowned. She'd thought him further along by now. His gaze lowered and settled on her mouth.

'I didn't think it was possible but you have an even more seductive laugh than Lily. You should let it loose more often, Rosie.'

She swallowed, heat battling a completely un-expected surge of jealousy. 'Who is Lily? One of your local *innamorata*?'

The watchful panther look became even more intent. 'The wife of my closest friend.'

'Oh. That sounds…uncomfortable.'

He smiled. 'I'm not attracted to *her*, just her laugh. It set the standard. Until now.'

She shook her head, at him and at herself. For some reason he had decided she needed to be won over. She wasn't certain why or for what, but she would have none of that. That would be a bad, bad mistake.

'I give you credit for fashioning your com-pliments with the skill of the glass blowers of Murano, but surely you could gain more by em-ploying your arts elsewhere?'

'Gain?'

The warmth had evaporated from his voice and

she flushed again, this time with shame. She'd been cruel and for no other reason than he made her uncomfortable.

'I apologise, Lord Wrexham, but I don't care for compliments. Not that I often receive them, but still… I prefer not being noticed. For any reason, good or bad.'

She'd given him a wide opening and she waited for the counterattack, her cheeks hot and her heart thumping. She'd dealt with far worse in her life, but she felt as exposed as a crab who'd just shed its shell.

'I wish you'd call me Dominic.' There was no acrimony in his voice, and a wholly different heat joined the fray.

She shook her head. They weren't in the quiet alleyways of Venice now. All she had to do was look about her and see that she did not belong in his world except in so far as her role required.

'You're a very stubborn young woman,' he said and turned away, inspecting the crowd.

'And you are a very stubborn young man.'

'I'm thirty-five. Hardly young.'

'I'm twenty-eight. Hardly young either.'

'You wear your years better than I do, Rosie.'

She smiled. 'That's not true, but thank you.'

'You see? That wasn't so hard.'

'What?'

'Accepting a compliment.'

She shrugged.

'And up go the battlement and fortifications,' he murmured and returned to observing the crowd.

She watched his profile, more puzzled than ever. The more he revealed, the more obscure he became. It was unsettling and she disliked being unsettled.

'Don't you ever tire of flirting, Lord Wrexham?'

'Does a prima donna singer ever tire of singing or a pianist of playing?' he answered without looking at her. 'I'm good at it, it isn't hard, and it's expected of me.'

'But a singer probably derives enjoyment from her art. Do you?'

His chest rose and fell, just enough out of rhythm to be telling.

'Or is it merely a matter of survival for you?' she prodded, and he turned to look at her.

'Everything is a matter of survival in the end.'

'That is no answer, or perhaps it is.'

He gave a grunt of annoyance. 'What do you want? A confession that it bores me half to tears sometimes? I dare say an opera singer practising her scales is bored with that part of her art as well. And yet she practises her scales for far many more hours than she sings upon a stage. So?'

She couldn't help smiling. 'Are you singing now? Or is this the slogging part?'

'If you think this is flirting, my performance is truly abysmal.'

'Oh, no. It is masterful. I notice you tailor your charm to your object. Perhaps this is one of the arias in your repertoire.'

'I am *not* flirting with you,' he snapped.

'Honesty can be very charming, especially when rare,' she noted calmly, rather pleased to have annoyed him so. She watched his temper teeter on the edge, but then that same honesty seemed to spread over the rest, his eyes lighting with laughter.

'You truly are a menace, Phoebe Brimford. And annoyingly observant. I dare say you will say it is my fault for needling you in the first place.'

'Oh, *I* never say *I told you so*. I am above such pettiness.'

He laughed. 'An absolute, abominable little menace. In answer to your question, on some exceedingly rare occasions I very much enjoy flirting. Unfortunately, that is usually when my performance is at its worst.'

She didn't tell him he was wrong. That this performance, if it was that, was indeed masterly. She might have achieved her aim of exposing a little more of his inner workings, but with each lever and cog revealed she was being drawn in, some fabric of her caught between the wheels, tugged deeper and deeper into the mechanism. She could feel it as firmly as a tide dragging at her feet.

His eyes narrowed. 'I wish I could read that twisty mind of yours, Rosie. I have a feeling it would be a revelation.'

She was saved from answering and from the burst of fear and heat deep inside her by the trill of the piano. A Scarlatti sonata swept in from the adjacent salon and she turned to listen, her heart beating hard.

'How beautiful,' she managed, and Dominic took her arm lightly.

'Let us go to listen, then. Your aunt is fully occupied in any case.'

She didn't resist and he led her out into the corridor, which was empty but for footmen carrying trays. She hesitated, but his hand curved over her arm, not pressing, just…warm.

'Trust me, I know the best place to listen in peace.'

Trust me.

An absurdity, but she followed anyway. After all, she liked places to listen in peace. Her speciality. And she could use some peace to calm the sudden clamour of her nerves.

The wall at the end of the corridor was covered by a thick burgundy curtain from ceiling to floor and Dominic pushed it aside to reveal a modest door that had been covered with the same gilt-embossed wallpaper. It led to a narrow veranda along the side of the palazzo where light and music streamed out, the shadows of the guests etched on the balustrade like dark fingers reaching into the night. She took a step towards the light, but his hand tightened.

'No, this way. It is even better.' His voice was a warm promise and the hairs on her nape rose. It was foolishness incarnate, but she followed again. Up steps that hugged the outside of the building guarded by an iron railing and onto the veranda on the floor above the salon.

'Listen,' he murmured.

The windows of the room behind them were dark and shuttered and they seemed to float above the small canal flickering with the lights from the palazzo. Only a few feet beneath them were guests and lights and noise, but up here they were in a separate world—darker, quieter…safe. The last sensation made no sense, but she could not chase it away. Didn't want to.

Listen.

For a moment all she could hear was her heart and then the music pushed its way in.

Downstairs the rumble and murmur of the crowd had dulled those beautiful notes, but it was as if they'd risen above the clouds where only the lightest birdsong reached. Here the Scarlatti was as pure as water bubbling up from a mountain spring. She leaned on the balustrade, soaking in the music as it rose, broken now and then by the faraway call of the gondoliers.

The pianist continued with Mozart, a tribute to

the city's conquerors, then a lovely French ballad full of joy, and finally a Russian tale of passion and yearning.

Like the food and wine Dominic had offered, the music robbed her of her edges. She hadn't felt so full or so empty for a long time. Not for years and years. Perhaps not ever. The strange fear that had struck her fell away and for once she was completely at peace with herself and with the strange, damaged man beside her. When it stopped and the applause broke her dream, she turned to him and smiled.

'Thank you, Dominic. That was a lovely gift.'

He was facing her, his hip against the balustrade, but for once she didn't mind his scrutiny. Nor the silence that stretched. She was content.

Finally, he spoke. 'I'm not a completely useless fellow, then?' His voice was more gruff than rough and the increasingly familiar surge of pity at the waste of him coursed through her. She held out her hand.

'Not useless at all. You've been very kind to me and I've often been ungracious. I'm sorry.'

He took her hand. 'I don't think *kind* is the word.'

'It is the word I choose. It is kind to want to share something you enjoy with others when you have nothing to gain from it.'

'You think I have nothing to gain from it?'

'Nothing but in the sharing of that pleasure,'

she replied. 'As you did by taking me to the Schi-avantis. That was a kindness, too.'

'Perhaps I am trying to seduce you.'

She tensed a little, but his words sounded more an accusation than a suggestion and there was a sulky twist to his beautiful mouth as if he was struggling against the current of her words. The foolish part of her that kept stirring when he approached wished his words *had* been a suggestion. A kiss on a Venetian veranda between the starry sky and the indigo canal would be something more than a kindness.

'Perhaps you are finding it as hard as I to accept an honest compliment?'

'Have you ever been kissed, Phoebe?'

'Yes. Do you find that so unlikely?' She answered as abruptly as he'd asked, unsettled that his question had mirrored her thoughts.

'Not in the least,' he answered. 'I might have three weeks ago. You certainly did your best to present a thoroughly strait-laced front. Not any longer. Now I would be very surprised if you hadn't kissed someone in your twenty-eight sage years. But that's a problem, you see.'

'It is?'

'For me, not for you. You were wrong. Apparently my kindness does have an object at the moment. Right now I would very much like to join the list of the men you've kissed.'

The cool marble of the balustrade felt rough

under her fingers, its edges pressing into her palm. She should not be seduced, not by words, or smiles, or wary dark blue eyes.

'There are at least a dozen women in the salon below who would be more than ready to welcome your kisses and more. You needn't lower your standards on a whim, Lord Wrexham.'

He moved abruptly towards her. 'Don't. Don't you dare use me as a bludgeon against yourself.'

She was already flushed, but the heat that spurted up from her chest was almost choking this time. His swift defence of her almost felt as if she'd insulted someone important to him, and that alarmed her even more than her reaction to his suggestion.

'That is rather dramatic of you, Lord Wrexham. Why on earth would you think of kissing me if not on a whim induced by the wine and the music? I know I'm no beauty like your many lovers.'

'I don't have lovers.'

'Bed partners, then, if you wish to split hairs.'

'I don't. I meant what I said. I don't take lovers. Or bed partners. I won't say I haven't had liaisons, but unlike your aunt I mostly prefer to confine my risks to losing my father's funds and falling off bridges in a drunken stupor.'

She stared. In the dark his face looked like a statue carved into the marble pillars. She'd accepted that he didn't always enjoy flirting, after all, it must be exhausting to charm so many people, but this… He didn't look as if he was lying, but…he *must* be jesting.

'I see I've finally succeeded in shocking you, Rosie Prim.' His voice was sharp with self-derision and she pulled herself out of her surprise.

'Yes. I don't know if I believe you. Gossip often exaggerates, but it rarely fabricates completely.'

He shrugged. 'Believe what you wish.'

He was lying. He must be… Was he?

'But I don't understand. Why not…if you can…?'

'Why not bed someone if they're willing?' he completed the question for her.

'Well, yes.'

'Why don't *you* bed Banister or Clapton? They're willing enough.'

She was about to deny it, but honesty forced her to admit there was some truth to that.

'But that is different. They might be willing to…to bed me because as a companion to Lady Grafton I am considered available and probably cheaper and safer than a local courtesan, but that is not to say that I am willing merely because they are.'

'I don't want to bed someone because they're willing, either. And you're doing it again, talking about yourself as if you're unattractive. You do your damnedest sometimes, but it doesn't work. Men are simple creatures, love. Beauty is nice enough on a museum wall, but that isn't what starts most fires.'

If he was waiting for her to ask him what did start fires, she was *not* about to oblige. And she would *not* ask him whether he still wished to kiss her after she had thoroughly ruined the mood, either. Her role in Venice was not to join the ranks of the fools.

Say thank you and goodnight and return to the safe, noisy crowd, Rosie...

She shut her eyes and corrected herself. *Phoebe.* She was forgetting her own name. This was *very* bad.

'You needn't look like I am about to toss you into the canal, Rosie. I've never kissed anyone who didn't want me to. Come. I'll see you back inside.'

She allowed him to take her arm and guide her towards the stairs. He'd done his best to make his tone playful but she could hear the coolness there and...hurt. Her heart ricocheted between heat and an ache at the thought that she might indeed have hurt him. She didn't want that.

'Dominic.' She grasped his arm and he stopped, his hand on the knob of the wooden door, his profile gilded by light from the windows below. 'It isn't that I don't want you to kiss me.'

'You needn't explain. It was foolish of me to mention it.'

He sounded so formal her heart melted further.

'It wasn't foolish, and perhaps if I were someone else I wouldn't have…prickled up like that. But you must see that I was caught off guard.'

He shrugged, his hand still on the knob, but he didn't open the door, so she continued.

'I am not accustomed to being propositioned by…by…'

'By drunken sots?'

'Do not put words in my mouth. I meant… Oh, drat…by handsome men. Unless they *are* drunk and could not particularly care what they grab. And you are not like that. I do not know *how* to respond.'

'That's simple. Yes, thank you, or no, thank you.'

He was twisting the knob to and fro. She watched it, trying to gather her resolve to force both of them back into the corridor and sanity. Back and forth went the knob. Yes or no. Yes or no.

What had Milly said? Life was brutish and short.

She laid her hand on his. 'Yes, thank you.'

His hand froze under hers, clamped hard on the knob. 'Are you trying to save my feelings?'

'For heaven's sake, you are not a boy with a skinned knee.'

He smiled suddenly. 'I'm being even more of an idiot than usual, aren't I?

'*I* certainly am. Do you wish to kiss me or not?

Or was all this merely to prove to yourself you could...?' Her words were cut off as he caught her about the waist and raised her onto the balustrade. She squeaked in alarm. 'Careful!'

Her eyes were level with his now, dark as night and glinting with starlight. Her mouth went dry, the rest of her melted.

'I very, very much want to kiss you, Rosie.' His voice was low, almost a hum. His hands were firm but soft about her waist. 'That was all I was thinking about while you were lost in the music. You wear your pleasure like a shining halo. Like a goddess rising with the sun. I was aching to touch you and feel all that joy bubbling inside you just as I was aching to lick the *limoncello* from your lips at the Schiavantis'.'

Her tongue touched her lower lip and she could have sworn she caught the bittersweet tang of the limoncello there. She was aching, too, just from his words, the heat he wasn't trying to mask. Her gaze dropped to his mouth. It was still beautifully formed, but that wasn't what caught her attention. It was the soft swell of the lower lip, which he used so well when he was sulky, and the pale line just beneath it from an old scar.

She touched her fingers gently to that line, tracing upward from it to the border between the new stubble and softness of his cheek and upwards to the uncompromising cheekbones. He didn't move as she explored, but his breath was short and shallow.

It was very bad. She knew it. Liking him was very bad. But she *did* like him. She looked up again. His eyes were still fixed on hers, wary and waiting. He seemed almost...scared. Though she knew it could not be true, she didn't want him to be, and without thinking she smiled.

He exhaled a sharp breath and pulled her towards him. Her arms instinctively went about his neck, which was a good thing because the impact of having her body pressed against him was far more powerful than the music and the limoncello combined. The ache she'd been carrying inside her like a fist burst its dam, flooding her with heat and the conviction that this was right. So very, very right.

'This is a little mad,' he said, his voice shaky against her hair, and she didn't know if he was referring to kissing her or doing it on a balustrade high above the canal. Both felt mad and yet both didn't.

She leaned her head back to look up at him and his hand settled very gently on her cheek, his eyes black as pitch in the darkness but as hot as a desert sun, searing her. If he'd pushed her off her perch right then, she might not have even realised it until she hit the water beneath. But all he did was bend his head slowly and touch his mouth to hers.

His kiss was surprisingly soft at first, his mouth brushing gently against hers, shaping, testing. His tongue touched the centre of her upper lip, a gentle invitation to open her mouth and she did. Her tongue met his, briefly, a tingling sensation like touching a galvanic machine. She shivered, her arms tightening about his neck as she pressed upwards, opening her mouth further against his. She wanted that again, more.

He groaned, his hand shifting down her back, curving over her behind and bringing her even closer. Close enough to feel the hard pulsing of his erection against her. This was another galvanic shock and her body jerked against his, greedy heat racing through her. He wanted her. It wasn't words. He wanted her and she…she wanted this… *him*…

She slipped her fingers into the warmth of his thick, dark hair and kissed him back as she'd imagined, tasting him as he tasted her, delighting in the pressure of his mouth on hers, her nerves bursting like fireworks as he caught her lower lip between his teeth, suckling it and caressing it with his tongue. She heard a deep thrumming moan and realised it was hers, as if her body had taken hold of the reins and she was nothing more than a shocked presence clinging to her saddle.

She let her hands roam as his did, feeling the tense ridges of muscle in his back, slipping under his coat to find the warm linen, curling her fingers into it as she dragged it from his waistband. The urge to touch him was as elemental as thirst. Still, her fingers hesitated before brushing the skin she'd revealed. They curled away from the contact, then settled, capturing his responsive shiver. He broke off the kiss, but didn't move away, his mouth against her cheek, his breath hard and fast.

'Do that again,' he muttered. She did, the lightest sweep of her fingertips, gathering textures and sensations, revelling in the velvet of his skin over hard, tense muscles. Beautiful.

Her hands lost their boundaries, merging with him, pressing and brushing as she mapped his back, his every responsive shudder, the sounds he tried to keep behind clenched teeth and failed. Each one peeled back another layer around the hard core inside her, and she felt them fall away with a mix of excitement and fear. She'd never felt anything like this. Never even known she was capable. But here, suspended above the canal, inches away from slipping into darkness, only his arms holding her safe on the balustrade…

Even in the uncharted territory of this pleasure, a little voice was calling out for her to stop, that the hard fist at her centre had to be kept safe…

She almost managed to withdraw when he cupped her face and raised it, his gaze dark and luminous as a starved wolf's. It was an unequal battle and all thoughts of safety faded, her eyelids shivering closed as he bent to kiss her with a hunger as hot and menacing as a beast and as beautiful as joy. His hand fisted up the fabric of her skirt, slipped under it, curving over her bare leg, his palm blazing hot against her, his thumb caressing the sensitive skin of her inner thigh, moving closer and closer to the thudding ache she knew was at the core of her growing agony. It was so right... The surge of incandescent excitement spreading out from that contact, the heat gathering at her core like a stoked fire. She was pulsing with it, with his touch, his taste. With him...

She pulled herself closer and he groaned and for a moment they were unbalanced, and finally self-preservation awoke. She grabbed for the balustrade, her eyes opening. They didn't fall. Probably hadn't even been in danger of that. The sensation of vertigo and falling had been something else entirely. But they were both frozen, breathing hard.

Very slowly, as if before a weaving snake, Dominic withdrew his hand. Her breath shuddered as even that contact crashed through her like discordant cymbals.

Madness. She shifted sideways, slipping off the balustrade and out of his reach.

'I went too far,' he said to the building opposite.

She wanted to say something light, sophisticated. What would Milly do? Laugh? Coo? Compliment him on his prowess? She had no idea what one did when one's world had been rocked by a kiss. She didn't want to say anything. Or for him to say anything.

'I must return. Goodnight, Dominic.'

There, that was sensible and calm. But as she walked past him, her hand reached out before she could stop it and her fingers brushed his sleeve.

Chapter Twelve

The light of day was a strange thing. It was possible to have one thought at night and a completely different one simply by dint of shining a little sunlight on it.

Dominic stared at the stripes of light cutting across the fresco of Daphnis and Chloe on the wall. He'd forgotten to close the curtains when he'd fallen into bed. Or rather, it had been too hot to close them. He'd needed the night breeze to cool him down.

That damned kiss.

How the *hell* was he going to face her now?

He could hardly remember rejoining the noisy crowd of the palazzo. The aftermath of their embrace had been worse than being drunk—he'd been steaming with unsatisfied lust and yet euphoric, a foreign combination that he couldn't really remember now it was over, like the tail end of a dream.

His body did, however, remember that it wanted her. He'd woken with a raging erection, still tangled in confused dream images of floating high above the canal, his body entwined with hers, her amber hair streaming around them like the wind and her eyes gleaming gold with laughter and pleasure. Then they'd suddenly plunged into the canal, surging through the water like mating dolphins, the water warm and smooth as liquid silk as it cocooned them together.

He wished he could have stayed in that dream rather than face reality.

He forced open his eyes, scattering the images, and focused on the fresco. It depicted a shepherd and shepherdess managing to copulate while playing the pan pipes. This was the best bedroom other than the Contessa's, but he'd always found the painting rather dull. He imagined generations of di Benedettis might have masturbated to its erotic promise, but it had done nothing for him and it did nothing now. That conflagration on the balcony might feel as if it had altered him in some elemental way, but it clearly hadn't affected his response to nude art.

He sat up, scrubbing a hand through his hair. He was being ridiculous. That kiss might have been a surprise, but there was no need to make too much of it, either to himself or to her. After all, all he had done was live up to his reputation. All that talking about flirting and how empty it was... Perhaps this was some form of cosmic revenge for being far too honest with her? A lesson to keep his mouth shut and his eye on the game?

The less he made of it, the less there was of it.

This assertion fell flat. Try as he might, there was no possible way he could convince himself nothing at all extraordinary had happened on that balcony. For the first time in his life he had been knocked on his back by lust. It was as if his whole life he'd been living a lie. A strange, muted lie. Like a dog raised in a cellar being suddenly released onto a wide, sun-drenched field swarming with plump rabbits. It was...overwhelming. He wasn't certain at all that he liked feeling this way. He was absolutely certain he didn't like knowing this might sneak up on him again and there was nothing he could do to prevent it.

No. There was something he *could* do. He could keep away from Phoebe. He *would* keep away from Phoebe. His reputation wouldn't be harmed by being caught *in flagrante delicto*, but hers would. She deserved better than being dragged into his sordid little world merely because his body had woken from hibernation.

A soft knock interrupted his uneasy thoughts and the ageless di Benedetti caretaker Emilio entered.

'Signor Crawford is waiting in the library. I gave him coffee.'

Dominic glanced with surprise at the clock on

the mantelpiece. He'd overslept and missed their rendezvous. For the first time in years. Even when he was out all night, he never slept this late.

'Hell. I'll be right down.'

Sebastian was sprawled in Dominic's favourite armchair and a half-smile curved his mouth when Dominic hurried in.

'So this is what they mean when they say the worse for wear. Either you had one hell of a night, or you had one *hell* of a night, Dom. Did it have something to do with Lady Grafton's companion?'

Dominic hoped he wasn't flushing. 'Why would you say that?'

'Perhaps because I saw the two of you slip in from the balcony last night.'

'I was showing her the view of the canal.'

'A courtesy which required your shirt to be untucked?'

Dominic cursed his friend.

'It's none of your business, Sebastian.'

'It is if you miss our meetings. I was worried someone had pushed you into a canal. Possibly the clever Miss Brimford.'

'Why does everyone associate me with falling into canals?'

'Probably wishful thinking, old friend. It isn't like you to be distracted.'

'I'm not. That was an aberration.' He changed the subject. 'That was quite a successful night for

Montillio's. Your new croupier-cum-entertainer was very well received. I dare say your cousin was pleased with your creation.'

Sebastian swirled the coffee in his cup as if he could read the future of his and his cousin's gambling house in the dregs.

'Yes. I admit I thought he was introducing her too soon, but she did well last night.'

Sometimes Dominic couldn't quite read Sebastian, but he knew when his friend was holding his cards close to his chest. They'd worked together in the past and Dominic had been happy when Marcus had sent Sebastian to Venice under the guise of opening the Montillio Casino. It was a perfect cover for their activities and had the added benefit of allowing Dominic a home playing ground where he could safely rack up losses to the house bank.

Sebastian rose and poured himself more coffee. 'So, let's discuss how we stand now that we've eliminated Farnsworthy and Darlington from the list of suspects.'

'We're down to the Claptons, father and son. They were always the most likely. We've baited the hook, so now it is time to see which of them rises to it.'

'If anyone is selling state secrets to the Austrians I would very much like to pin it on George Clapton, but so far all we know is that he's a nasty bit of goods with a small mind and grabby hands.

Not someone I'd expect the likes of von Haas to trust to keep his mouth shut about selling state secrets.'

'Still, we cannot ignore him. I know he's running low on funds, and now Sir Henry has kicked him out of the house he doesn't have easy access to his father's documents.'

'He'll be back in Papa's home during the Consul's ball the day after tomorrow. He might make a move them.'

'I'll keep an eye on him.'

Sebastian eyed him with a faint frown. 'No distractions this time?'

Dominic clenched his jaw, more annoyed at himself than Sebastian.

'No. I've had my fun.' The words burned even as he spoke them and he went to refill his own cup.

'Is something wrong, Dom?'

There was true concern in Sebastian's voice and Dom grimaced at his cup, but he kept his voice light as he spoke over his shoulder. 'All this concern because I kissed a lady's companion? I'm reputed to have had sex with half of Venice. What's one kiss more or less?'

'I'm not a member of your audience, Dom, remember?'

Dominic sighed. He wasn't in the mood for an inquisition. He wasn't in the mood for much. He knew he'd made a mistake. A string of mistakes.

'I never should have taken her to the Schiavantis' in the first place,' he muttered to himself.

'You took her *where*?' Sebastian demanded, sounding far more shocked at this than at the admission Dominic had kissed her.

'What does it matter? I came across her at Martelli's bookshop and she was hungry.' Damn, now he was reduced to twisting the truth. But at least it served to distract Sebastian.

'What did you eat?'

'Rixi e bixi.'

Sebastian sighed beatifically.

'Thursday. Wait a moment.' He frowned abruptly. 'Martelli's bookshop was closed on Thursday. His godson's wedding. I know because Giovanni had to attend as well.'

Dom cursed himself, again. 'I took her on Tuesday, but then Giulia and Matteo insisted she come back for *rixi e bixi* on Thursday.'

'They insisted.'

'They liked her.'

'They aren't the only ones, apparently. What the devil are you playing at, Dom? This isn't like you.'

'I know, damn it. I've never made such a fool of myself in my life, and my whole façade is based on playing the fool.'

Sebastian smiled. 'Don't be so hard on yourself. In fact, it's nice to know you're human and can end up with your entrails in a twist like the rest of us.'

For a moment Dominic considered confiding in Sebastian. But what the devil could he say? That for the first time in his life he was desperate to bed a woman. A woman he had no right to take advantage of. Who thought him weak and a waste. Yet she still liked him despite her disdain for what she thought he was. This conviction made his heart speed up even more. Like a damn fool boy. It was ridiculous yet it felt…good. He'd never wanted to be *liked* before. It had never occurred to him it could feel…necessary. Damn, this was foolishness incarnate.

'It doesn't feel *nice*.' He poured himself some more coffee. 'It's a damn nuisance. And ill-timed. Until this issue is resolved I should stay well away from her.'

'Agreed. In fact, perhaps I should be the one trailing Clapton—'

'No,' Dominic interrupted. 'The whole point of my role as drunken fool is that no one takes me seriously, so I'm given free rein. You start wandering around the British Consul's house and Clapton the Elder will want to know why. Don't make a mountain out of a molehill. I might act like it, but I'm not a complete idiot. At least not yet.'

Chapter Thirteen

I want to go home.

Had Phoebe been in a good mood, she would have smiled at the childish thought that was throbbing in her head like a bad tooth. But she was not in a good mood. Now that Milly had slipped out of Sir Henry Clapton's ballroom on the burly arm of Alexei Razumov, Phoebe's role for tonight was reduced to her least favourite occupation of waiting patiently while others did the work. She was usually good at waiting, but tonight she was tense and unsettled and everything that made it abundantly clear that kissing Venice's *enfant terrible* had been a serious mistake.

For heaven's sake, Phoebe. What had you been thinking? Or rather, why *hadn't* you been thinking?

Dominic was clearly regretting it as well. As far as she knew, he'd not returned to the Gioconda since then, and even when she'd spotted him entering Sir Henry Clapton's ballroom with Mr Hibbert an hour ago he hadn't once come near her.

He hadn't even looked at her.

It was no excuse that he'd arrived late, as always, and drunk, as always. Both he and Hibbert had clearly begun their evening elsewhere, and with gusto. They arrived close to the stroke of midnight, looking a little worse for wear. As usual the women didn't seem to mind. Dominic had already gathered a little crowd of them, like colourful petals about his dark centre. He was smiling down at them and she could hear their laughter from here.

Well, if one was to learn a lesson, it was best learnt fast and hard. She ought to be thankful to him for that.

'Miss Brimford?' Phoebe turned at the voice behind her. A blank-faced footman was addressing some point above her left eyebrow. 'Lady Grafton is unwell. A maid is waiting by the stairs to take you to her.'

Phoebe went into alert. This was not according to plan. Had that lug Alexei harmed her when she'd tried to coax him outside? Tense and ready, Phoebe hurried in the direction the footman indicated and found a maid waiting in the corridor, a rather sullen expression on her round face as she watched Phoebe approach.

'Where is Lady Grafton?' Phoebe asked and the maid curtsied, looking even sulkier. She turned and hurried down the corridor, clearly in a hurry to return to her own business. Phoebe's mind rushed ahead. Had something gone wrong and Milly had had to feign illness?

The maid opened a door at the end of the corridor and Phoebe hurried into the gloom.

'Milly? What...?'

She felt rather than saw the movement. She turned in time to see the maid's grin, the glint of a coin in her hand, just before George Clapton entered and closed the door behind him.

'Alone at last.'

Several sensations swept through Phoebe at George Clapton's slurred words. The first was relief—this had nothing to do with Milly or their mission. The second was alarm—a drunkard was unpredictable and therefore always dangerous, no matter what weapons one possessed. The third was annoyance—with herself at being caught off guard. Here was proof of the price of being distracted with trivialities. The fourth, and fifth, and sixth sensations were frustration, impatience, and anger. This was not the first time men had thought her fair game—poor, plain, without recourse. A low-hanging fruit for them to pluck to assuage their wayward cocks.

She pulled herself back from all of these reactions, concentrating only on what mattered. 'I think there must be some mistake, Mr Clapton...'

'Oh, no mistake. You needn't play coy with me.

I know how your aunt gets by. Saw her slink off into the shadows with that drunken Cossack. No reason why you shouldn't have some fun yourself. Couldn't do it back at the Gioconda, though. Too many busybodies. But now we're on my turf and Father's busy with the guests we've time for some quick fun.'

'No, we haven't, Mr Clapton. I am not interested in any *"fun"*, quick or otherwise. Kindly stand aside and allow me to leave.'

His sandy brows lowered. 'No point in playing the prude. I've seen the books you read. I keep thinking of you, in your room, letting down your hair, in bed with your books…touching yourself…' His breath shortened, his voice tightening but still heavy with wine. He shoved his hand deeper into his pocket, making no attempt to hide what it was doing in there. 'You can touch me instead.'

Phoebe supposed the proper thing to do for a true dried-up spinster would be to shriek or faint, or both, but that was risky on far too many levels. She compromised by picking up a square-based candlestick from a table. It glinted dully in the darkened room.

'The only thing I shall be touching you with is this candlestick, Mr Clapton. I am afraid you have a very mistaken opinion of me.'

He laughed, the bastard. 'Is that how you like it? A bit of rough?'

'I would say the edge on this candlestick is rather more sharp than rough. Shall we test it?'

His laughter faded as the veil of spirits lifted a little, and the sulky frown pushed forward again. 'Don't be a prissy fool. I know you're not an innocent. Not living with that promiscuous doxy. And I've seen you making up to Wrexham, too. Not that he'd touch a plain meg like you, not when he has all those beauties panting for him. You'd do well to take what you can. I'll make it worth your while. You look like you could use some pin money to buy yourself something pretty.'

She hefted the candlestick, so damn tempted to swing. 'Stand aside, Mr Clapton—'

They were both caught off guard as the door swung open, catching Clapton on the behind and propelling him forward a couple of stumbling steps.

'Where the devil does he keep the...? Ah, there you are, Clapton. You'll know where the brandy is, won't you? Be a good fellow and point... Oh, hello there, Miss...ah... Miss Primbroad... I say, why are you waving that candlestick?'

The last part of Wrexham's ramble was rather less slurred, as if it had penetrated his alcoholic haze that he'd intruded on a less than pleasant moment. Clapton cursed, but Phoebe didn't lower the candlestick. Nor did she answer the rhetorical question. Dominic moved deeper into the room, squinting at them.

'I say. What's afoot? Trouble? Are you misbehaving, Clap?'

'Go away, Wrexham.'

'Don't think I care to. Not at all the thing, making women brandish candlesticks. Take a hint, man.' His tone was still singsong, but there was something hard beneath and Clapton cursed again. Drunk or sober, Dominic had quite a few inches on him, not to mention muscles.

Dominic grinned and rubbed his fist. 'Shall I deck him?' he asked no one in particular.

'No. I would rather do that myself.' Phoebe raised the candelabra another inch. The urge to wreak revenge on this pompous bully was so tempting she had to grind her teeth together to stop herself from snarling. She had never been closer to forgetting who she was… No, who she was *supposed* to be.

Dominic laughed and came to stand beside her, leaning against the table. 'Very well, then. Aim for the head. It's thick enough.'

Mr Clapton did snarl. 'You drunken sot. You'd best stay out of my way.'

'Happy to. Never liked you anyway.'

'I don't want you to like me.' Clapton all but spat the words.

'Lucky, that. I don't think Miss Brimford likes you either. Do you?' He turned the wide-eyed question to Phoebe and she shook her head.

'No.'

'Short and to the point. That's two against one, Clap. You're not wanted here.'

'May I remind you this is my home!'

'Not really. Belongs to the Crown. So be a good chap and toddle off, will you?'

Clapton's gaze locked with Phoebe's. Her arm was beginning to burn. Finally, he stomped out of the room, throwing over his shoulder, 'You're welcome to the dried-up hussy. She wasn't worth more than a toss in the dark, anyway. If that.'

Phoebe remained there as the door snapped behind him, her heart thudding and ears ringing.

'You can put it down now.'

She started a little. Dominic's voice had changed, softened. She lowered her weapon onto the table and clasped her hands together.

'I ought to have beaten him to within an inch of his life,' Dominic said without inflection and cupped his hands around hers, which she realised were shaking with fury.

'No,' she said and cleared her throat before continuing. 'Then it would have been about you. And in the end, I was the one who sent him running.'

He smiled, but briefly. 'That you did. He's a squirmy little coward. That type is the worst. He chose the wrong person to bully. Would you mind very much if I found another excuse to deck him, though?'

She tried to smile at his attempt to lighten the mood and shook her head. 'I don't think you ought to. That might lead to trouble with his father and you never know when you might need the services of the English Consul.'

'You mean in general or me especially?' She didn't answer this attempt at coaxing humour so he continued. 'You ought not to worry about other people's welfare all the time.' His hands were warm around hers, his voice, too.

'I'm not. I don't,' she mumbled. It wasn't even the anger and fear that was making her mind stumble, it was his return to this unexpected, unwanted softness and the very foreign sensation of being…safe. It made no sense. If there was one thing she *wasn't* in this man's company, it was safe.

Still, it was such a *wonderful* sensation.

Such wonderful hands.

Large, long-fingered, a little rough, with a scar shaped like a starburst just above his wrist. The urge to turn her hands in his, brush her thumb over that small patch of pale, shattered flesh was so strong she was scared she might act on it.

'I'll see you back to the palazzo.' His tone was tense and she looked up. He'd changed again, dropped that light-hearted mask, revealing something hard beneath.

'Lady Grafton…'

'Can take a flying leap,' he replied. 'If she chooses to disappear all the time and leave you to your devices, it's time you paid her back in kind. I'll tell one of the servants that you felt faint or something and returned to the palazzo to rest.

'It will have to do. Come.'

She didn't protest. She could hardly insist they send for Milly. And besides, why protest when this was precisely what she wanted right now? To return to her room and sink into a dreamless sleep…

No. She glanced up at him as he led her out into the corridor.

Not sleep.

Foolish, foolish Phoebe.

Chapter Fourteen

With everyone still at Sir Henry's, the palazzo echoed like an empty ruin. At this hour the very few servants only came when rung for, and even then grudgingly unless they were well paid like Milly's maid, or well bullied like Mrs Banister's.

'This place is gloomier than a crypt,' Dominic said with a frown, his voice low. 'I'll go and rouse your aunt's maid.'

She shook her head. 'She is away with her family today and so is the cook. There's no one in the palazzo but the Banisters' maid and valet and I have no intention of summoning them. I am perfectly fine.'

He frowned. 'I don't like the thought of you upstairs alone. Perhaps I should have a cautionary, ah…word with Clapton after all.'

'No, please don't. I don't think he is at all interested in me, really. It was merely his vanity.'

'Oh, he's interested. I've seen him watching you.

Him and Banister. Very differently, though. Don't allow your lack of vanity to blind you, Phoebe.'

She flushed a hot red and shook her head. He took her hand again and guided her up the stairs, his hand tight on hers. When they reached her door he stepped inside and inspected the lock.

'No damned key.'

'It doesn't matter...'

'The hell it doesn't.' He glanced about the room and she did as well, hoping she'd not left anything indelicate lying about.

'Spartan,' he murmured. 'But your bed is larger than mine. Unfair. Well, we'll manage. I've slept sitting up before.'

'You cannot be serious!'

'As serious as that candlestick you were swinging. I don't trust Clapton not to turn nasty. What the devil do you think he will do now? Unless he decides to bed some poor maid, he will mostly drink himself into a resentful fury at the double insult of you rejecting him and me witnessing it. He'll not forgive you for that. And unlike yours truly, he's a brute when he's drunk. I've seen him at his worst in the small hours. If it weren't for his father, the Luzzattis would have happily fed him to the fish only a few nights ago. I'm afraid that, given your choices, you are better off with me as gooseberry until his ardour and the wine wear off. Now ready yourself for bed and I'll bring another blanket and pillow and set myself up in your chair. Ten minutes.'

'But I couldn't possibly fall asleep with you in the room.'

He paused at the door and threw her a smile over his shoulder. 'I agree it's going to be a challenge. But we'll have to manage. I'll tell you a bedtime story.'

She stared at the closed door.

Mad.

Her heartbeat echoed in the silence of the room like the drums of battle. She unclenched her hands. She could still feel the pressure of the candelabra in her hand—the cool, smooth surface, its reassuring weight.

She wished she'd swung it. But that would lead to consequences. Another reminder that wishes were all well and good in one's mind; they were not to be indulged in the real world. Such as wishing Dominic would do rather more when he returned to her room than guard her door. Oswald had been right—the dangerous moment had arrived and the real test was whether she could separate these two parts of her and protect both. She would have to try.

She went about her nightly preparation by rote, only pausing as she pulled a pin from her hair and watched it unroll over her shoulder. Her hair was one of her few vanities, but it made no odds. She was still, as that worm Clapton had said, nothing more than a plain Meg.

An ache, sudden and foreign, thumped inside her chest. Not her heart—something deeper—as if she'd long ago swallowed a box and whatever had lain dormant inside it had just given a sharp kick.

She pulled another pin and another thick tress slipped over her shoulder. What had Dominic said? Fox colours? He was being generous to her brown hair but she supposed in the sun it did have glints of fire.

Like her. She just needed some light shone on her.

She pulled out more pins, placing them on the small dressing table with its cracked paint. Then she raised her hands to braid it as she did every night, but stopped. No, not tonight. Instead she merely tucked one side behind her ear and went to change.

Her simple gown did not require a helping hand like Milly's, and she soon slipped it off and laid it out.

Ten minutes.

She went to the ewer and pitcher of water and readied herself for bed, with a little more attention than usual.

She wished she understood Dominic. He was such a mass of contradictions. Was he being nice merely because he presumed she was upset and unsettled by what had occurred? Or was the memory of that kiss still there despite the way he'd ignored her earlier?

She took one last look at herself in the mirror. The ten minutes were almost up. She touched the little pearl pendant that hung from a plain silver necklace to nestle between her breasts and turned away from the mirror just as a soft knock sounded, followed by a hushed whisper.

'May I enter?'

She opened the door before she could reconsider. He was still dressed, though he'd slipped off his coat, crushed cravat, and boots, and he carried a blanket and pillow and chair. The corridor, which led only to her and Milly's room, was empty and dark and for a moment it felt as though he was being formed from the very essence of the night. She moved back to let him enter, too confused to even realise for a moment that he hadn't moved.

'Your... Do you sleep with your hair like that?'

She touched her hair again.

'I haven't had time to braid it,' she lied.

He drew a deep breath and entered, arranging his chair and hers to face one another in front of the door and placing his pillow at one end. She inspected the arrangement.

'You shall never fall asleep on that.'

'I've slept under bridges, over bridges, in gondolas... You name it, I've probably slept there.'

'That is different. I dare say you were drunk. You aren't very drunk any more.'

'True. I'm trying to be on my best behaviour and not make a fool of myself any more than I have. I'll manage. I really have slept on worse.'

'During the war?'

He glanced back at her and away. 'Yes. If there is one thing a soldier's march teaches you it is to snatch sleep when you can, regardless of comfort. Shouldn't you braid your hair?'

'Why are you so worried about my hair?'

'Worried isn't quite the right word.'

'Oh, very well. I'll braid it.' What had she expected? For him to be overcome with lust at the sight of her hair? Ridiculous.

She sat on the side of her bed and set to work, fuming silently at herself. It took a moment for the quality of the silence behind her to penetrate her maudlin thoughts. He was still standing by the chairs, his hands unnaturally rigid by his side, his eyes half veiled by his long lashes. He was so still he looked like a statue, except for the expression in his eyes. She froze as well. Or rather, she went as still as he, but inside her a great furnace opened, the heat scalding and scorching its way along her veins.

For the briefest moment sane and sensible Phoebe tried to grab the reins, but was shoved mercilessly off the driver's seat by Rosie. She let her half-formed braid slip from her hands onto her chest, watching him as she teased one of the tresses free. Then another. His lashes flickered, lowered. He shook his head very slightly.

'Phoebe…'

Phoebe. Not Rosie. Her little flash of bravado flickered and died and she turned her back on him again, cursing herself and him even more roundly than before. She'd thought she'd seen the same burning heat as last night in the deep blue of his eyes, but it was dark and she was an idiot…

A hand settled on her shoulder, warm and firm. She met his eyes in the mirror.

'I'm here to protect you, Phoebe.'

She shrugged his hand off. 'You're here to soothe your conscience. I thought you might as well make yourself useful at the same time.'

He laughed faintly, but colour slashed across his cheekbones at the contempt in her voice.

'You are truly unique, Rosie Prim. If I did… I would be no better than Clapton.'

'There is no comparison. He forced his attentions on me. You are not forcing me. I am offering. If you don't wish to, all you have to do is say so. Yes or no.'

She hadn't meant to taunt him with his own phrase from last night, but when his eyes met hers again, narrowing, there it was—that heat. She hadn't been wrong. She swallowed, her thighs pressing harder together.

'Oh, I want to, Rosie.'

'Then why not?' she demanded, her voice far more uncertain than she would like. She dropped her gaze to the pile of pins on the dressing table and picked up her braid, wishing she was beautiful and seductive like Milly. Just for one night she wanted to know what it felt like to let go…to feel passion. Abandon. It was not right to go through life hiding from that side of herself, was it? Even agents of the Crown had a right to pleasure. Why must she deny herself something so essential to humans that it stood at the centre of literature and music and…and everything?

Just for tonight. Then she would be herself again. Sensible Phoebe. Oswald's agent. The insubstantial Zephyr.

Why not?

If Dominic could summon his wits he was quite certain he could provide a thousand and one reasons why not. All he had to do was remember them. Even one would do. The problem was he hadn't encountered this situation before. He'd never had to contend with someone who could make drums beat through his body with her laughter and then make those same drums fall into total chaos with a wistful look. It was like waking up in someone else's body—unfamiliar, disorienting…

And *there* was his reason why not…

'I told you. I don't take lovers. I'm not a…a warm person.'

It worked. He watched her face in the mirror and saw the two serious lines appear between her brows. Good, he needed serious Phoebe here to counter Rosie and his own fraying sanity.

'So you said when we were at Montillio's, but I don't even know what that means.' Her voice was sulky and he very much wanted to lean down and kiss the curve of her shoulder where her plain nightgown was slipping a little. Instead he focused on the truth once more.

'It means I can do without…this. Physical relations. I've never found it as compelling as most men. I don't mind the game and I've learned to play it well, but mostly it isn't worth the bother. I was always cold.'

She looped a long strand of hair around her finger, frowning at him in concentration. She looked…adorable. His stomach gave that strange inward twist again that seemed to be a reaction it had developed solely for her. In truth he didn't feel cold right now. He didn't feel like himself at all. He felt about to combust like a ball of crushed, dry paper tossed onto a fire of his own making.

'I don't quite understand,' she said, her voice both prim and uncertain, but her eyes flickered to his and then stayed. 'I thought you said… But… Do you mean to say…you…uh…cannot…?'

She floundered and he couldn't help it, he laughed. 'I can, that isn't the issue.'

'Then is…is it that you prefer men? I have seen the way they watch you, just as much as the women do. You needn't be afraid to tell me. I know I am not experienced like Milly, but that does not mean I am ignorant or…or a prude or anything.'

He felt a little prudish himself right now, which was ridiculous. He owed her the truth, which was strange, because he didn't owe her anything. Right now, with her big golden eyes branding him he felt compelled to answer. Both her and himself.

'I don't… Usually I'm… God, this is hard.' He took a deep breath and plunged in. 'I don't prefer anyone, Phoebe. I won't say I haven't used the fact that both men and women appear to be attracted to me, but the truth is that I am mostly…indifferent. I can take it or leave it. Mostly I leave it. I know what people say about me, but I'm not a passionate person. I do my damnedest to ensure I give pleasure when I do, well, have, uh, relations, but usually I prefer to do it myself. It's less of a bother, and even then I can do without it for long periods. In any case, I think it boils down to the fact that I don't like people very much. Most people at least.'

He was sinking deeper and deeper into embarrassment, but he had to be clear that his reluctance had nothing to do with her.

'But kissing is different?'

'Different from what?' he asked, confusion joining his embarrassment.

'Well, you said you wanted to kiss me…on the balcony…at Montillio's. Is that different for you from—' she cleared her throat 'from copulation?'

He ought to lie. It would be so much simpler. He opened his mouth, fully intending to try. But the words stuck and he gave up.

'I have no idea. I don't usually enjoy kissing either. There are exceptions. Apparently you're one. A substantial one. The truth is I'm so damn hard right now I don't think I'll be able to sit down. But that doesn't change the fact that…'

She turned towards him, her hair fanning out over her shoulder and chest, catching what little light the candle on the mantelpiece bestowed on the room. 'That what?'

That what, indeed? What on earth was wrong with him? For the first time in so damn long he was aching to bed someone. Aching. It was utterly foreign… *Frightening.*

'You don't want to bed a drunkard.'

She huffed and stood abruptly, stalking past him to pick up a dressing gown that hung from a peg by the wardrobe.

'Pray do not tell me what I want or do not want.' She shoved her arms in. 'Have the courage to tell me what *you* want or not. Now it has been a long, long, long day and I'm exhausted. Good night.'

She blew out the candle and slipped under the covers, her back to him, her hair dark against the pillow.

Dominic stared at her. How the devil did she always manage to put him at a disadvantage? He ought to go to his makeshift bed and prove that he was indeed capable of sleeping anywhere, even with a raging erection.

He made it to the chairs only to turn back to the bed, where he sat down carefully on the edge. She said nothing. He placed his hand lightly on the pillow, close enough so that the tips of her hair brushed the side of his little finger. The tingle shot up his arm and he grimaced. He was as sensitive as a babe.

He closed his eyes, hoping for some answer from within, but the only things inside him were thumping heat and need and an almost sick feeling of impending loss.

A hundred voices ganged up on the one voice that was begging him to raise the cover, slide in, gather her warmth against him. He was bound to ruin this. It was beyond his experience. It was wrong. Let her sleep…

'Phoebe.'

She turned in the darkness, her eyes luminous and dark.

'I'm not much for courage in these matters, but

the truth is that I do want you. But not like this. Not while I can still hear that bastard's voice in my head and see you clutching the candlestick with fury in your beautiful eyes. I want you to want me because you do want me, not because part of you wants to erase what happened tonight. Do you understand?'

She breathed deeply and sat up against the headboard, her mouth a downward bow as if she was about to cry. She rubbed her eyes.

'I'm too tired to argue with you, Dominic. Perhaps you are partially right. I *do* want to erase it. But I find it a little insulting you think I would… well, offer myself to you simply for that reason.'

'Not simply, and not only for that reason. But that is the reason why my conscience won't let me do anything about it tonight.'

Her mouth quirked. 'Any other night but this?'

Excitement bubbled up inside him, the childish, vivid kind he'd forgotten was possible.

It would be more comfortable to remain where he was, safe in the limited confines of his limited sexuality. Where he knew what to expect and what not to expect. And then there was always the risk he would discover that all this heat and excitement amounted to nothing different at all when it came to the act of sex. Just more of the same lukewarm pleasantness he could easily do without.

He had no idea which outcome he preferred. But he did know that once Pandora's box had been opened, it would be hard to close it without at least peeking inside.

He nodded, slowly. 'Any other night but this.'

She stared at him, her lips parted. 'Are you jesting?'

He ought to be, but he couldn't. Didn't want to. He shook his head. 'I know I jest about many things, but not this. But I don't think we should discuss this now. As you said—it's been a long day.'

He rose and she sighed and twitched her blanket aside.

'Very well. Lie down. You'll be more comfortable than on those chairs.'

He shook his head. 'No, I won't.'

She took one of her pillows and plumped it in the middle of the bed.

'There. Imagine this is the Grand Canal. You on one side, me on the other. I promise I won't ravish you in your sleep. Though if you snore, I might kick you. Now lie down and go to sleep. I'm tired.'

She turned her back on him again and snuggled under her cover. For a long moment he merely sat there. Then he lay down very carefully on his side of the bed, staring into the darkness. She was very quiet and he wondered if she had indeed fallen asleep. If so, he envied her. She shifted a little and he froze. If she argued her case further he wasn't at all certain he would have the strength…

'Thank you for worrying, Dominic,' she said softly, her voice muffled by the cover.

He closed his eyes and breathed out. Being noble was overrated.

Chapter Fifteen

Dominic had not considered that he would misbehave while asleep, but clearly his unconscious mind had taken advantage to toss out all his conscience's good intentions. When he opened his eyes he was wrapped around Phoebe, the Grand Canal pillow crushed between their bodies. Their fully clothed bodies, he noted with a mix of relief and regret. For a moment he stayed right there, his arm holding her against him, his face buried in her silky hair. His body was already ahead of him, throbbing with anticipation. He couldn't remember the last time he'd felt so at peace and so in agony at the same time.

This was new, too. Waking to the sense of rightness and yet feeling utterly unfulfilled. More colours for his growing palette.

The rattling of the doorknob knocked over his mental easel, especially when it was followed by Lady Grafton's voice.

'Phoebe? Are you awake? What is wrong with your door?'

He froze even as he realised that the reason for the doorknob rattling was that someone had placed the chair under the knob. And it hadn't been him.

Clever Phoebe.

Clever Phoebe was wide awake and off the bed like a shot, dragging her cover with her.

'Nothing is wrong with it. I locked it,' she called out, her voice hoarse and her cheeks blazing. 'I shall come to your room in a moment.'

They listened to her aunt's departing footsteps. Then she pointed a peremptory finger towards the curtain by the wardrobe that served as a dressing and bathing corner.

'Wait there until I am certain there is no one in the corridor.'

'No need for that.' He rose, holding his pillow strategically to shield the evidence of his discomfiture, and headed for the window.

'Where are you going?' she whispered as he placed one foot on the ledge.

'To my room to change and then to San Polo. If I don't come to *calcio* practice ahead of the game, Donatello will have my head.'

Milly was waiting for Phoebe, arms crossed and eyes narrowed.

'Why did you lock your door?'

Phoebe took a deep breath and gave a very abbreviated version of George Clapton's amorous overtures and Dominic's appearance. She hated lying to Milly, even by omission, but she wasn't quite ready to tell Milly that Dominic had shared her bed, however innocently, or that she had woken cocooned in the warmth of his arms. And she was certainly not ready to tell her she had somehow found the daring to proposition him. Where on earth had *that* Phoebe come from? Perhaps Dominic had been right that George Clapton's attempted attack had knocked her off balance.

Except that she'd wanted Dominic before that and she still did. Her skin lit and her insides crackled like gunpowder every time she thought of what might have been, what might yet be…

Any other night…

Her breathing charged ahead and she struggled to calm it and complete her tale. Milly's winged brows drew closer and closer together, her eyes narrowed with anger.

'I wish you *had* conked that slimy slug over the head, Phoebe. Though it is probably best you didn't. At least not until we're done here. Then I'll happily do it for you.'

Phoebe smiled. 'That is sweet of you, but threatening him was bad enough. Never mind that now. Tell me how it went with Alexei instead.'

Milly sighed and sank onto the armchair, kicking off her slippers. 'Ugh. He's another noxious slug, always drooling over my jewels as he moans about his miserly father and ugly wife. Poor woman. I shan't have any qualms about framing him for stealing von Haas's documents. It is good we are coming to the end of this mission. Between him and Clapton, there are too many toads in this swamp...' She paused, her sharp gaze fixing on Phoebe. 'By the way, just how *did* darling Dominic come to be there so fortuitously?'

Phoebe frowned. Now Milly mentioned it... Only moments before he had been surrounded by a bevy of attentive beauties in the ballroom... And suddenly there he was.

'I... I don't know. He said something about searching for brandy.'

'There was plenty of brandy on hand in the card rooms. Enough for a battalion. I know because Alexei was enjoying it earlier. Did he follow you?'

'I don't know. I can't imagine why. I'm not certain he even knew I was there that evening. He certainly seemed surprised to find us in that room. I didn't think of it at the time.'

'I dare say you didn't if you were reduced to brandishing a candelabra. Perhaps he saw you rushed out of there by one of the slug's minions and he's seen that manoeuvre before and came to the rescue. If so, that is impressively chivalrous of him.'

Phoebe went to the sofa and sat down. It might be nothing at all. Perhaps he *had* noticed her called away and… For a moment she could almost feel him standing behind her, his eyes dark, brooding, watchful. Milly wasn't methodical, but she had very sound intuitions about people. When she smelled a rat it was best to check under the sofa.

Phoebe let the thought enter and settle. She'd already accepted that Dominic was a mass of contradictions. And lies. Perhaps there were more than she'd even realised. She'd attributed her difficulty in seeing him clearly to the unfortunate attraction that afflicted her, but perhaps it was not that. Or not merely that…

'What are you thinking, love?' Milly asked in tones utterly unlike those she employed in public.

'I don't know. You are right that something is off about him. I can't put my finger on it, though.'

'You will. You always do. What do you always tell me? Don't push against a door that won't open. Let it be and search for ways around it and often it swings open of its own accord. Right now we shall concentrate on making you as pretty as a picture for our excursion to the royal gardens with your icy giant von Haas this afternoon. You shall have quite a bit of him over the next few days, no? Charming him at the gardens today and keeping an eye on him at the Imperial residence ball the day after tomorrow while I sneak into his office. A delightful evening's excursion.'

Phoebe smiled. There was nothing quite as familiar and comforting as plotting a break-in. That was all she must concentrate on at the moment—charming von Haas sufficiently to discover how best to enter the Procuratie without being caught. Everything else must be set aside.

But once they were done she would take her fate in her hands and try and seduce the most desired and elusive and confusing man in Venice.

Phoebe let out a long breath. She must be quite, quite mad.

Chapter Sixteen

All men were boys. And slightly mad.

This was Phoebe's conclusion as she stepped onto Campo San Polo the following day. Or rather pressed and shoved her way through the roaring, rumbling, and cursing crowd.

Why had she even come? This was no place for a foreign woman to wander. Only an idiot like her would have come here on her own.

An idiot or a woman bent on propositioning one of the players.

She hadn't even told Milly where she was going. After their successful afternoon enjoying von Haas's gracious hospitality at the Giardini Reali, which had included a short tour of the Procuratie buildings themselves, she reasoned she'd earned a day off. Especially given what awaited them tomorrow.

Milly was well accustomed to Phoebe's need to spend time alone and knew she thought best while prowling. Usually Phoebe would wander until her mind cleared, absorbing the streets and alleys, and then return. But today she left with a destination in mind.

She was going to Campo San Polo to watch grown men play a game she knew nothing about other than that it involved a ball and apparently a great deal of violence.

Why? Because she was a fool and she wished to see Dominic. She'd seen neither hide nor hair of him since he'd slipped out of her window the day before and a few careful questions had ascertained he hadn't slept at the Gioconda. No one found this unusual though, as Lord Wrexham was expected to hop between bedrooms.

Phoebe knew this image he portrayed was not strictly true and yet she didn't know what to put in its place. There was part of her that hoped watching him play football might give her a clue as to who he really was.

And whether she was mad to be considering propositioning him. Again.

She let out a frustrated huff and several men looked over their shoulder and made way for her, eyes wide. Apparently there were advantages to being a foreign woman in this tangle of shoving and cursing men and Phoebe took full advantage to make her way mercilessly to the front of the crowd.

She reached a line of makeshift wooden fences

that enclosed part of the square and the cheering crowds. To the right there were several groups of people standing high on tables or on two large stone wells, and all around people filled the windows, calling out encouragement or curses.

Phoebe spotted Dominic immediately and almost as immediately regretted it. He stood some ten yards from her, hands on his hips, laughing at something one of the players was saying. He wore vivid blue breeches, tall dark boots, and nothing else.

Phoebe swallowed.

His muscled arms and chest were slick with sweat and bronzed by the sun to a lovely pale wood colour. His hair was dark with damp and the sun picked out traces of mahogany, like a fire smouldering deep below the surface. There were smears of dirt along his back and even from here she could see a livid bruise on his shoulder. At one point he must have been wearing a shirt because its tattered remnants hung from his belt like a storm-torn sail. A blue ribbon was tied around his left arm, its tails fluttering. He looked like a pirate after a battle that had ended in his favour.

This was *such* a mistake.

She truly did not need these images engraved into her mind. She had more than enough to torture herself with. She forced herself to inspect the rest of the square. A knot of other players seemed to be arguing with a man she surmised must be the game's official as he was the only one wearing puffy black and yellow striped breeches.

There was another man in the discussion, but this one was dressed as fine as any dandy and Phoebe recognised Donatello Luzzatti. He appeared to be playing peacemaker, his hand gestures calming, and soon the reds and blues moved away and the judge raised a leather ball. Signor Luzzatti ambled back towards the crowd and before she could withdraw he caught sight of her and turned in her direction, his gaze intent.

There was an audible murmur from several men beside her and they slipped away, leaving her for a moment as exposed as Andromeda tied to her stone by the shores of Joppa. Phoebe's heart was already pounding uncomfortably and now it accelerated further, this time with apprehension. But as he reached her, Signor Luzzatti's face lit with a charming smile.

'My dear Miss Brimford. You came!' he said, quite as if he had extended an invitation himself. 'You shall witness a triumph. Our friend Domenico is in good form and he and my boy have done well this day. Come, you shall sit with me.'

Phoebe had no choice but to follow, the crowd parting for them like a sinuous Red Sea. He led her to a raised tribune halfway down the square and shooed away a plump official so she could take a seat next to him. She thanked him, very self-conscious to be watched by so many of the crowd, but just then there was a cry as the judge set the ball in motion once more and no one wasted another thought for her. Including her.

It was horrible. And strangely, unnervingly, beautiful.

First, everyone seemed to want to kill Dominic. Well, everyone looked as if they wanted to kill everyone else, but it was only Dominic's fate that worried her in the slightest.

And the mystery of it was that they all seemed to be having a marvellous time trying to kill each other. And all for a silly, dirty leather ball.

Men.

'There were once bullfights here,' Donatello said, raising his voice above the cacophony. 'The last one was twenty years ago, but then a bull in a frenzy attacked the tribune and the cowardly officials decided that was that, no more bulls. So now we have this. But it is better, yes?'

Phoebe watched the mayhem before them— men running, cursing, pushing, falling, taking swings at each other.

'Better for the bulls,' she muttered, but thankfully his son Pietro had just kicked the ball into the opponent's tent and the cheers drowned out her words.

Totally against her will her mind began following the horrid little ball, her body straining and flinching as if she'd become that round sack of leather. She began to see that different players had different roles. There were burly fellows who tried to block and stop others and capture the ball from them, and then agile, swift players who ran with it and tried to kick it into what she gathered was the object of the game—a tent-like structure with the enemy's coloured flag on it. Dominic and Pietro Luzzatti were in the latter camp. Pietro was slight and swift as a fox, slipping between the others as if he was greased, which perhaps he was.

She registered all this, but her attention was wholly on Dominic.

It wasn't by choice. She did her best to detach her gaze from him, but it was drawn back each time. He and Pietro appeared to control the last stage of every battle. Every time he took possession of the ball it felt to Phoebe as if the red team converged on him like a swarm of wasps and her stomach tangled into a knot of knots.

He was quick, but it was his calculation that was more effective than his speed, he seemed to always gauge where there were openings, and when they closed on him he passed the ball with precision to Pietro, even if he was halfway across the field. The moment the ball left him so did the swarm and Phoebe could breathe again.

It felt like *hours*.

Finally, Donatello glanced at his pocket watch and muttered.

'Five minutes to the hour. Come on, Pietro.

One more for your father.' He glanced up at the sky. 'For you too, Father.'

By some signal the players were also made aware of the time and there was a rush of renewed energy. The blue team secured the ball just feet away from their tent and it was passed along with more brutality than usual. She tensed when it was passed to Dominic and she watched him weave, his gaze scanning the players, searching for openings, giving orders to the men assigned to keep his path clear.

She could sense the moment he felt Pietro was well positioned behind a wall of blue players preparing just for this. But just as he was poised to kick the ball an enormous bull of a man crashed through the two men protecting him and, with a roar of rage audible above the din, threw himself towards Dominic like a starved lion being let loose from a cage. Phoebe's body clenched in total panic. Dominic was large and well-muscled, but being tackled from behind by a roaring beast would surely kill him.

She cried out and Signor Luzzatti shushed her just as two equally well-endowed fellows tackled the incoming man, inches away from Dominic and seconds before his leg shot out, raising the ball into the air and carrying it over a wall of men and directly towards the running form of Luzzatti's son, who with a deft twist of his foot sent it into the tent.

The crowd rose as one with a great roar and an answering chorus of boos from the red team. Luzzatti was on his feet, stamping them like a delighted boy, cheering at the top of his lungs. A chant of *'Pietro i Domenico!'* set up, louder and louder. Phoebe found herself on her feet, too, laughing and cheering with the rest.

'Bravo, Dominic!'

There was no possible way he could have heard her voice amidst the din but just then Dominic turned, the sun coursing over his bare chest like a spray of gold tossed at him, his hand halfway through scrubbing back his damp, tousled hair.

Her breath caught mid-cheer.

A great rushing sound replaced the cheering crowd, a biblical wind filling the world and muting everything else. Goosebumps rose on her arms.

She was saved from herself by the judge calling the end of the game. The crowd streamed into the *campo*, clapping backs and cheering. They picked up Pietro and carried him to the tribune, where he laughed up at his beaming father. They surrounded Dominic as well and drew him and the other players to the tribune to receive Donatello's blessing.

'I brought you a gift, yes, Domenico?' Donatello motioned to Phoebe. She felt ridiculous and was certain she was blushing like a schoolgirl, but the men standing around them appeared delighted at this unexpectedly medieval twist to their victory.

'Give your lady the ribbon!' Someone called out and the others chimed in. Dominic's gaze caught hers, the blue as vivid as the silk ribbon adhered to his arm.

'It is a trifle damp, but all in a good cause,' Dominic said as he tugged it loose and held it out. A shiver of fear struck her as she looked down at the slash of blue laying across his palm. She ought never to have come. What had she been thinking? Why hadn't she been thinking? This was foolish, dangerous...

'You're about to shame me before half of Venice, which shall promptly inform the other half, you know.'

She looked up swiftly at his words. He was still smiling, but the wariness was back in his gaze. She knew she hadn't the strength of mind to be sensible, not when he looked like that—caught between happiness and hurt. She took a deep breath and held out her hand.

'I shall be honoured to carry your team's colours, damp or not. Thank you, Dominic.'

His chest rose and fell as he took her hand. His hands were rough with grit and yet as gentle on hers as if he'd picked up a chick fallen from a nest. Hers shivered a little in his and she called it to order. Calm.

He tied a blue bow about her wrist and then

raised her hand to his mouth. His lips were warm, his breath still fast and hard and a shiver of pure anticipation raced through her. Then he raised her arm a little to show the crowd, which set loose a cheer almost as loud as at the winning strike.

They stood there, amid the mix of Venetian nobility and citizens, engulfed in the exuberant chatter, but all Phoebe was aware of was her hand in Dominic's as he helped her off the tribune and that he did not let it go. It was shockingly improper. Her being here at all was shockingly improper. It went counter to everything her image was supposed to portray, to all of Uncle Jack's and Oswald's training, and yet she couldn't find it in herself to care.

Later she would be proper Miss Brimford once more and at night she would become the Zephyr once again. But right now she was only Phoebe who was bursting with joy that he was holding her hand as if it was the most natural thing in the world. Right now she was…happy.

So this was love.

She could almost hear Milly answer her, eyes rolling.

'I don't know about love, but it most certainly is some marvellous lust. I mean, just look at his chest. And those shoulders… And his arms… I mean, good *lord*, child!'

It is more than that, I'm afraid, Milly.

Love had tackled her like that great big lion

man, throwing her hard to the paving stones, and it kept kicking her where it hurt just when she thought she was beginning to pick herself up again.

But it was also wonderful.

Dominic turned from his animated discussion with the Luzzattis, who kept clapping him and Pietro on the back, his gaze catching hers, a drop of perspiration slipping from his temple over his sun-warmed cheekbone. His eyes narrowed and for the briefest of moments his tongue just touched his lower lip, reminding her what it felt like on hers. Her stomach clenched, followed by a rush of heat setting up a pulsing tattoo between her legs and turning her breasts tender and tingling. If he'd wanted to kiss her right then, she probably wouldn't have said a word, couldn't have.

His hand tightened, drawing her closer, and when he bent towards her she turned her face up, stupid and hopeful.

'There's nothing for it but for you to come to the celebration, Phoebe. Donatello and Pietro will expect that now. But stay close to me at all times; after that little show the crowd will know not to touch you for fear of upsetting Donatello, but they'll soon be good and drunk and they can be…handsy.'

She nodded, his practical words waking her abruptly from her sensual stupor. She nodded again, this time to herself. Wake up, fool. Enjoy it for what it is, but remember what it isn't. This was not the time or the place to start believing in fairy tales.

As they followed the Luzzattis, someone tossed Dominic a white linen shirt and she watched in regret as he slipped it over his head. But he took her hand again, this time threading his fingers through hers.

They had not far to go. An old, rather bare palazzo had been set up as a banqueting hall and long tables were loaded with food and drink. The Luzzattis had pride of place and she and Dominic were seated next to Donatello and across from Pietro.

There was a great deal of laughter and drinking and toasts, and Phoebe had a marvellous time, not least because her thigh was firmly pressed against Dominic's under the table for most of the meal.

While Dominic and Donatello talked in a mix of Venetian and Italian so swift and idiomatic it hurt her head to try and untangle it, Pietro leaned forward and, with a shy enthusiasm that was as charming as his father's bolder version, began telling her in near perfect English all about his plans to study galvanism in Bologna, giving her a full lecture about electricity. When he waxed enthusiastic about the implications of Hans Christian Oersted's experiments, his father and Dominic also stopped to listen, Donatello alternately rolling his eyes and hanging on his son's every word with evident pride.

Dominic watched with that intent yet veiled look in his deep blue eyes, a smile curving his beautiful mouth, his hand resting lightly on his thigh and his fingertips on hers. That sign of possession was just a further aphrodisiac to her addled mind. She wanted to lean against his arm, her head on his shoulder. She wanted…

When the singing began Dominic whispered something to Donatello, who nodded and grinned, waving his hand in dismissal.

Dominic took her hand again. 'Come, time to leave before we're called on to join the chorus.'

Outside the clouds had gathered into full-bellied darkness and the air smelt of rain. She raised her face to the breeze, drinking in the blessedly cooler air. Every one of her senses was at its fullest.

When he hailed a gondola she wanted to protest. She wasn't ready to return to the Gioconda just yet. At all. But she said nothing, afraid that if she said anything at all it would be something very foolish. He didn't speak either, but he didn't let go of her hand as they sat.

The rain began lightly—a shiver of drops pricking the surface of the water. She raised her face to its coolness, laughing as the clouds burst under their own weight and the rain came quick and hard. The gondolier grinned at her, and Dominic put his arm around her, tucking her against his side. As protection from the rain it was rather futile, but as another blow to her armour it was masterly.

She sank against him, turning her head so she could breathe in his scent—sweat and rain and that deep, dark musk that kept pulling at her like the call of her own personal opium den.

She was about to speak when the gondola stopped before an arched door in a brick wall. She didn't know where they were and didn't care, and when Dominic helped her out of the gondola she followed him through the door and into the garden of Eden. They ran through the rain towards a Moorish palazzo at the far end of the garden, passing bloom-heavy rosebushes and a gazebo smothered in vines whose tendrils danced wildly under the rat-tat-tat of the storm. The building was as beautiful inside as out. It was nothing like the Gioconda's long-decaying splendour. Here the candle sconces gleamed, gilt banisters bracketed a grand staircase, and above them the ceiling was a masterpiece of cherubs and angels and clouds, as if the heavens had been trapped here.

She stood for a moment looking up, her soggy dress dripping audibly on the pale-veined marble floor.

'It's beautiful.' Her voice was a hoarse whisper and he turned to her with a smile just as a man in livery appeared from behind the stairs. Phoebe stepped back in alarm, but Dominic caught her elbow and delivered a series of instructions to the footman including the mention of baths. Phoebe held back her panic until the man disappeared.

'I cannot stay here. I shouldn't be here at all. I certainly cannot *bathe* here.'

'Why not? You'll have a far nicer bath here than in the cracked hip baths and tepid water at the Gioconda. And once your clothes are dry and this biblical storm lets up, I shall see you safely back to your aunt. Meanwhile I shall send a footman with the message that you are visiting with the Contessa di Benedetti.'

'The who?'

'The owner of this palazzo.'

Phoebe looked around her. 'Oh. Is she a…a friend of yours?'

'She's a little more than a friend.'

'Oh.'

'She is my cousin,' he clarified.

'Oh!'

'And seventy-three.'

'Oh…'

'I'm tempted to continue this just to see how many variations you can extract from a simple *"oh"*.'

She flushed. She felt transparent and strangely… young. She wasn't certain she liked feeling like this. It felt raw.

It felt…true.

He held out his hand. 'You'll feel better after a hot bath.'

She placed her hand in his and for a moment they stood there. His hand tightened, but then he turned and led her up the stairs.

Chapter Seventeen

Dominic was right. She *did* feel better after a hot bath.

Especially a hot bath in a large claw-legged tub set in the middle of a cosy boudoir warmed by a crackling fire. Phoebe dried herself and slipped into the elaborate purple and gold dressing gown the maid had left when she'd taken away Phoebe's soaked clothes. She sat down at the mahogany dressing table and began brushing her hair with a heavy silver-backed brush, watching her almost unfamiliar reflection as her hair slowly dried, turning from dark to light. She felt like a medieval queen.

There was a tap on the dressing-room door and, expecting the maid, Phoebe bade her enter and paused in mid-stroke, all her post-bath languor disappearing in an instant as Dominic stepped over the sill. He wore long, dark trousers and a white linen shirt and nothing else. The light of the fire turned his eyes black and gold and accentuated the shadow of the corridor behind him so that he seemed to materialise from darkness.

The devil coming for her soul.

Why not? He already had her heart.

All the warnings—remember who he is, remember what he is, and mostly—remember who *you* are—went up in a puff of sulphurous smoke.

Any other night must…*must* be tonight.

'You look like you belong here, Rosie,' Dominic said, surveying her from her head to her bare feet. 'A Venetian princess with fiery eyes ready to command us lesser mortals.'

Her heart hitched but she laughed. 'And here I was, thinking you looked like the devil come to claim my errant soul.'

'Huh. That's not very nice. Besides, your soul is far too pristine to interest any devil.'

She looked away and went back to her brushing. It should not matter that that was what he thought of her. After all, that was what she wanted people to think of her. Her efficacy as a spy depended upon it.

He sat down on the matching chair beside her and brushed her cheek with his fingertips. 'What did I say wrong?'

She shook her head. 'Won't your cousin be upset I am using her dressing gown and brush?'

'Gina will only be upset she was not here to meet you…' He paused as the maid re-entered with a tray and set it down on the table beside her with a smile at her and a wider one for Dominic. When she was gone Dominic poured Phoebe a glass of wine and she drank a little and picked up the brush again, tugging at a damp knot.

'Here, I'll do that.' He took the brush from her and turned her gently back towards the mirror, drawing her damp hair over her back as he shifted his chair to sit behind her. Her shoulders clenched but she said nothing. She had never liked people brushing her hair. Her mother had done that when she was little but she'd always been hurried and abrupt, always half-listening to Phoebe's father's movements in the next room and jumping up when he called. Phoebe preferred doing it herself. She almost hoped there would finally be something she could dislike about Dominic's touch.

The brush pressed against her back as he worked slowly on the ends, raising them to the warmth of the fire.

'Shall I stop?' he asked, tracing a finger along the rigid line of her shoulder.

Yes.

'No,' she answered, but she was still waiting for the surge of resentment to strike.

'Drink your wine.' His words were as soft as his touch and she did as she was told. Her scalp and back tingled with something between alarm and surrender, and she could see it in the face reflected in the mirror and tried to chase it away, but it only made it worse.

She focused instead on his reflection beside hers. With his lashes lowered in concentration his face fell into stern lines, the impersonality of the glass accentuating how handsome he was. Unfairly so. Next to him she looked even less remarkable. Just another face in the crowd when his must always stand out. It was a barrier between them, but even more she felt it as a burden he must carry with him wherever he went. She closed her eyes to shut out both of them, the fire warm and orange against her lids.

'Did you enjoy your visit to the Giardini Reali yesterday?'

His voice was soothing, but her eyes opened of their own accord, trying to read in his face what she sensed in his voice. She was beginning to recognise the tell-tale signs of his moods, but she wasn't certain where he was now. He seemed both relaxed and tense at the same time, and there was something in his question she could not place.

'Very much, but it is not as pretty as your cousin's garden.'

His mouth quirked in a smile. 'Did von Haas bore you to death?'

'Not at all. We discussed the rise and fall of the Republic of Venice and he showed us the changes Napoleon made to the Procuratie when he was there, and the lovely ballroom in the imperial residence designed by Giovanni Santi.'

'He took you on a tour of the Procuratie?' There was surprise and still that other, harsher undertone in his voice, and she tried to untangle it as she answered.

'He did. It was very kind of him.'

'There you go, using that word again. Von Haas and "kind" have never met. Do you like him?'

Was that jealousy in his voice? And if it was? It felt…good. Foolish good, but good. Power came in many and strange forms. This form was new to Phoebe.

'Herr von Haas has been kind to me. Why shouldn't I like him?'

His fingers tightened in her hair, not painful, just… It felt good, too. That sign that she could elevate his tension. Foolish Phoebe.

'I've been kind to you, too, Rosie.'

It was a childish thing to say and she couldn't help smiling. 'I like you, too.'

He shifted a little closer, his eyes narrowed. 'Why did you come to the *campo* today?'

'Because I was curious?' She'd meant it as a statement, but it crept up into a question. She cleared her throat. 'I once went to watch a bullfight when in Arles. It made me quite ill.'

'You didn't appear to be suffering from any… indisposition today.'

'I *was* nervous. It looked quite as if you were all trying to kill each other.'

'And yet it was a surprisingly tame game. Not even one broken bone.'

'Someone tore your shirt off.'

'Ah. That was the ladies, not the players.' She could hear his grin and shook her head but couldn't help smiling.

'Oh, vanity, thy name is Dominic.'

'So you were merely cheering because the game was over?' he prodded and she shook her head again.

'No. I was happy you won. You looked…' *joyous, alive, beautiful* '…happy.'

'I was. Am. I was happy to see you, too. For a moment I thought I was seeing things.'

'I didn't mean to intrude. I was planning to watch for a moment and leave, but Signor Luzzatti saw me and demanded I join him on the tribune. In truth I was afraid to say no.'

'Your instincts are sound. Donatello doesn't often hear that word. In fact, it even occurred to me that Donatello had brought you to pressure me into doing my best.'

'Is he that conniving?'

'Worse.'

'He seems nice.'

'He's as nice as von Haas is kind. Pietro is nice, but Donatello is that breed of beast that smiles as he plucks your eyelashes out one by one.'

She shivered a little. 'I am glad he is fond of you, then.'

He paused combing to brush his hand over her shoulder. 'So am I. I would rather *you* be fond of me, though.'

'You know I am. I would hardly be here otherwise.' Her words were a little hurried and he didn't answer, his hand resting on her shoulder, his fingers just touching the bare skin beside the lapel. Then he removed it and continued brushing. She took her glass and drank some wine. It wasn't wise, but then neither was she, apparently.

'Your hair is like silk.' His voice flowed over her the way the wine flowed inside her. 'It's damnable you cannot have it down all the time. I want to see it blowing in the wind, slipping over your skin. Damn, I want to see it slipping over mine...' There was a faint snap as if he'd closed his teeth on those words. 'Sorry, Phoebe. Forgetting myself here. I've never played lady's maid before. I could become accustomed to the role.' He didn't seem to expect a response, which was lucky because she couldn't think of any. Couldn't think at all past the melting of her body. He continued, his voice musing, 'You're not accustomed to having your hair brushed, are you?'

She shook her head.

'Hmm.'

She straightened. 'What does that mean?'

'Nothing, sweetheart. Don't turn, I'm not done yet. There's still a little more to dry.'

A sharp comment hovered on her tongue and she swallowed it. He sounded so comfortable and yet she was a confused jumble of nerves and need. It wasn't *fair*.

He reached past her to lay the brush on the dressing table. He was very, very close; her already tingling back could feel his warmth through her dressing gown. The urge to lean back was so strong.

He rubbed his cheek against her hair, his breath moving warmly through it, caressing the side of her neck like a kiss. His fingertips just brushed the pattern of the brocade dressing gown along her thigh. 'I liked the way you rested your leg against mine in the banquet hall after the game, Phoebe. It felt so damned good.'

She stifled a whimper.

'Just that line of heat against me,' he continued. 'I wanted to curve my hand over your thigh, under your skirt, just gently, like this...' He eased the edge of the gown aside, revealing the line of her thighs pressed together. He traced his finger up that line, from her knees almost to the dark curls hidden by the shadow of the dressing gown. He straightened, drawing a deep, unsteady breath. 'Damn. I told myself I'd behave. This is not going as planned.'

His tone was light but she heard the strain beneath it. He was fighting this as much as she. She turned. His pupils were dilated, the blue pressed back against an indigo wall. His jaw clenched as their eyes met and he looked away. 'You are a very bad influence on me, Phoebe Brimford.'

It was an absurd thing for someone like him to say, but it calmed her a little.

'You are a far worse influence on me, Dominic. And I wanted to touch you, too. Under the table. Before that. When you came to the tribune. No, before that. When I saw you standing on the *campo*. And when I saw that giant of a man throwing himself at you, I wanted to rush in there and stop him.'

There was a streak of heat along his cheekbones as he smiled. 'I'm very glad you didn't. Strozzato is something of a juggernaut and if he so much as ruffled your beautiful hair I'd have had to take measures.'

'I don't need you to protect me, Dominic. I understand why you wouldn't…that night…and I admit that perhaps you were right that it was ill-timed. But I wanted to do it before that cad Clapton made an ass of himself and now in the light of day I still want to. If you don't wish to, then tell me and I shall leave and not bother you again…'

Her words ran aground as he turned her fully to him, his knees apart to make room for her legs, his hands curving under her bare thighs as he slid her forward. The movement dragged at the gown, uncovering her legs further. She grabbed a fist of the fabric before she was bared altogether, but that merely drew his gaze downwards, his lashes shielding her for a moment from the scorching heat of his eyes. It didn't help. Now she could look her fill without being pinned by his gaze.

'You *know* I wish to, Phoebe. All you have to do is look down to see how much,' he murmured, his fingers brushing gently on the sensitive skin of her thighs. Her muscles clenched as her gaze followed his invitation to look. He wasn't trying to hide his arousal and she couldn't hide her response, either. Her whole body was one big answer.

She swallowed and looked up and he nodded, slowly, as if they had just sealed a solemn pact.

'Lean back.'

'What?'

'Back.'

She did as she was told, her elbows on the dressing table, taking her weight. He traced his finger along the lapel of the gown, just skimming her skin. It was so light, but her flesh lit from within at its passage.

'These colours suit you, Rosie. Fire and passion. Everything you keep bottled so tightly inside.'

That was what it felt like, something bottled so tight it might explode...*would* explode. It could not be released safely. It was frightening, but not as much as forcing the cork back into the bottle. She couldn't imagine that.

His finger reached the meeting of the lapels and descended, the gown parting without resistance and revealing the shadowed valley between her breasts, their creamy swell.

'A thing of beauty...' he murmured as he slipped both hands under the fabric, warm and strong on her ribs, his thumbs brushing against the weight of her breasts. He was breathing through his parted lips and she was barely breathing at all. She watched in embarrassment and excitement as the pale rose of her nipples tightened and darkened, echoing the almost painful core inside her.

'Phoebe...' His voice had darkened, too. 'Do you know what you are doing to me?'

She shook her head and he moved forward and her knee came into contact with his crotch. He was hard and thick, his pulse beating against her. Because of her. An inner scale began tipping inside her, turning heat and fear to power.

He smiled rather as a wolf might smile at a lamb. 'That's what you are doing to me. I dreamed I woke up next to you this morning as well. It was a disappointment to find I was fondling a damned pillow.'

'Lucky pillow.'

He gave a surprised laugh. 'Phoebe mine, you are unique. You completely upended me. What the devil are we going to do about this?'

'This, I suppose. Until you grow tired of me or I must leave.'

His smile faded. His hand closed on the sash that held the dressing gown closed and he pulled. The fabric tautened and softened as the knot gave way, the silk slithering against her skin. Her legs snapped together, not to deny him, but because she couldn't help it. Her muscles seemed to be outside her control. She wished she'd insisted on the maid bringing her a shift to wear under the gown, but it was already too late, the sash slipped free with a hiss and the heavy fabric fell open, revealing her from neck to toes.

He breathed in, deeply, his gaze roaming over her, scorching her as it went. Embarrassment, excitement, panic, need, uncertainty—she felt so many conflicting, frightening things that her mind just went numb and she sat there like a mannequin, her hands gripping the edge of the dressing table like a condemned woman in the docks waiting for a verdict.

'I need Rosie to make an appearance soon,' she said shakily.

He looked up, his gaze focusing a little out of the haze, but he was still breathing hard. 'Rosie?'

She nodded. 'She is better at asking for what she wants.'

'I'd rather have both of you here. Shall I summon her to join us, then?' he smiled, his gaze softening, and her foolish heart all but leapt into his lap. She nodded.

'Very well, Phoebe mine.' He slipped his hands under her gown, curving over her shoulders. His hands were warm and strong, his fingers firm against her back as he eased the gown down her arms as well until it was nothing more than a pool of warm colour cascading around the chair. Now she wore nothing more than the blue ribbon on her wrist, which she had not removed even in the bath. His gaze settled on it, his breathing turning tight and harsh. He reached out and traced its span.

'I'll start by asking for what I want, Rosie. I want you spread out on my bed wearing nothing but my ribbon. I want to explore every inch of you, map you with my fingers, my mouth, my body... I want every cell of your body to remember my touch...' His gaze locked onto hers. 'What do you want, Rosie?'

She searched for words and failed. Instead she leaned forward, almost tumbling into his arms, her hands about his nape, her lips parted and hot against his.

'This... You... I don't even know...'

He picked her up, carrying her into the adjacent room and setting her down on a bed at least three times as wide as her bed at the Gioconda. Then he straightened, a very piratical smile curving his mouth.

'That's more like it,' he murmured. 'Who said dreams don't come true?'

She couldn't help laughing, her hands reaching for him of their own accord. He tugged off his shirt and trousers and with a groan between agony and ecstasy spread himself alongside her, his body warm, his leg slotting between hers, hard and heavy. She liked that weight, wanted more of it, wanted him on her, imprinting her with more than a ribbon.

'I love your weight on me,' she whispered, shifting against him like a cat. 'This is what I wanted. To feel you with all my body.'

'Hello, Rosie. I'm glad you could join us,' he murmured, nuzzling the warmth between her neck and her shoulder. His erection hardened against her thigh, pulsing and pressing, and without thought she slid her hand down his chest, over the hard bone of his hip, the cusp of his thigh and over the pulsing heat of his cock, the lightest of brushes up the length of the shaft and back before closing on the velvety heat. He shuddered, groaning.

'Not too fast, we want Phoebe with us, too.'

She laughed, absurdly pleased that he liked her touch. 'Phoebe is here, she's just…'

'She's just what?' He kissed her neck, licked the sensitive spot just below her ear, and then caught the lobe gently between his teeth, teasing it with the tip of his tongue in a way that she felt all the way to her nipples. They hardened and the tingling swept lower, gathering between her legs again, calling out for attention. He couldn't have heard, but he shifted, kissing his way downwards. Her mind leapt ahead and panicked.

'She's frightened…'

She should have kept silent. He stopped, his hand hovering above her curls.

'Phoebe is only frightened because she's the smartest, most sensitive darling I've ever met.' He brushed her mouth softly with his. 'I hope you won't be offended, Rosie, but I like her even better than I do you.'

Her heart thumped hard and tears stung at the corners of her eyes. 'Rosie is offended.'

'Rosie knows I adore her too. She's just as protective of you as I am, Phoebe. Do you know what I want now that my first wish is fulfilled and I have you in my bed?'

She shook her head.

'You asked me once if I was a virgin and, though I haven't been one for close on twenty years, I'm feeling pretty virginal right now. I'm afraid of cocking it up, literally and figuratively. I promise to take precautions, but I want to make love to you more than Donatello wanted to win the *calcio* tournament.'

'That much?' She laughed, running her hands up his back, and down. His words should have sent her into a flat panic, but they did the opposite, her muscles relaxing, her body moving almost unconsciously against his.

'More. I don't understand what the hell you've done to me but I don't care any more. I just want you. Are you certain you want to go ahead with this, Phoebe? I need you to tell me you want this.'

She nodded, reaching up to brush his thick, dark hair back from his brow, sinking her fingers into its warmth, drawing his head down towards her. She spoke against his mouth, his lips warm and firm on hers.

'I want you, Dominic. On me, inside me. I just want you…'

He groaned, turning on his back and bringing her with him, his arms almost painful around her as a shudder coursed through him. She nuzzled the curve of his neck, delighted with the power her words had on him.

'You're shivering,' she whispered against the rapid pulse below his ear. 'Are you cold by any chance?'

'Are you laughing at me, Rosie Prim?'

'A little. I don't know how, but I feel very daring. This isn't like me at all, you know. I've never done anything like this, but it feels right. To touch you.'

He cupped her cheek with his palm, his eyes dark and intent on hers. 'It feels like heaven. If I'd known what I was missing all these years I would have come looking for you a lot sooner, sweetheart.'

Phoebe didn't answer; she couldn't even begin to find the words, or if she could they were too dangerous. She didn't even want to think them, she didn't want to think anything at all, just feel. She turned to brush his palm lightly with her lips. 'I love your scent,' she whispered against his skin as her hand trailed down his chest again. 'What is it?'

His voice sank lower along with her hand. 'What? Nothing. Soap. I don't know.'

'I love it. Every time you loomed over me it was like someone pulling a string up my spine.'

'That doesn't sound very comfortable.'

'It wasn't,' she murmured. 'It was anything but comfortable. It unsettled me and I told you before that I do not care for being unsettled.'

Dominic laughed at her chiding tones, but he was losing a battle to remain calm. Her voice, her hands, her body shifting again and stripping away his control. He didn't like being unsettled either. Part of him wanted to let it happen, but in another part something deep and hard was snarling in fear, like a cornered rat.

He tried to concentrate on her words and not on his rising panic. 'Did I loom over you a lot?'

'It felt like it. Reading my books over my shoulder. Poking fun at me.' She spoke against his fingers, each word a puff of warmth. A rumbling groan was building up in his chest, the need to tighten his body around her, imprint himself on her. Had he loomed over her? He had, without even realising it. Enjoyed teasing her, enjoyed the way she pushed back—firmly, but without either the poison or the honey he was so accustomed to drawing. What a fool he'd been not to recognise the pit he'd been digging.

'I like your taste in books,' he managed. 'And you always bristled so adorably when I poked fun at you and then you demolished me.'

'I did not.'

'Every time. Hibbert is keeping count. It was the highlight of the last fortnight—prodding you and being demolished. Better than *calcio*.'

'High praise, indeed.'

'I think… I think this was what I was aiming for all along.' Oh, God, he should shut up before he said something even more embarrassing.

'Is it awful of me to be grateful to George Clapton? I don't think I would have dared tell you how much I wanted you otherwise,' she said, her voice muffled as she opened his hand and pressed a kiss to his palm. His arm tightened about her with remembered fury, possessive, deep, jealous…foreign. He gritted his teeth until the wave passed, stifling all the idiotic things his mind was thinking. Like telling her if that bastard ever so much as looked at her again he would kill him with his bare hands. Idiotic and childish and as hot as the lust pounding away at him like a blacksmith's hammer. He pulled her back even harder against him, his mouth on her hair, breathing her in.

'Phoebe.' His voice was a cracked gasp of need and she turned in his arms, her hair a fan of warmth on the pillow, her lips parted, her amber eyes half hidden by her lashes. He wanted to imprint this image on his mind forever. But he also wanted, desperately, to kiss her again.

This kiss wasn't the same as on the balcony. She didn't hesitate and he was too far gone to worry. She turned into him, her body melding with his, her legs parting a little to allow his to press upwards between them, bringing her even closer until her breasts were crushed against his chest. He let out a breath of agony and pleasure as he absorbed the heat of her body, the coursing of her pulse, her breath. He brushed his hand up from her waist, over her arm, her shoulder, lightly over the pulse at her neck. He cupped her cheek, capturing the lobe of her ear between his fingers, soft and supple, and turned her head to meet his kiss.

Her sigh was like a homecoming—warm, relieved, inviting. Her kiss was something else entirely. It was all Rosie. She might not be experienced, but she held nothing back.

He closed his eyes, sank into the foreign clamour of his body slipping out of his control.

Strange words hovered and batted against his insides like the death dance of moths about a fire.

He set them free.

'I want to be inside you, Phoebe. Up to my hilt. I want your body to close on me like a fist. I want to keep you here all night, in the same agony you've been keeping me in all week. Until you can't bear it any longer. Until you come apart.'

'I'm already in agony.' She shivered against his hand, straining closer. 'I don't know what to do. I want to climb out of myself. What should I *do*?' There was naked desperation in her voice and he dragged her closer as he leaned back against the headboard. She shifted against his erection, gasping in a deep breath as he stroked the core of her pleasure. Her hair cascaded over her shoulders, framing her beautiful breasts, moonlight outlining her face and shoulders.

'That's right, move against me. Find your pleasure. I want to see you come. God, Rosie, you're beautiful.' She shook her head, but was too far gone to shy away from his words. She rocked on him, her thighs contracting and easing as she rode against his erection, his fingers. He wanted so badly to be inside her. All it would take was a shift of his hips, hers, and he would lose himself utterly.

His free hand clenched hard on the softness of her behind. Her eyes focused a little between her narrowed lids, her teeth sinking into her lower lip.

'Again…'

Oh, hell. He obeyed and she bucked against his hand, her fingers digging into his shoulders.

'Touch your breasts,' he commanded, throwing good sense to the wind. She ran her palm over her breast, cupping it, her thumb brushing over her nipple. Her head went back with a little mewl.

'I felt that between my legs, inside me…where you're touching me.'

He bent forward, taking the offered nipple into his mouth, suckling and licking, her hands threading through his hair as she coaxed him. Her sliding against his erection was unravelling him, too. Now he no longer wanted to be inside her. He didn't want anything but what she was doing right now, her damp heat hard and slick against his erection as she rode him.

She came with a long, shattered whimper, her body tensing, her pubic bone pressed hard against him. He held still, capturing each diminishing shudder that rippled through her. Her lashes fluttered and she drew her lower lip slowly between her teeth, her tongue caressing it as if capturing the last taste of ecstasy. It took every ounce of his determination not to groan and crush her to him and pull her down hard on his erection until he found that same ecstasy.

Instead he held himself still as he watched the shades of pleasure pass from joy through to sweet calm, her mouth soft and curved, her eyes closed, just the faint hint of that line between her brows telling him Phoebe was still there, thinking, worrying, but calmer now. He settled her on the bed, slow and careful. He almost felt as if he was inside her—could feel how sensitive her skin was, how any touch was almost unbearable. He himself was still one thudding ache.

She sighed and shifted towards him and his body jerked as her thigh brushed the hard heat of his cock. Her eyes opened, sleepy and warm. And then her hand closed on him, cool and firm.

He breathed out slowly. 'Wait.'

'It felt so good, riding you like that,' she murmured, her hand shifting gently against his heat. 'I never imagined anything could feel so good.'

He shook his head, not at anything in particular, merely because his brain was slowly melting, everything gathering around the slow, sleepy movement of her hand. It fisted, closed, released. He groaned.

'Am I hurting you?' She didn't sound very worried.

He shook his head. 'No. Don't stop.'

'Can you also…climax from touching? Like you did to me?'

'Yes,' he bit out.

'Of course,' she murmured. 'That is how you pleasure yourself. Will you show me how?'

'This is a thousand times better. Just…just do what you're doing. Don't stop.'

She raised herself on her elbow, her leg draping over his, her hair a tumble of warmth on his shoulder. He wanted to but he couldn't keep his eyes open, sinking into the agonising bliss she was wringing from him. She seemed to be exploring him, caressing his shaft with her palm, the back of her hand, the tips of her fingers, her hand sweeping away to trace the lines of his thighs, the sensitive skin between them, his abdomen clenching as she bent to kiss the soft skin below his ribs, and his body practically leapt off the bed as her tongue flicked his nipple as he had hers.

'I loved when you did that, and then breathed on it and did it again. Like this. Do you like it?'

'I love it,' he groaned, feeling the tail end of the reins slip from his hands. 'I love everything you're doing. I want to be inside you more than I want to be alive, but I don't want to stop.'

'Then don't.'

'I have to, sweetheart, just for a moment at least. Despite appearances, I'm a very cautious fellow. We need protection.'

'Protection… Oh! Of course. Show me how!'

He laughed at her command and obeyed. The slumberous curiosity with which she watched him only made him more desperate. He lay down beside her and pulled her into his arms again, trying to anchor himself to a safe point before he let go of his moorings. He'd done this often enough in his life and yet it felt different. Important. For the first time he felt the act was not merely being done to him or by him, but together. He'd not even known there was a difference.

It made him all the more determined not to rush. He put a lead on his lust and concentrated on exploring her again, his hands curving over her warm skin and lush curves. Soon her little whispers of appreciation or praise were doing as much to tear down what remained of his defences as her own enthusiastic exploration of his body. Nothing had ever excited him as much as watching her succumb to pleasure. He wanted to end his agony, but even more he wanted it to last forever now he'd found it. She was hot and slick against his fingers and he took his time, caressing her to a new pitch of need, her body arcing against him, her eyes half closed. He wanted to see her come again, but this time while he was deep inside her so he could feel her hold on him.

He held himself still at her entrance, half exultant and half terrified of hurting her. Her fingers scraped down his back, his sides, urging him closer. He pressed in gently, regretting even the sheath that separated them. He bent to kiss her, long and slow, teasing her with his tongue and lips as he moved slowly, gently, each movement a little deeper, each thrust sending a wave of pure scorching pleasure through him, pushing him further and further away from safe harbour. The still sensible part of him kept waiting for her to stiffen in pain, but she merely urged him on, her hands roaming his body, her nails sinking into the muscles of his back and adding to his spiralling ecstasy.

When he was fully inside he held himself still, absorbing the feeling of being enveloped, held hot and hard by her. Then he splayed his hands around her hips and brushed his thumb over her clitoris at the juncture of their bodies. She tightened about him with a moan.

'Yes, touch me right there. I can feel it…everywhere. Do that again.'

He did as he was told, his beautiful agony growing as her body pressed and bucked. He had no idea what rhythm she was searching for, but the uncertainty of each movement only made him wilder with need. In the fog that was his brain he only knew he was heading into uncharted territory—terrifying and beautiful. He let his body lead, drawn by the pleasure of the friction between them, finding a new, joyous rhythm. Then she froze, her legs clamping hard around him as she shuddered through a long wave of pleasure that drew him in and without warning his world cracked and shattered, tossing him over the edge of the earth. A great wave of joy grabbed him, emptied him out and filled him until he was nothing but light and peace.

Chapter Eighteen

He must have slept. It felt like days but was probably nothing as dramatic because the fire was still bright and cheerful. Phoebe was asleep and Dominic was wrapped around her as he had been the night he'd shared her bed. Except that she was blissfully naked and warm against him and his hand was cupping her breast.

He stayed right there. He couldn't remember the last time he'd felt so at peace.

Died and gone to heaven.

If that was what it was, he was fine with it. Except he didn't want Phoebe to die, not for many long years. She deserved better. Certainly she deserved better than him.

His hold tightened. Right now he didn't want to think sensible thoughts. Right now all he wanted was to explore this magical new landscape again.

And again.

Forever…

'Dominic?' Her voice was husky and deep as she turned in his arms.

'Sorry, did I wake you?'

She shook her head. 'I was dreaming.'

'So was I… No, wait…it wasn't a dream.'

She smiled and tucked her leg between his. 'I dreamt we were falling off Montillio's balustrade into the water, but I wasn't afraid.'

He smiled at how her dream mirrored the one he'd had after their kiss. 'That doesn't sound like sensible Phoebe.'

'Sensible Phoebe doesn't dream. Not those dreams anyway.' She traced a line below the purplish bruise across his shoulder. 'Does it hurt?'

'Nothing hurts right now. My body is singing too loudly for anything else to be heard.' A thought occurred to him and he stiffened in a mixture of embarrassment and concern. 'I should be asking *you* that. Did I hurt you?'

Phoebe frowned, puzzled. She ought to be embarrassed, but she felt too comfortable with him to turn prudish yet.

'No. It didn't. I'd expected it to be painful, but when you… Well, when you entered, I was too…lost in the moment. Is it strange that it didn't hurt?'

'I have no idea. Perhaps it only hurts when you're not ready. I think we were more than ready.'

She hummed in agreement, moving against

him, enjoying the textures of his body. 'I was so ready I felt like I was bursting from my skin. But it was strange. Having someone inside me. Strange but wonderful. I loved the feeling of you stretching me, filling me…'

Needing me.

He wrapped his arms around her, holding her tightly, and she stilled as they both seemed to teeter on the edge of something. She had no idea what: a warning? A promise? Both?

Then he pulled away and sat back against the headboard, one hand holding hers lightly, his other clasped about his raised knee. His gaze was abstracted, focused on the window. It was still damp with rain and there was nothing but grey beyond. The heavens warning her.

She sat up as well, reality finally beginning to pull her out of her beatific stupor. All too soon she must leave Venice. She'd left so many places, but this time when she left she would be taking something valuable with her and leaving something even more valuable behind.

She could understand greed now, wanting to take and keep. She knew she couldn't, but she wanted just a little more of him. She wanted to know him in more than the biblical sense. Even worse—she wanted him to know her. She'd never suffered from vanity, but now she wanted Dominic to know she was not merely a meek companion, a victim of life and circumstance. She wanted him to see what she'd achieved in life…

To see *her*. Phoebe the Zephyr.

But Phoebe the Zephyr was the first to know better.

She finally pushed back the fog of lust and dragged her spy's instincts back from the depths they'd sunk to. There would be no telling anyone, let alone a man like him—he might not be the drunkard she'd feared, but his proficiency at perpetuating that lie only made it worse. Someone like him, a habitual, calculated liar living on his wits and occasional winnings, a close friend and confidant of the local criminal family… She'd met men like Dominic in her life. Clever survivors who found the weak points of whatever system they occupied and made the most of them, often serving local men in power. They were chameleons, manipulators. Useful and dangerous…

It was damnable that Oswald did not have someone in Venice she could approach for information. He'd admitted that this was a weak link in the chain he'd wrapped around the continent. Haas had disposed of one of the Foreign Office's men several years ago and made it very clear he would have no qualms doing so again. As far as Phoebe knew, since then all missions to Venice had been handled by people like her and Milly—transients.

She could always contact Oswald's agent in

Rome or wait until Oswald or one of his deputies arrived in Verona ahead of the Congress. Someone was bound to know more about Dominic. The son of a duke would not go disregarded by the powers that be, if only because of the potential for embarrassment.

There could still be no future for them, but she still wanted to know the truth. It mattered.

She looked down at their joined hands.

'How did you come to live in Venice, Dominic? Was it because of your cousin?'

He glanced at her. 'Didn't Agatha Banister regale you with all the gossip?'

'She said your father sent you away. That doesn't sound very likely.'

'Why not? He makes no secret of the fact that he can't stand the sight of me.'

Her heart clenched, but she didn't let him divert her. 'That might be true, but what I meant is that it doesn't sound very likely that you would allow him to dictate to you.'

His mouth quirked. 'True. I left because I was in debt. Gambling. Venice is cheaper and more forgiving towards my kind. Perhaps I'll have to leave here, too, one day.'

His answer was too quick, and again his words rang false. She of all people had no right to resent him for lying to her, but the heat beginning to bubble inside her was definitely anger. She pulled the cover up about her and he moved towards her, his hand curving over her leg, warm and firm.

'No, don't cover yourself. If you're cold, I'll warm you...'

'I'm not cold. What is your father like, Dominic?'

He stilled, shooting her a look that was both surprised and annoyed. 'You choose your moments, Phoebe.'

'There is never a good moment to discuss horrid parents,' she replied, and he gave a faint laugh.

'That's true. So let's not discuss them.'

That was a very definite line in the sand. She crossed it. 'Tell me anyway.'

'I don't wish to. Not good for my digestion.'

'You're not eating now.'

'I was contemplating dining on you again.'

That was a different tone—the flirtatious voice she'd heard him employ so often in the salons and casinos. It rang utterly hollow now she'd peeked over his walls.

'Gossip says he blames you for the estate falling into debt. I presume it was already in debt before you were even out of leading strings.'

The bed shifted as he rose and picked up his trousers from the floor, pulling them on with his back to her. She watched, yearning and sadness and angry determination mixing into a rather bitter brew.

Part of her wanted to let it go. So what if he

was lying? She did not need the truth from him; they had no future anyway. She opened her mouth to apologise, but he began speaking, his voice so toneless it took her a moment to understand he was answering her.

'When my grandmother was killed they took me from her house in London back to Rutherford. My father's first comment when they brought me to him was that I looked like a girl and a puny one at that. There was a woman standing in the room, very much with child. I didn't know she was my stepmother. I hadn't even been told he'd remarried. She stood there watching me, her hand on her belly. My father grabbed my hair and pushed me very close to her belly and told her that she'd better provide him with a better specimen of manhood than his useless first wife had managed. I remember his hand twisting in my hair, almost shoving me into her. She had both her hands on her stomach by then, as if she was terrified I might contaminate her.'

'I suppose she was more terrified of your father. If he was violent with you, he might very well have been with her.' She spoke softly, wary of interrupting. He picked up his shirt, shaking it out.

'Probably. Looking back, I can see she was hardly more than a child herself. She would have been all of sixteen when he married her and apparently she lost quite a few babes before she birthed my half-brother. She came with a nice dowry, too.' He glanced over his shoulder. 'It was gone by the time I was eighteen and not a penny of that could be blamed on me. All I had for those years were my school fees. I spent much of the time between terms at the house of a friend of mine who was two years above me. He was the youngest of a large family and his older sisters already had children of their own, and so Sherbourne Hall was always full to the brim with children and noise. It was hardly a house of vice where I could rack up debt.'

She blinked at the name, but said nothing and he continued.

'Then I joined the army directly out of school and though my father deigned to pay for my commission, probably hoping the war would do away with me, I doubt that brought the duchy to bankruptcy. My father did that all on his own. Like father, like son. In this case he was just like my grandfather.'

'You said your father was a model of rectitude.'

'He is. He's also vain and arrogant and adores being adulated. He was surrounded by sycophants who stole from him and drained his coffers. His steward and his agent bled him and the estate dry, mortgaged what could be mortgaged, and pawned the rest. And once matters became impossible to ignore they disappeared to South America. When I turned twenty-one the lawyers gave me my grandmother's jewels, which were the only thing she had managed to keep from my grandfather. She told me she hid them in the wall of her privy and took them with her when she was widowed.'

Phoebe smiled. 'What a marvellous woman.'

He didn't turn, but she saw the line in his cheek curve as he smiled and her heart squeezed, hard. She wished his Dommy could have lived a long and loving life so that Dominic could have grown up far from his father's vain cruelty and disregard.

'So it was easier to blame you for his mistakes?' she prodded gently.

'Don't make a martyr out of me, Phoebe. Where there's smoke there's fire. I learned how to make my way. I didn't have an allowance like the other boys, so I learned to win what I wanted at cards. Sweetmeats, books, whatever took my fancy. I had other ways, too.' This time the smile he shot her over his shoulder was cynical again. 'Some boys were willing to pay just to have me watch while they pleasured themselves. More if they could touch, but after a few times I decided I'd take the lower price. All I had to do was to stand there, like a dumb statue, just like I used to when the artists made me pose for their drawings at Dommy's house. People stared at me anyway—I reckoned I might as well get paid for it for a change. Easy money. Between that and the cards I had what I needed.'

She was very careful not to let her breathing show how upset she was, but the effort was only making the ache inside her worse. She knew all too well worse things happened to children, but she wished they didn't, and especially not to him. She wanted to wrap herself around him as if she could reach through time and cocoon him from the reality that had been forced on him.

She thought of herself at his age, living between the drops of her father's righteous anger and her mother's meekness and the knowledge of her future closing in on her. Of being stripped down to the value of her body as well, if only as a vehicle to be impregnated for the good of God's Flock. But she had had Milly and then Uncle Jack, who had given her the strength to break away and choose her own path.

'Did your friend know any of this?'

His smile lost its harsh edge and he turned back to her. 'Marcus was furious with me when he found out. I told him I needed the money and he said I was worth more than that and hired me to translate his Latin texts for him.'

'He had you cheat on his class work?'

'I thought he did, but it was just a ploy to save my pride. Marcus has a gift for languages and he certainly didn't need my help. Two years later when I was in the same class as he'd been when I began translating for him he handed me all the translations I'd done for him and told me I already had a whole year's worth of class work. He'd kept it for me. I was furious with him.'

'Why?'

'Because I felt he'd acted out of pity. All that time I'd been so proud he needed my help, that I'd earned that money fairly... Discovering he was being noble and didn't need me at all hurt me more than anything. I think I sulked for a month.'

'Poor boy. He must have been upset, too.'

'Why would you think that? One would think he would have been glad to be rid of me.'

She shook her head. 'He sounds very attached to you. You said he was the youngest in a large family. It sounds like he wanted a younger brother and he'd rather adopted you. How did he make amends and convince you to stop sulking?'

'Perhaps *I* apologised.'

She laughed and shook her head again. 'Too stubborn. I doubt you'd learned to be charming yet.'

There was reluctant amusement in his gaze, and traces of that vulnerability that kept chiselling away at her good sense.

'I came back to my room one day and tucked into the book I was reading was a sheaf of notes with my latest class assignment in Latin in his writing. There was also a note from his mother reminding him to invite me to stay with them for the summer. I burned the Latin translation but kept his mother's note.'

'Why on earth did you burn it?'

'Because if anyone had found it, he would have been in trouble. The teachers knew my Latin was excellent, that I had no need to cheat, and they might have thought Marcus was trying to curry favour with me for... Well, for carnal purposes. It would have damaged him two-fold. He wanted to prove he trusted me. I went and told him I'd burnt the translations and that he was an idiot and that he could tell his mother I would come for the summer.'

'And what did he do?'

'Nothing. He just nodded in that annoying way he has and told me not to forget to bring my cricket bat. And that was that.'

'Were you in love with him?' she asked before she could stop herself. His brows rose a little but he didn't look offended.

'I love Marcus dearly, but I was never in love with him. He is part of who I am, the better part. He is the only person I truly trust.'

She nodded. She understood that at least. 'Sometimes that is enough.'

'True, clever little Phoebe. Who do you trust?'

For a moment the word 'you' rang in her head. An absurd lie, or a foolish wish. She set it aside. She might be living a momentary fantasy, but she knew what her life was and what it wasn't.

'I trust Milly.'

'Your aunt?' He sounded sceptical but she didn't take offence.

'Yes.'

'Is she the sister of the uncle you mentioned?'

She hesitated. Was this how it happened? Little drops of truth leaking through the cracks in her defences?

'No, my father's sister.'

'The religious zealot.'

She nodded and he frowned.

'I've never heard of Lord Grafton. Where did she meet him?'

She'd started this catechism, she could hardly object to it. And there was nothing to be uncovered there, not truly.

'He was my father's friend. Part of God's Flock.'

'God's Flock. That sounds rather ominous.'

'It wasn't pleasant. Milly was wed at fifteen. Lord Grafton was sixty-three. Luckily a few years later he had an apoplexy. I was fourteen by then and my number was coming up...'

'Your number?'

'My marriage number. All the girls had a pledge number and when our number drew near the men would bid on us. Milly got word to my uncle and he spirited us away.'

'You were to be married at fourteen. By auction.' He'd become more and more still and there was definitely a menace to him now. Each word was sinking deeper and deeper.

She shrugged, hugging her knees and trying to think back. For the first time she felt an urge to set those long, dark years out in her mind like pages torn from a book. She knew she was the same person as that girl, but she didn't feel it. Sometimes she thought that girl was far stronger than she.

'Not married yet, but the pledge preparations and cleansing rituals would begin at fourteen and continue until the marriage. I knew what was waiting for me and I had no intention of discovering the joys of being pledged. I planned to run away and I told Milly, and she convinced me to let her try and find Jack, my uncle. He used to come when I was young and before the Flock separated from the world. He tried to convince my mother to leave my father, but she wouldn't hear of it.

'I'd always liked him and he would smuggle books to me even though girls were forbidden to read anything but scriptures. I didn't believe he would come, but then one night Milly knocked on my window and he was with her and I climbed out of the window and that was that. She took great risks for me. I was still a girl and might have been forgiven, but women who disobeyed were labelled evil and kept in the cellars of what they called God's House. They were chained to their beds at night. All the girls were taken down there once a month to witness them being chastised.'

'Bloody hell. You're inventing this, aren't you?'

'I'm afraid not.'

'Does this place still exist?'

'Someone set fire to God's House a year after we escaped. Five women died there. After that the local magistrate could no longer turn a blind eye to what was happening and the Flock was encouraged to seek other pastures. Most of them, including my parents, planned to start afresh in Virginia, but luckily their ship went down in a storm with everyone on board. Milly calls it divine retribution.'

He sat down beside her, tucking his hand into her clasped ones. Her hands were cold against his warmth and he frowned down at them, unlocking them and rubbing them between his.

'What do *you* call it, Phoebe?'

'A relief. I would have hated the thought of them beginning again elsewhere. Of the girls and the women they would have harmed in the name of God. I rather like the idea of them being swallowed up in a storm and digested by the elements. Very biblical. I'm a very unnatural person, I'm afraid.'

He raised the back of her hand to his cheek and the warmth of his skin and the roughness of his stubble chased along her nerves. Fear struck her hard. Every one of his gestures was pressing a wedge between her and some part of herself that kept her safe. He was like a forbidden book, like a glance through a prison window at rolling hills and a gleaming sea beyond. One could not unsee, unread, unfeel such things. He was now part of her.

'I'd say unusual rather than unnatural,' he murmured, brushing his mouth over her knuckles. 'Clever *and* brave. Your story trumps mine by several leagues.'

'It isn't a contest.'

'No. Life rarely is, but we do tend to make it one. I thought your aunt was nothing more than a doll stuffed with self-indulgent fluff. Clearly I owe her a profuse apology.'

'Don't you dare say a word to her or to anyone. I told you this in confidence.' Panic made her voice too fierce and the tension returned to his face, and with it the mocking smile that had irked her from the beginning.

'Thank you for making that clear, Rosie,' he drawled as he retreated to the window. 'I shall try to watch my tongue when next I'm drunk. The same applies to you. I won't appreciate any additions to the already rampant gossip about me.'

'Yet you seem to delight in it. You certainly do nothing to discourage it.'

'Ah. Here comes the sermon. Sharing my bed doesn't give you any rights to lecture, sweetheart.'

'I would never presume to stand between a man and his folly.'

'Of course not. You think you're above all that nonsense. Well, you may have escaped one prison, but you've confined yourself to another.

How long are you going to continue to hang on to your aunt's coat-tails, hiding from life in your books and convincing yourself that men are being pleasant to you because they're *kind* and *nice*? You think *I'm* indulging in folly? Well, have a look at yourself, Phoebe.'

'My sharing your bed doesn't give you any rights to lecture me either, Lord Wrexham,' she threw back at him. 'And you're worse than a fool, you're a…a damned monument to wasted intelligence. Now, if you don't mind, I really must return to the palazzo. Thank you for a most entertaining afternoon.'

'You're very welcome. I dare say that was why you came to San Polo in the first place. Some light entertainment before you return primly to your chosen cage, yes?'

The words stung, but they were true enough. She had not only chosen her cage, she had put a great deal of effort into building it. She would not abandon it for a man whose way of life both tantalised and angered her. To contradict him would be to open a door she was not ready to pass through.

She took a step towards the door. 'I should go.'

'Yes. Once you dress I shall see you back.'

'Only to the bridge. I think it wise we are not seen together.'

She hadn't meant it to sound quite so cold. Or perhaps she had. This escape into sensual madness might feed her fantasies for years to come, but now it was over. She was not built for love and pain.

For the next few days she needed her mind clear and concentrated only on her duties. And once her duty here was done, she and Milly would be off again.

Dominic shrugged as well, a mocking smile tugging at the corner of his mouth. 'Definitely wise, Miss Prim. Our paths will part at the bridge. And—as you just said—thank you for a most entertaining afternoon.'

Dominic watched the slim, prim figure cross the bridge.

He wanted to go after her, let slip some of the fury bubbling inside him.

He felt used. Like the whore people thought he was. Except it was worse, because he'd shown her more of himself than he had to anyone in years and years. He'd even told her about Dommy and Marcus and...

And in the end, as he'd suspected, it made no odds. In the end, for all her insight and compassion, she'd treated him like all the others. As a body to be used and discarded. He'd served his purpose and now she could return to her safe little shell until the itch caught her again. Well, he was damned if she'd scratch it with him next time. Hopefully once she left Venice his body would return to its hibernation. Even if it didn't—he would be a damn sight more careful in future. He might be a tad dense, but he learned his lessons eventually.

He ought to be grateful she expected nothing of him beyond his services in bed. She'd understood the limits of these encounters better than he did. Sensible Phoebe. It was absurd that a lady's companion was acting far more sensibly than he.

His conscience pricked through the fog of anger and resentment. Phoebe had been many things before she was merely a lady's companion, and she had every reason to be sensible. Neither of them had had the best start in life and hers had been hellish. She had every right to wish for the security that her aunt provided. He certainly had nothing better to offer her but an empty title and even emptier coffers.

He had every reason to be sensible, too. He was not in Venice to explore his late-blooming sexuality. He was here at the service of the Foreign Office and his brief was currently to discover whether their own consul was selling political secrets to the Austrians. His attempt to search the Consul's office had been interrupted by his concern about Phoebe being drawn away by Clapton's little trick, but he still had a chance to discover the truth. To do that he must be completely focused for the next few days.

After that...

After that he would put his mind to whatever

task Marcus set him. That was the nature of his occupation. It was *his* nature. He enjoyed what he did. It had given him a twisted sort of dignity in his aimless life after the end of the war left him adrift, unwelcome in his home and cut off even from the meagre funds his future title promised. And there were others involved, too. He had no right to let the reins slacken because his body had decided to come of age twenty years late.

He turned his back on her and headed towards his next destination. The rain had stopped long ago and the paving was beginning to dry, which was a good thing. If he was forced to make his escape along a ledge tonight, he preferred it not be wet.

Chapter Nineteen

'Phoebe Brimford!' Milly's voice was sharp and Phoebe started, the brush slipping from her hand and hitting the floor with an angry clack. She picked it up and set it carefully on the dressing table, avoiding her image in the mirror.

'I'm ready. Shall we begin?'

Milly stood with her hands on her hips. She was dressed in a gown of deep red satin, her dark curls piled high and threaded through with golden ribbons. She looked like a Greek goddess. And like most of the Greek gods she looked displeased.

'You were not listening to a word I said.'

'Yes, I was, Milly. You said Mrs Banister is downstairs and it is time to go.'

'Well, perhaps you were listening, but this isn't the first time you've been miles away recently. You are only like this when something is wrong. Since I am about to risk my neck I would appreciate your sharing your concerns with me.'

Phoebe shook her head and pressed the lid down firmly on the bubbling stew of hurt and guilt and loss.

Two days had passed since the most wondrous afternoon of her existence. Two long, empty days. She wasn't in the least surprised that Dominic was avoiding her; she'd behaved atrociously towards him. She'd brought down her drawbridge on his foot when he'd been kind and gentle with her. It wasn't his fault she was a coward, yet she'd punished him for it. She'd made him believe she regarded him as everyone else did, which was unforgivably cruel.

Yet side by side with her pain and guilt was the knowledge he'd not been any more honest than she had. Believing something firm and solid and trustworthy lay beyond his lies and games might be nothing more than a wishful fantasy. After all, Dominic was also a survivor; he knew how to attune his lies to his listener's ears. She'd known men who could lie without guile or compunction and tell you they were innocent while holding the knife still embedded in their victim's heart.

Her heart and even part of her mind cried out that Dominic was not like that, but precisely because she didn't want to be wrong about him, she had to consider she might be. For all she knew his show of vulnerability was a brilliantly orchestrated act.

No. She didn't believe it. He'd been honest with

her and she'd kicked him because she was a coward. She owed it to both of them to apologise and that was precisely what she would do once this night's work was behind her.

Not that he would forgive her. Not that he *should* forgive her. He'd bared his deepest vulnerabilities and she'd made him believe she'd used him like everyone else…

'Well?' Milly prodded, and Phoebe dragged herself into the moment and forced a smile.

'I'm sorry, Milly. It is nothing. I promise you I am fully present now.'

Milly hesitated. 'Do you wish to tell me what is wrong, love?'

'Perhaps it is merely that I am not comfortable with us switching roles tonight,' Phoebe replied, hoping a half-truth would do for now. Eventually she would tell Milly all, but not yet.

'We've already had this discussion,' Milly said, adjusting her gloves. 'I shall depart with Razumov for a night at the club and you shall attend the ball with the Banisters and keep an eye on von Haas. This way we are both accounted for, yes?'

'Yes, but you shall have all the burden of breaking into the Procuratie and ensuring Razumov is out of the way for the night, while I shall be nothing more than another wallflower at the ball.'

'I am beginning to think you don't trust me, Phoebe. I assure you I am still young enough to manage a night's activities on my own.'

'You know I trust you. You're the only person on this fair earth I do trust, Milly.'

'Likewise. Now, let us go to it before Mrs Banister departs for the ball without you. It's time to tie the knot on our Venetian affair.'

Phoebe had fully expected her share of the evening's work to be a big dose of boredom.

After two hours in von Haas's beautiful ballroom with its white and gilt walls and massive crystal chandeliers she decided boredom was not sufficiently appreciated. She would have far preferred boredom to the feelings that beset her as she watched the spectacle being played out by the windows overlooking the canal.

It had been hard enough witnessing Dominic's flirtations at Sir Henry Clapton's ball. Tonight it was excruciating.

To be fair, he'd warned her. Told her not to believe men could be *kind* or *nice*. He'd called her a bloody idiot.

He'd been right on all counts.

Watching him as his dark blue eyes devoured the two beautiful women beside him, she found both her intellect and pride were torn—she'd truly believed him when he said his attraction to her was unique. But what had she expected? The inebriated flirt was a side of Dominic she had seen too often to dismiss simply because she'd discovered other aspects of him. He might say what he wished about being attracted to plain Phoebe. It might even be true, but it was only part of him. The other part that fed on being adored by women and men and depending upon them for his survival was back on full display.

As Phoebe watched surreptitiously from her wallflower's corner, a footman with a tray of wine moved past and was recalled by Dominic, who took a glass rather too abruptly, spilling some of the wine. The taller of the two women, an Austrian noblewoman with flaxen hair, touched his arm and said something, possibly the exhortation Phoebe had made herself—please stop.

He laughed and leaned in to whisper something in her ear, an intimacy which caused the other woman's luscious mouth to settle into a jealous pout. She caught his arm, trying to pull him towards the dance floor, but her action destabilised him and the rest of the wine spilled onto her dress. She shook her skirts with an annoyed moue, but Dominic just wandered off, no doubt in search of the wine-bearing footman.

'Disgraceful,' Mrs Banister scoffed. 'It is a wonder that wastrel is invited, though I dare say that is due to his father. Shocking, quite shocking, don't you agree?'

Luckily Mrs Banister's attention was claimed just then by another Englishwoman and Phoebe was saved the need to respond. Against her better judgement she kept track of Dominic's laughing progress through the room, and when he slipped through the thick curtains that masked the servants' entrance her bitter hurt gave way to surprise. If he wished for wine, there was plenty to be had right here. If he wished to find a servant to help him tidy up, the men's retiring rooms were in the opposite direction. Ditto if he was feeling ill…

Phoebe called herself to attention. Dominic was not her concern. Her only concern was her mission. By now Milly had probably completed her clandestine visit to von Haas's office, which meant Phoebe need no longer keep an eye on von Haas. Soon Mrs Banister would tire and they would return to the Gioconda and that would be that.

Phoebe stared hard at the servants' entrance, waiting for Dominic to reappear.

Damn the man.

With the practice of many years, Phoebe melted into the oblivious crowd and slipped through the curtains as well.

The grand ballroom on the *piano nobile* had been full to the gills with nobility and royalty, glittering like the chandeliers and chattering like a flock of jewelled parrots. But beyond that bubble of power and privilege, the corridors lay still and dark, only a few of the candles in the ornate sconces lit.

Phoebe had a clear map of the buildings in her mind and she knew where this landing gave access to. The stairs to her left led to the kitchens, but the door opposite her led to von Haas's personal living quarters. She listened for a moment and then gently turned the knob. It *should* have been locked, and yet it wasn't. She glanced at the keyhole, trying to make out any tell-tale scratches. But if the lock had been sprung, it had been done neatly. It was none of her business, and yet…

She slipped into the darkened corridor beyond, trying to convince herself that Dominic had descended to the kitchens for some reason. But just as she was about to return she saw a shiver of dark on dark under one of the blank doors at the end of the corridor and her heartbeat shot ahead in a mixture of dismay and fear and anger.

She knew precisely where von Haas's personal study was. And she knew who was now in it.

Chapter Twenty

Dominic held the candle above the fireplace and smiled.

Well, well, well.

'Thank you, my dear von Haas, for being so arrogantly predictable,' he murmured. He snuffed out the candle and was just setting it back in its place on the mantelpiece beside a vulgarly jewelled ceremonial sword when he heard it. Just a whisper of fabric against wood. Whoever it was was right outside the locked door.

Even as surprise struck him that he had heard nothing before that, he was already across the room, raising the latch on the window. He'd oiled it the moment he'd entered the study, but before he could even raise it the door opened. His shock grew. He'd *locked* the door as soon as he'd entered; he was certain of it.

Or had he? Had his anger at Phoebe looking through him with cold disdain thoroughly clouded his judgement? Whatever the case, this was bad news.

He slipped his hand into his pocket, closing around the knife. Then he armed himself with his fool's smile as well, but the words he'd prepared fell away and for a moment all he could do was stare.

Phoebe shut the door behind her, her gaze moving from him around the room and back.

'What did you take?'

'What?'

'What did you steal?'

'Steal?'

'Don't play me for a fool, Lord Wrexham. You are in von Haas's personal study. In the dark. What did you steal?'

She looked quite different from the woman who'd been plaguing his thoughts over the past few days...weeks. Her eyes looked black, as if night had robbed them of their fire. They still glistened, but there was no softness there, not a smidgen of the passion or vulnerability she'd shown so openly only two days ago. That, more than anything, unsettled him.

He cleared his throat and did his best to slur the words. 'Why would you think I was stealing?'

She raised her hand and began ticking off items on her finger. 'You've been exiled and cut off by your family. You have expensive habits and yet you also seem to be able to honour your gambling debts. And then there are the rumours that the carnival thief escapes over the rooftops, which I have seen you do.'

'You've seen me escape over a roof?'

'I've seen you climb out on a ledge narrower than your boots three storeys above the canal. And now I've seen you examine what appears to be a very expensive jewelled scabbard. Even if von Haas has the crown jewels of Austria in his possession, stealing from him on his turf is beyond rash, it is suicidal.'

He glanced at the scabbard next to the candelabra he'd replaced. Yet he'd been across the room when the door opened... He remembered the swish of fabric against the door that had warned him. Had she been watching him through the keyhole?

He considered telling her he was waiting for one of the women he'd been so ostentatiously flirting with in the ballroom, but discarded that idea before it was even fully formed.

'If he *did* possess the crown jewels of Austria it might be worth a try, but as he doesn't that is a moot point. And I had no intention of stealing anything. I was looking for his private stash of excellent whiskey Castlereagh sent him. A whole crate of the finest Scotland can produce. One of his fellows told me it was sitting in his study collecting dust. I didn't think he'd mind.'

'Why on earth do you think I'd believe such nonsense?'

'Because it's the...'

She waited, but for the life of him he couldn't say it. The lie just wouldn't come.

She'd broken him. Like a clock stuck just before striking midnight. He tried another tactic instead.

'Just what were you doing following me in the first place? Did you think I'd slipped off on a tryst with one of my many paramours?'

She made a faint sound, like a kitten hissing. 'I'm not so easily diverted, Lord Wrexham. But while you're busy thinking of a better lie I suggest we return to the ballroom. I would rather not be caught here with you.'

She stalked out and he followed, feeling for all the world like a naughty schoolboy. His success in finally confirming who had betrayed the trust of the Foreign Office felt rather less impressive now he'd been caught out by a lady's companion sneaking up on him with nary a sound... What the devil was happening here?

She stopped at the door to the servants' landing, listening. He stopped as well, cursing inwardly at fate, at Phoebe, and at the servants he could hear clunking up the stairs. They'd taken too long and the second supper was about to begin, which meant the stairs would be crowded with traffic for the next quarter-hour.

He nudged her aside, taking the key from his pocket and locking the door again before hanging it back on the small hook beside the door frame. He pointed towards the main stairwell leading down to the hallway below. It would leave them exposed for a few moments but it couldn't be helped. Phoebe followed without a word, but he could feel her glare burning a hole between his shoulder blades.

It was sheer bad luck that just as they had almost reached safety the doors to the ballroom opened. It was instinct that made Dominic open the first door they passed and slip inside. Perhaps if Phoebe had kept walking and claimed she was looking for the ladies' retiring room the incident would have passed unremarked, but she must have had the same idea as he, for they both found themselves on the other side of the door in a small, dark sitting room.

It wasn't dark enough, though. The light under the door was sufficient to make out Phoebe's disapproving form and folded arms. He shook his head at the whole situation and kept his attention on the voices outside the room.

Of all the lousy luck…

'In there? Are you certain it was Miss Brimford?'

'Well, naturally I am not certain, Mr von Haas, but just as I was returning from the, ah, retiring rooms I am quite certain I saw a figure dressed in the precise shade of blue she wore slip into that room…with a *man*.'

'Mama…' Rupert Banister's plaintive voice was interrupted by von Haas's impatient tones.

'I sincerely doubt someone of Miss Brimford's sensibilities would be likely to engage in such behaviour, Mrs Banister. However, if it would calm your concerns, I shall show you…'

Dominic looked about the room, but it offered no recourse, not even a window. He turned so that his back was to the door, pulling Phoebe into his arms just as it opened. A convulsive shiver ran through her and his arms tightened as he bent his head to hers, his lips moving against her temple, down over the crest of her cheek, as he said the most banal and utterly unfounded words he'd spoken in a long, long time.

'Trust me.'

If Phoebe hadn't been so angry at Dominic and even more so at herself, she might have laughed.

Trust me.

She'd never trusted anyone less. Yet even knowing he was a liar and a fraud, her body was responding without restraint to the heat of his body, his scent, to the warmth of his breath on her cheek. She held herself very still, hoping against hope that his stratagem would work.

She doubted it.

The door opened and the brief silence was broken by an all too familiar voice.

'Ha!' announced Mrs Banister in tones laced with immense satisfaction. 'What did I tell you?'

'Go 'way,' Dominic slurred without turning. 'We're busy.'

'Wrexham.' This single word was pronounced in von Haas's iciest voice. Dominic glanced over his shoulder and wavered, but his arms were like steel bands around her.

'Von Haas,' he said with fuzzy amiability. 'Be a good fellow and run along. Shan't be long.'

Von Haas broke into a fluent and brutal dissection of Dominic's morals and wit in German. Dominic listened with apparent amiability as he kept Phoebe shielded from view, but his fingers were digging into her waist.

'I don't speak Austrian, von Haas, but that doesn't sound good. Do a fellow a favour and run along, spare the lady's blushes.'

'*Lady...*' von Haas muttered, in English this time. 'You may be my guest tonight but don't bring your doxies into my private rooms, Wrexham.'

'Not nice to call a lady a doxy, old boy.'

Von Haas gave a snarl and moved into the room and Phoebe knew there was no possible way she would leave unrevealed. She raised her chin and took a step back.

'I agree, Herr von Haas. Even a doxy should not be called that, especially not in her presence.'

'Miss Brimford!' von Haas exclaimed, and

Dominic's hand tightened convulsively around her waist.

'Well said, sweetheart,' he said merrily, but there was an edge to his voice.

'What are you doing here? With *him*?' von Haas demanded, his voice dripping disgust, and Phoebe cleared her throat, avoiding Mrs Banister's shocked gaze.

'I apologise for abusing your hospitality, Herr von Haas. I think… I think I had best return to the ballroom.'

'Not yet, sweetheart,' Dominic exhorted. 'It's early yet. We'll find somewhere else…'

'Unhand her, you decadent wretch!' Lady Banister snapped, her ivory fan aimed at Dominic's chest. It took that accusation for Phoebe to realise Dominic still had an arm around her waist and she moved away. It also brought Rupert Banister out of his stupor. He took a step forward.

'I want a word with you, Wrexham. Outside.'

Dominic gave a strange little laugh and took back Phoebe's limp hand. 'For pity's sake, can't a fellow propose in peace? Do be a good chap, von Haas, and take your guests elsewhere. You are all quite *de trop*.'

Dominic's words cut short the burgeoning scene. Three faces stared at them in shock and disbelief. Three voices threw back the word in unison, each an octave apart, with von Haas as base and Rupert hitting the high note.

'Propose?'

If Phoebe hadn't been so shocked herself, she would have found the farce quite amusing. But she *was* shocked. She met Dominic's gaze and the fog cleared a little. His tone had been typically Dominic—light and just a little slurred—but his gaze was sharp and heavy with warning. She'd caught him out and he was locking her in. She could destroy him with a word, she realised. Tell von Haas what he had been doing only minutes before. It was the proper thing to do, legally and morally. She drew a deep breath.

'I told you your timing was off, Dominic,' she said, forcing herself to smile. He blinked twice, rapidly, his hand easing on her wrist, his fingers slipping between hers.

'I was never known for my tact, or my good sense, except in offering for you. What do you say?'

'I won't hear of it!' Lady Banister announced.

'You don't have to hear of it,' Dominic said amicably. 'In fact I would be only too delighted not to hear anything of you either. Now you're all welcome to leave so I can finally get on with proposing. So s*hoo*.'

Lady Banister visibly gathered herself together. 'I shall be telling Lady Grafton of your shocking conduct, young woman! Not that it isn't her fault entirely, but what may be excused in a widow of uncertain years cannot be excused in her companion. If you do not come away with us this instant, you shall find yourself in the street without a character and never find employment with a noblewoman again, respectable or otherwise.'

'Now, that isn't kind,' Dominic remonstrated. 'Phoebe has more character in her little finger than any of your so-called respectable noblewomen. Besides, she won't need employment. One day she'll be a duchess. They're unemployable anyway.'

Phoebe sighed and slipped her hand from Dominic's. 'We shall talk tomorrow, Dominic. Good night, Herr von Haas. Thank you for your hospitality and my apologies for abusing it.'

'What she said, von Haas. Aggie. Banister. Night all,' Dominic said and turned to Phoebe, briefly touching her cheek with a light brush of his finger. 'I think it's best you go with the dragon and her pup and I'll come to the Gioconda tomorrow so we can continue this without a Greek chorus chiming in. Dream of me, will you?'

He sauntered out, not waiting for an answer, which was lucky because the only response that occurred to her was hardly suitable for polite society.

Mrs Banister lectured her all the way back to the palazzo. Lord Wrexham's morals and prospects and manners were abused roundly, but she dwelled longest and with great vigour on Phoebe's foolishness in believing his intentions to be honourable.

'He may be a rake and a wastrel but the Wrexhams are among the most distinguished families in England. He shall never deign to marry a woman past the first bloom of youth and without a penny to her undistinguished name. The very idea is laughable. You have nothing to offer—neither birth, nor looks, nor dowry. This is nothing more than the whim of a bored and spoilt libertine. You cannot be foolish enough to believe the blandishments of such a knave.'

Phoebe sat mutely, eyes downcast, and offered no defence either of herself or of Dominic. Rupert Banister stared pointedly out into the canal, looking for all the world like a sulky pug. The gondola ride could not have lasted more than ten minutes, but it felt as if they had travelled to Rome and back at the very least.

When they reached the palazzo she hurried to her room, Mrs Banister's tirade still trailing her up the stairs. Once alone she wrapped herself in a blanket and sank onto the side of her bed with a groan. She had never, in all her years working for Sir Oswald, made such a hash of such an easy assignment. She hoped very much that Milly had done a better job with hers.

The very worst was that nothing she had learned today made any difference. It should have killed all her foolish feelings for him, but they were still there, aching worse than ever.

Chapter Twenty-One

Phoebe had no idea how long she'd been staring at the cracked wall of her room when she heard the whisper.

'Don't scream.'

She had no intention of screaming, or at least not with fear. Though several times over the past hour as she'd remembered those fateful moments with Dominic she'd wished she could give a good howl of anger and frustration.

'Surely this could have waited until the morrow?' she told the shadow moving towards her from the window.

He held up his hands and his voice was calm, neither drunk nor playful. 'I don't know that it can. Von Haas might come to speak with you and he's an early riser.' He stopped by the bedpost at the bottom of the bed, his eyes catching the meagre light from the windows in a vulpine gleam.

'What *are* you, Lord Wrexham?'

His teeth flashed. 'I think we've gone a few leagues beyond common proprieties, Phoebe. You really ought to be accustomed to calling me Dominic.'

She fisted her hands in her blanket. He was trying to charm her for his ends. Strangely, that calmed her. *This* she could cope with.

'Very well, *Dominic*. Go and jump in the canal.'

He gave a low laugh and sat down on the side of the bed. She scooted back further and he raised his hands again.

'I promise I won't touch you. But I need to know if you shall tell von Haas you found me in his study.'

'Thereby disclosing I was there as well? Do you take me for a fool, Lord Wrexham?'

'Not in the least; pity about that.'

'I don't happen to think so. I'd rather not be a fool.'

'I don't know. I rather enjoy the experience. It's freeing.'

'You're not denying this…you…this is all a sham?'

'Which part, sweetheart?'

'Oh, *stop* it.' The bed shifted a little beneath his weight, but he didn't speak, so she continued. 'You're the carnival thief, aren't you?'

'Are you planning to tell von Haas that?'

She leaned back against the headboard. Strange that she felt even more disappointed now than

268 The Wrong Way to Catch a Rake

she had with the thought that he was a drunkard.
It made no sense. After all, drunkards rarely escaped the siren call of the spirits. While thieves…
well, that depended. On why they stole, what they
stole, and from whom.

In this case from the most powerful man in
Venice.

Utter folly.

She took a deep breath, setting aside her anger
and trying to think clearly. At first she'd accepted
Dominic's reputation without question—that of a
charming, spoilt, impoverished, pretty nobleman
spiralling into ruin. Just another charming fool.
Was it all a façade to shield the activities of the
carnival thief?

Yet stealing from von Haas did not fit that pattern. Could it have been a crime of opportunity
and arrogance? Finding himself in the Imperial
residence, he'd not been able to risk temptation?
No, another man might have been foolish enough
to consider it an exciting dare, but whatever Dominic was, he was no fool. If she took that into account, the only explanation was that he had been
in search of something other than valuables. The
question was: what?

'Before you make any demands of me, I want
to know what you were searching for in von
Haas's study.'

Once again all the charm drained away and that
other man stepped forward. He hadn't moved and

yet she felt as if they both had. Then, slowly, he reached forward and wrapped the tip of her braid round his finger. Her scalp tingled, and not with alarm, not that kind of alarm anyway. She wished she were wearing a more substantial nightgown than a thin cotton slip. She didn't look down, but she could feel her breasts grow heavy, her nipples tighten. She gritted her teeth, willing her body to behave.

'I have never, ever had such a stroke of bad luck as having you step into my neatly arranged world, Miss Phoebe Brimford.'

Well, *that* was flattering.

'The feeling is entirely mutual, Lord Wrexham.'

'Dominic.'

'Dominic,' she parroted before she could think better of it.

He smiled and her antagonism gave a whimper of defeat. Whatever he was—drunkard, thief, or worse—she was in trouble.

'Do you work for the Luzzattis? Are you a rebel?' she demanded.

'None of that matters at the moment. The only thing I need to know is what you plan to tell von Haas tomorrow.'

'I don't owe you anything. Certainly not an answer.'

'I know that. But I am asking none the less. Nicely.'

'Or?'

'Or...?'

'What will you do to me if I don't answer?'

He stroked the tip of her braid with his thumb and gave a wry smile. 'Not a thing. You know that.'

Damn him. She could have dealt with threats. She had no idea what to do with capitulation.

His gaze fell and he let out a long breath. 'I've cocked up royally, sweetheart. The point is, I'd appreciate some warning if I must leave Venice precipitously. That is all. You'd have to come with me, though.'

'What?' she gasped.

'We are betrothed, after all.'

'You aren't serious.'

'As serious as *rixi e bixi*. You do realise my proposal was made in front of the local potentate and the prime gossip of the English community in Venice? That has more authority than having the banns read in church. News of our impending nuptials is likely spreading through Venice even as we sit here, ah, negotiating.'

'Given your reason for making that offer, I didn't take you seriously. Nor will they. They saw you were drunk.'

He shrugged, the same whimsical smile curving his mouth. 'You were caught embracing me in a darkened room and you did say we would continue our discussion elsewhere. Not much of a denial, darling. You could have slapped my face and stormed off. Or hit me over the head with a candelabra. Clapton would have appreciated that.'

Damn him again, he was right. She'd condemned herself as much as him.

'I think you *are* mad, Lord Wrexham. Even if that is true, I have every intention of jilting you.'

'That isn't kind.'

'I am quite certain you shall give me full reason to.'

'No, no, I shall be a model fiancé and husband. Reformed rakes and all that.'

'That's a right load of codswallop.' She snorted and he laughed.

'That's a very un-duchessy thing to say, Rosie mine.'

'Precisely. Why are you so calm about this?'

He sighed. 'Resigned, not calm. The moment you found me I should have hustled you out of that room and made my own way out of the window as planned. I allowed myself to be distracted. My mistake. A bad one, admittedly, but mine. I retrieved it as best I could, but I couldn't protect you.'

'I don't need you to protect me. And this is all a moot point. As I said, it is always a woman's prerogative to change her mind.'

'It is also unfortunately a woman's fate to be tarred with the worst of any scandal, which is precisely what that Banister harpy is likely brewing even as we speak. I might be a useless fribble, Phoebe, but there is one thing I always do, eventually, and that is pay my debts of honour.'

'I am not a debt,' she snapped, and his mouth twisted as he reached out to touch his finger lightly to her fisted hand.

'No, of course not; that was a bad choice of words. But… Would it be so awful? We get along well, you and I. You know the worst of me and you don't appear to hate me, at least not until I did what I did last night. And then…there is this…'

His hand closed over her fist, raising it to brush his mouth over her knuckles, then turned it over to do the same to the sensitive inside of her wrist. It was the lightest of touches, but it wrenched at something deep inside her. Her eyes burned as she watched his dark head bent reverently over her hand. As if he truly cared.

He remained like that for a moment, his breath unsteady against her skin. His voice just also a little unsteady when he finally spoke.

'Every time I touch you I fall deeper into this hole, Rosie. It's becoming very uncomfortable.'

Uncomfortable? It was *agonising*.

She made another grab for sanity. 'Lust isn't worth sacrificing the rest of your life offering a marriage you don't want.'

'Who said I don't want it? I think we could manage quite well together. I never considered marriage; or rather I did consider tying myself to an heiress at some point, but in truth I doubt I would ever have been able to bite that bullet. I'm just not that ruthlessly practical. But this is different.'

Different how? she wanted to ask, but he raised his head and picked up her braid again, slipped his fingers between the tresses and untwined them.

'Consider the advantages, sweetheart. The duchy might be drained, but you'll be pleased to hear my father couldn't completely break all the trusts set up by Dommy's clever father. As my wife you'll have around a thousand pounds a year. That should keep you safe and clothed if your aunt decides to move on. I don't like the idea of you being dependent on her.'

She shook her head. This was all too strange and unrelated to anything in her life, and why was she even considering it? Madness must be contagious.

'Dominic. No.'

His fingers had continued to unravel her braid, but they stopped, resting lightly on her shoulder. His gaze rose to her, his eyes narrowed and slumberous with heat.

'Why not? These past couple of days staying away from you... It's been damn hard. I know you made it clear you don't think much of me beyond my value in the sack, but for me you've become something of an addiction, Rosie. And even if that's the only thing you truly appreciate about me… You *do* like this, don't you?' He stroked his fingers through her hair, fanning it over her shoulder.

Words choked in her throat, fighting for release:

You're wrong—it is far from the only thing.

You're also right—I *do* like this. No, I *love* this. I love *you*.

She tugged her braid from his grasp, trying to find resolve, sanity…safety.

'There is no point in this discussion until we know whether Mrs Banister will gossip.'

'I'm damned if I'm having my fate determined by the likes of Mrs Banister.'

'I see. You would rather have your fate determined by the turn of a card. Or worse.'

He shifted away a little as well. 'Is that it? Your preacher parents come home to roost?'

'No, Dominic. It is that we are fundamentally different.' Frustration entered her voice as she continued. 'I don't understand you. I would have thought you would be delighted not to burden yourself with a wife of no particular birth, beauty, or resources. I admit this…this attraction between us is—other than being rather mystifying—is compelling. However, as we have already crossed the Rubicon, I am willing to continue to…well, to continue *that*. While we remain in Venice. I would think that would be sufficient for you.'

'Sufficient.'

'You *know* what I mean. Why on earth are you being so stubborn?'

'Why on earth are *you* being so stubborn? Have you truly thought through the benefits of what I am offering? I may not have much, but as my wife you would certainly have more than you can hope for as a lady's companion. You would have more than enough to live on for the rest of your life. So long as *you* don't take up gambling.'

She pressed her hands together. 'Dominic, I am a lady's companion, daughter of a provincial vicar. My grandfather was a provincial doctor. I am not suitable material for a duchess.'

'I don't give a damn if you're one of the Sultan's concubines. I know who you are and you're a far better prospect for a duchess than I am for a duke if I do happen to outlive my father. You are certainly leagues better than any milk and water miss he would like me to wed. And more importantly... I like you.'

He said the words as if he was tossing himself off a bridge. They were hardly a declaration of undying love, but she felt as if he'd bared his soul to her. Amidst all his lies she could still sometimes discern a clear truth. He liked her. Dominic truly liked her and somehow knowing that all but broke her heart.

Her breath shuddered in and out. 'Dominic, please listen to me. I shall let this...this engagement stand. For now. To lend it plausibility I shall hint to von Haas that I stand to inherit my aunt's money…'

'No!' The word was immediate and harsh. 'Damn it, Phoebe. There you go again, insulting both of us.'

'You are in no position to preach to me, Dominic. Those are my terms. Also—you will not mention marriage to me again.'

'That will be a tad hard if we are engaged.'

'You know what I mean. When we leave… When my aunt and I leave… I shall find a way to call it off and that will be that. Until then I want you to stop whatever it is you are doing here. No more sneaking about and climbing in and out of windows. I mean it, Dominic.'

He made a strange sound, half-laugh, half-grunt, and shoved off the bed. He strode to the window and she half expected him to leap out of it and transform into a raven, but then he returned to sit beside her. Closer this time, his thigh pressing against hers.

'Very well. For the moment we'll agree to disagree. I'm not in much of a position to negotiate, am I? So for now I'll court you like a proper duke's son and try my damnedest to keep my hands off you and the gossips off both of us. In a week we'll depart for my cousin's house on Capri. It's on a beautiful beach and her neighbour is a charming, widowed count your aunt can flirt with to her heart's content. We'll have some privacy there so I can ravish you at night and work this out during the day. Meanwhile we continue as we are.'

'Don't think I didn't notice you didn't agree to my conditions about not sneaking about. You must think me a complete fool if you believe I can be so easily distracted with promises of islands and beaches.'

'I think you…' She heard the rasp of his stubble as he scrubbed his hand over his mouth, as if stifling a profanity. She could almost feel him thinking, trying to find some way to put her in a box and tuck her out of the way.

'Get off my bed.' She shoved his thigh with her foot. It was childish. His hand closed on her ankle and even through the blanket she could feel his strength. Then his hand slipped up to her calf, shifting the linen against her skin. His hand was hot. Or she was hot.

His head lowered, a shock of dark hair falling over his brow, the shimmer of moonlight catching on the hard line of his cheekbone and jaw.

An ache, harsh and frightening, cleaved through her, contracting her lungs. It wasn't anger, or fear, or even that annoying, persistent lustful need. It was a different kind of fear altogether. It was like her uncle's horary, the planets shifting into their new alignment, and this new dark planet was shoving its way into the centre.

'Can't you tell me, Dominic? Has it something to do with the Luzzattis? Have they a hold on you and are forcing you to steal things?'

'Is that what you think?'

'I don't know what to think. No, they wouldn't have you steal from von Haas. Not unless…'

'Unless what? I'm curious what tale your fertile mind will construct for me next.'

His head tilted, a smile softening his mouth. All the while his hand was softly moving along her calf, his fingers slipping under her knee to caress the warm skin beneath. If he was trying to distract her, he was doing a very good job.

'Is it political?' she asked, clinging to her resolve, trying to read something, anything, on his handsome face. 'Are you or the Luzzattis involved with the Carbonari rebels? Is that what you were searching for in von Haas's rooms? Something to help them against the Austrians?'

'Damn, I like that image you're painting of me, Phoebe. A rebel with a cause. The only problem with it is that Donatello doesn't give a damn about politics. At least not that kind of politics. The only power he cares about is his own. He hasn't an ideal to his name other than the sanctity of his family. You'll have to try again.'

'This isn't amusing!'

His hand stopped, tightening, and again she saw the curtain lift a little. 'You said I must think you a fool. You couldn't be further from the mark.

I think you are the most intelligent, observant person I've ever met. I also think you must have been put in this world to turn mine on its head. In my wildest dreams I would never have imagined… What the devil am I going to do with you, Phoebe?' His voice was low and hoarse, the plea in it dragging along her sensitised nerves.

'Get off my bed,' she managed, but her voice was as wobbly as her insides. She didn't know what to think either. Her mind was a chorus of discordant voices, as if the whole of the Rialto fish market were trying to hock their wares inside her head. She wanted…she *needed* quiet so she could think. 'Get off,' she said again, more emphatically.

'I should. I know I should. I *will*.' He let go of her leg and stood but didn't move away. She could feel his gaze on her, a physical scraping against her nerves. 'You'll be the death of me, Phoebe.'

'Don't say that.' Her voice shook and she almost reached out to draw him back down beside her. 'I won't tell von Haas anything, Dominic. He will think what anyone would think—I'm a sad, bored spinster only too delighted to be seduced. Nothing more.'

'No, he won't. Von Haas is no fool. And he wants you.'

'Don't be ridiculous.'

He laughed. 'Too late for that. Next time you see me sneak into a room, don't follow.'

By the time she untangled herself from the sheet he was out of the window. By the time she reached it, heart in her throat, he was nowhere to be seen.

Chapter Twenty-Two

The small stone bench by the sea offered a lovely view of Giudecca under the noon-time sun. It also offered privacy.

'Now that we are alone,' said Milly, pinning Phoebe with her dark eyes, 'what the *devil* happened last night?'

'Nothing—'

'Nothing?' Milly interrupted. 'You call becoming betrothed to Lord Wrexham *nothing*?'

'Well, not really, but—'

Milly held up her hand. 'Agatha Banister, the biggest, loudest busybody this side of the English Channel, barges into my bedroom at an ungodly hour of the morning when I had barely had two hours' sleep and announces that you have been ruined. That she witnessed Lord Wrexham *accosting* you—her words—at von Haas's soirée, and then he announced your betrothal.'

Phoebe waved her hands as Milly's voice

rose. 'Please hush. Dominic was merely saving his skin. I found him rifling through von Haas's belongings and then... Well, the long and short is that von Haas came in upon us and Dominic claimed he was proposing. It was a master stroke of distraction, damn him.'

'*Why* did you find him rifling through von Haas's belongings?

'What?'

'Why did *you* find him? Don't tell me you too were fool enough to go rifling around von Haas's belongings yesterday of all days.'

'No, no, of course not. I followed him. Dominic. Wrexham.'

'Why?'

Phoebe's throat was tight with shame. Milly rarely took this tone with her. It was especially hard because it was well deserved.

'I thought... I think he might be the carnival thief. Or working for the Luzzattis or the Carbonari rebels. Or all of the above.'

Milly's mouth pursed. 'And, believing that, you still thought it wise to follow him?'

'I wasn't certain. And you must admit that if that is true, we ought to know.'

'Why? It doesn't affect us in the least. For all I care there can be a dozen thieves denuding the local aristocrats of their jewels. What I do care about is that you allowed yourself to be distracted by a triviality merely because it might have involved Dominic. That is not like you and it is definitely not like you to be caught in the act. And in *such* an act. You were there to keep von Haas in sight while I stole documents from the Procuratie and planted them in Razumov's rooms, climbing over fences and through windows dressed like a ruffian... I am too old for such nonsense.' Milly's voice descended into an unaccustomed snap and Phoebe winced.

'You're quite right, it was a mistake for us to switch.'

Milly sighed, relenting. 'It wasn't a mistake. It would have been impolite and out of character if you did not attend von Haas's function after his gallantry towards you. But it *was* a mistake to follow Wrexham. I know you've grown fond of him, but no matter what he truly is—a gambler, a drunkard, a thief, or a rebel—you cannot protect him. You do know that, don't you, Phoebe? We almost died trying to protect Jack and in the end it was all for naught.'

Phoebe took Milly's hand and they sat in silence for a moment. She knew seeking salvation for anyone but oneself was hubris. And yet...

Milly patted her hand. 'Never mind. We've dealt with worse. But you must tell me exactly what transpired so we can plan ahead.'

Phoebe nodded and told her most of what had transpired, including Dominic's visit later that night to negotiate terms with her.

'Capri, eh?' Milly sniffed when Phoebe closed her tale. 'Generous of him to throw in a charming Italian count. Like a bone to a dog.'

'I've put us both at risk. I'm so, so sorry, Milly.'

'I'm not chastising you, Phoebe. I'm worried for you. And I dare say a little frightened. I've been following your lead for so long it is disorienting to see you step off the path you yourself set. As your faithful sergeant, I feel obliged to raise the alarm.'

Phoebe tried to smile, but she was frightened, too. 'You are hardly my sergeant.'

'Of course I am. I have not the mind to pull it all together. I enjoy being told what to do and I enjoy doing it.' Milly's gaze narrowed. 'And don't change the subject.'

'I didn't, you did.'

'So I did. Well, I'm changing it back. What shall you do about your betrothal?'

Heat and cold clashed inside Phoebe once more. What should she do? What *could* she do?

'I shall wait. I don't think von Haas shall mention it. He will likely consider the whole affair, and me, beneath him and avoid both. Luckily we no longer need him. Mrs Banister is the real problem, but with any luck lecturing both of us will satisfy her.'

'Unlikely. This is too juicy a titbit to keep to herself. But aren't you forgetting Wrexham?'

I wish I could. Phoebe almost said the words

aloud, but not even to Milly did she want to reveal that much. She wasn't ready for that. Part of
her still hoped this was rather like the influenza
and she would wake up the next morning cured.

'He shall do as I ask.'

'You are that confident in your power over
him?'

'Not at all. But he is feeling guilty and therefore
inclined to try and make amends. And whether
he is a thief or a rebel or merely one of Luzzatti's
pawns, the last thing he wants is to call attention
to himself.'

'My dear, his façade is all about calling attention to himself.'

'Not this kind of attention.'

'True.' Milly sighed. 'It is all so complicated.'

'No, it isn't. It cannot be. This is what I am,
Milly. I cannot even imagine what it would mean
to be anything else. Not without losing myself. I
fought… *We* fought too hard to become what we
are for me to toss it away because for the first time
in my life my body has gained ascendancy over
my mind. Oswald warned me it could happen and
when that day came I might have to choose. In
the end this is a choice between what I have and
some…some fantasy.'

'Becoming the future Duchess of Rutherford
is quite a fantasy.'

Phoebe groaned. '*That* is a burden I most certainly don't want. A title means nothing to me.'

'But Dominic does.'

Phoebe breathed in and out. She wished so much that she could lie.

'Yes, he does. I...care for him. I want him to be happy. Or content. Or something. I want him...' Her breath cut her off before she could complete her thought and it didn't matter because that was the truth. She wanted him. To be with him. It felt...so right. Not even knowing it would destroy so much of what she had so painstakingly built could change that conviction. But thoughts and actions were two utterly separate things.

She cleared her throat and continued. 'I want him to have a good life. But I cannot give that to him any more than he can give that to me. Because what I have now is *already* good. And it is *mine*. I won't give that up for what may very well be an infatuation. After all, everyone appears a little infatuated with him, so why not me? Perhaps in a year or so I shall think fondly of him but heave a sigh of relief that I was wise enough to walk away. I have done what you told me to—created memories to sustain me.'

'There is a vast difference between creating memories and finding a man who you feel bonded to through your heart, Phoebe. You and he... I was there at your birth, love. I could not be closer to you even if you were my own child.' Milly placed her hand on Phoebe's, her voice shivering a little. 'Please don't lie to yourself, Phoebe. I am an expert on infatuations, but I have only ever loved one man in my life and I carry that knowledge with me always. *If* you choose to walk away, then admit what it is you are walking away from. Make that choice knowing that you are in love with him and that what you have with him is unique. If you hide from that, it will follow you around like an arrow in your back that you cannot reach.'

Phoebe didn't answer. She couldn't. It was true.

A ship sailed by, unfurling its topsails as it headed towards the open seas. She wished she could hail it and climb aboard. It didn't matter where it was headed. As long as it was away from temptation.

'It makes no odds,' she managed at last. 'Even if I was willing to throw away everything I have built, why would I risk it all for a liar? Because that is the only thing I am certain is true about him—that he lies about who he is and what he does. I don't even *know* him, Milly. For all I know he may be doing to me what I have done to von Haas, only a thousand times more successfully. He might be Luzzatti's puppet or just a common thief. Whatever he is hiding, he *is* hiding. He asked me to marry him, to tie my future to his, without any attempt to explain or justify his actions. I am merely to trust him like a dumb, blind little mouse because he asks me to and smiles at me and… The more I think of it the more infuriating and disrespectful and *outrageous* it is.'

'I admit it does sound rather bad when you put it that way. Still…'

'Still?' Phoebe prompted, almost hoping that Milly might magically find a way out of this fog without her either losing her heart or herself. But Milly merely shrugged.

'No, you are quite right. If it was someone like Rupert, then it might have been possible to keep to our work without giving the fellow up, but Dominic… No, I cannot see it. He is too clever to hide our activities from indefinitely and…well, whatever he is up to, chances are it won't mix well with being an agent of the Crown. You *would* have to choose.'

Phoebe let those words settle. That was the core choice: Dominic—whoever and whatever he was—or the life she had created. The person she had fought to become. The only person she knew how to be.

She drew a deep breath, hoping that something, anything, would come to her rescue. But in the end it was simple. She could not have both.

'I *earned* who I am, Milly. I will not give it up. I cannot. He likes me, I *know* that. It isn't merely the…the passion, but there is something between us that makes us both…comfortable. Not just with each other, but with ourselves. I think that is why he is willing to wed someone so utterly outside his sphere. When we are together I can see him so much more clearly than when he is with other people. It is like putting on spectacles when my eyes are tired and those smudgy lines gather into words. I don't know why he is like that with me, but he is. I think… It is absurd in a way, but… I think he feels safe with me.'

'And so he should.'

'No, he should not. He does not trust me with his truth and I do not trust him with mine. We could never go forward like that. And I didn't even mention that his best friend is Lord Sherbourne.'

Milly straightened. 'What? Good lord. How did I miss that?'

'He doesn't precisely advertise the fact, but they are even more than friends; Lord Sherbourne appears to be something of a big-brother figure to him.'

'Of all the awful luck. Oswald might be able to take advantage of you being a duchess, but I doubt he would appreciate you marrying the best friend of the director of the Foreign Office's spies. Does Dominic know what Lord Sherbourne's occupation really is?'

'I doubt it, but it is even worse than that. Lord Sherbourne saw me.'

'Saw you? When? Where?'

'Six years ago. In Oswald's private office in London. After we returned from Hamburg. It was only for a moment, in passing, but he looked right at me. His kind don't forget faces, even faces like mine.'

'No, but there's no reason why he would think you were one of Oswald's agents, is there?'

'Would Oswald meet a nondescript young woman in his private office? And then the same woman is introduced to him as Dominic's fiancée? You must see this is an impossible situation. The whole idea is so preposterous that I can't imagine why I even have to raise objections to it.'

'I can. Because you don't want to lose either of your selves. Not the Phoebe you worked so hard to create, nor the Phoebe you discovered with Dominic.'

Phoebe let out a long, shaky sigh. That was it, she supposed. 'No, I don't. But, as you said, I must choose none the less. It is as simple as that.'

As painful as that.

'We're done here, Milly. I shall play his game for the duration of this week and then break this so-called engagement. It is time to move on.'

She tipped back her parasol and raised her face to the caressing sun. Perhaps if she just kept going, walked right over it, this ache would fade as most everything else did in life. She hoped it would, because right now it was wrenching at her like a tiger's paw shoved through her chest, talons sharp into her thudding heart. But the pain could not change reality, or the choice she had to make.

A week with Dominic and then she must leave.

In all the nights she'd lain awake over the years, worrying and planning for the morrow, Phoebe had never imagined her downfall would come at the all-too-gentle hands of a handsome, seductive, lying heir to a dukedom.

Chapter Twenty-Three

It took Phoebe two days to realise that being openly engaged to the most desired and reviled man in Venice for a week was her worst idea ever.

Every moment spent with her new betrothed was pressing a knife deeper into her heart, an organ which should have been sufficiently dried up to offer greater resistance, but was proving as mushy as overcooked peas.

If she had an ounce of sense or self-preservation, she'd bundle Milly into a boat and leave Venice right away.

It didn't help in the least that she was now famous.

The same way a five-legged goat or a flying pig might be famous. The same element of fascinated disbelief appeared in people's eyes whenever she and Dominic were together, which Dominic ensured was often.

She told herself it was important she be seen

with him so that she could find the right time and opportunity to jilt him in a convincing manner. Apparently her ability to lie was now extending to herself. It wasn't merely that Dominic wasn't giving her any reason to do so, but also that she wasn't even looking.

Yet despite her growing confusion and misery, she was also happier than she'd ever been. Which was confusing in itself.

So she did her best to justify her madness. What was a week in the grand scheme of things? She'd earned this time, hadn't she? A week of living the fantasy life of a younger, prettier, simpler woman. A normal woman with normal pursuits and wishes and plans who was being wooed by the handsome son of a duke. A charming, clever, lying, scheming…

She pushed those thoughts away and fixed her attention on the concert Dominic had brought her to this afternoon at Chiesa San Toppoli, where a young man was now singing Handel's *Ombra mai fu*.

She glanced at Dominic's profile, wondering if he too remembered that long-ago day at the Gioconda. Probably not. For her it had been the day she'd taken her first steps down this path, but for him it had likely been just another day of pulling the wool over the world's eyes for reasons she still could not fathom. She'd tried to trick him into revealing his secrets, but he'd sidestepped all her attempts or offered that most infuriating palliative of all: *Trust me.*

She trusted him as much as she trusted herself. Which at the moment meant not one smidgen.

Yet here she was, seated beside him on the hard wooden pews, her hand tucked in his and his thigh pressed against hers in a manner that would have drawn strict condemnation from Mrs Banister had she been present, which, happily, she wasn't. The daytime crowd in the small church was mostly local Venetians who weren't in the least scandalised by physical proximity, and soon Phoebe relaxed into the pure pleasure of the music and being so close to the bane of her existence.

Because, in the end, Dominic made her happy. And often more than happy. Sometimes even ecstatic. A state of mind and body she had not realised was possible. All he had to do was smile at her and her insides lit like one of the electrical mechanisms Pietro had described that fateful day in Campo San Polo.

'I stand by my earlier claim about love songs,' he murmured to her under the cacophony as the audience applauded the end of the concert. 'That must have been one hell of a tree. Did you like it?'

'It was beautifully sung. Thank you.'

'I thought we should commemorate the first day you deigned to speak to me. Or down at me.'

Phoebe laughed, absurdly pleased he had remembered. And there it was—that damned inner flurry of bliss, for all the world as if she was seventeen. And there, too, was the knife in her heart.

'You had me well fooled, Dominic. It was a masterly performance.'

His hand stiffened in hers and he sighed. 'It wasn't all a performance. I adored teasing you. It is like… One day I'll take you swimming on the other side of the lido. There are these big, swelling waves there. Sometimes you have to dive under them before they give you a good thrashing, and sometimes they just…pick you up. It's an amazing feeling.'

'What on earth has that to do with you lying?'

He shook his head and drew her to her feet. 'It has to do with you. That's how I felt when I tangled with your alternately sharp and soft tongue, sweetheart. Even ducking to avoid a thrashing was exhilarating. And when you went soft and worried it was like being picked up by those swells… I can't describe it. I'll take you there so you can see for yourself. But none of that was a performance.'

Phoebe didn't answer. Couldn't. Damn the man. Damn him. This was why she shouldn't press for answers—every time she did, he just pulled her in deeper.

He bent closer as they moved aside to allow the boisterous Venetians to exit first, his voice lowering further and further as he spoke until it was a subterranean rumble. 'You'll love it. The water is still warm from the summer, like liquid silk, and it wraps around you and picks you up... Or we'll go after dark when the waves are calmer, somewhere no one can see us. I'll strip you naked and hold you against me in the warm waves. Can you feel it? Your body pressed to mine, your legs hooked about me as the waves wash around us, my hands cupping your beautiful behind while I kiss you into oblivion...'

'Dominic!' she scolded as a trickle of perspiration ran down her back. Could she *feel* it? She was *aching* with it, her breasts already heavy and tight, her stomach a chaotic knot of lust.

Luckily he fell silent, but his hand was tight around hers and she could feel the tension thrumming through him as well.

'Let's go somewhere...private. My Venetian side draws the line at carrying through a seduction in a church.'

There was nothing she wanted more at the moment than to be carried through this seduction, but their engagement had had one unforeseen effect. She could no longer move about unobserved. It was one thing attending a church concert with her betrothed. It was another going with him to the di Benedetti palazzo to spend an afternoon of sin. Or to a lonely beach to spend a night of delight.

Milly had made those rules very clear to both of them.

He gave a sudden harsh sigh, as if she'd spoken aloud. 'Very well, I'll behave. I know that look.'

'What look?'

'Like you've found the perfect bridge.'

'What?' she asked, confused.

'From which to push me off.'

She couldn't help smiling. 'I have. The bridge of sighs. Through the window.'

'Ow. I hope you open it first. I would hate to damage the local art.'

'Yourself or the window?'

'Now, that is thoroughly mean, Rosie mine.'

'You'd be feeling mean, too, if you had people staring at you all the time...' He raised a brow and she corrected course, adding, 'In a critical... Oh, you know what I mean!'

'I do, and I'm sorry people are such idiots, but my God-like powers don't extend to correcting the mistakes of creation. This nonsense will die down if we ignore it. I won't even tell Milly she looks delightful for a future mama-in-law.'

Phoebe laughed despite herself. 'I dare you.'

Dominic smiled down at her. 'That's better. And speaking of honorary in-laws, Marcus, who is the closest thing I have to a real family, is due in Venice shortly, which is excellent because I want you to meet him.'

'You want me to meet him?' She couldn't keep the alarm out of her voice.

'Of course I want you to meet him. He's my

Milly. Don't look so terrified. He has a damned soft heart underneath that gladiator's exterior.'

'When…when is he arriving?'

'He and his wife are probably with his mother's family in Ravenna at the moment, but he should be here any day now.'

Oh, hell.

Hell, hell, *hell*. The last thing Marcus Endicott, Earl of Sherbourne, would feel when he met her was adoration. The universe could not have concocted a better jest than if it had been penned by the most mischievous of Greek playwrights. She followed Dominic in a half-daze, trying to consider her options, but there weren't any. Sherbourne's imminent arrival didn't truly change anything, it merely moved the inevitable closer.

It was time for this Zephyr to waft away once more.

She started in surprise when just before they passed through the arched wooden doors that opened onto the square Dominic propelled her into a small room, shutting the door behind them.

'Dominic…?'

'Just one more moment before we have to rejoin the world, Phoebe.' He brushed his knuckles over her cheek. 'You look so worried. Don't be. Marcus will adore you. He likes people with twisty minds as much as I do. And he likes people who seem to like me. You do still like me, don't you, Phoebe?'

She wished she could lie, but her skills failed her when her body and mind colluded against her.

'Of course I like you, Dominic. You know I do...'

Before she could think, she found herself picked up and planted on the simple wooden table set against the stone wall with Dominic's arm around her waist, his face buried in her hair, and his mouth warm against the sensitive skin of her neck. Her body, already teetering, shuddered with delight, and relief, and anticipation.

'I thought you said something about your Venetian side and churches...' she murmured, arcing her head to give him better access. Her time with him had slipped from days to mere hours and she did not wish to waste one moment of it.

'So I did, but then I remembered what you said about reading Fanny Hill in the basilica,' he whispered as his hands moved over her hips and waist to brush lightly against her breasts. 'No better place for the *stark naked truth*. And there is nothing as pure as this, is there?' His palm brushed over her breast, the fabric of her dress rubbing over her sensitised nipple. She moaned, her hands fisting in his coat, her legs clenching together against the need he unleashed. He pressed them apart, grasping her hips and pulling her against him, his erection hard and hot even through their clothes. What would it be like in the sea? With nothing between them but the warm water of the Mediterranean…?

'Nothing as pure as this,' he said again, his voice a harsh growl as his mouth closed on hers, nipping her lower lip gently and drawing another moan from her.

Pure, maybe, but there was nothing gentle about his kiss this time. It was ravenous, his mouth and tongue plundering and taking, giving her no time to think and barely to breathe. This was another part of Dominic, fierce, demanding, taking what he wanted…

She loved it. Loved being pulled along in the tide of his passion as it fed hers. Stark, naked lust. She wanted him to push her fully over the cliff of his desire, to spread her out on this plain wooden table and take her to heaven.

'God, Phoebe, I want you so damned much.' He spoke the words against her mouth, his voice as raw as she felt. She gave a cry and kissed him back, her fingers digging into his hair, its silk slipping between her fingers. She loved feeling him, tasting him, losing herself in him. She loved *him*.

'Why can't you marry me today, Phoebe? Right here. I'll go find a damned priest.'

His urgent words sliced her right down the middle.

One side cried out: *Yes. Today. Now. Before I can think.*

But the other side knew better. Their time had already run out.

* * *

Dominic regretted the words the moment they were out. Not because he didn't mean them, but because he did.

She didn't answer, but her hands tightened in his hair, her teeth scraping against his lip, turning his body into one big, desperate heartbeat as she all but brought him to his knees with her mouth and hands and the little whimpers that made his legs weak.

It was killing him that she could not see how right this was.

Please say yes, Phoebe. It's already swallowed me whole, let yourself be swallowed as well. Say yes...

Say yes... Yes... Yes...

'Phoebe. Say *yes...*'

She stilled, her breath coming in pants. He cursed himself again, trying to fight his way through the crashing waves of pleasure and pain. It was a whole new landscape, as foreign as a tangled jungle, except all the beasts set loose were from within him.

This feeling was even worse than the carnal urge she'd sparked in him. It went deeper, curling tentacles around something that had long been lost in some dank cavern, tugging it out with a great, ripping ache. Something powerful and weak all at the same time. Terrifying and exhilarating.

When she slipped off the creaking table he

didn't stop her, but he couldn't stop himself from holding out his hand. 'Is the thought so very awful, sweetheart? I know you don't think much of me—'

'Stop that,' she interrupted fiercely, but her gaze was firmly on the stone floor. 'You know that isn't true. And I don't regret anything that happened between us for a moment, Dominic,' she said in a voice more like her own, but still in that light, breathy tempo, as if she'd rushed up a flight of stairs. 'But there was never any possibility of taking this any further, despite your chivalrous instincts. I don't wish to step into the role of a future duchess. It is not who I am.'

'The only role on offer is that of my wife, Phoebe.'

She shook her head. 'That isn't true, or at least it is far from the whole truth. Please don't argue. I don't wish to discuss this. I have decided. It is my choice after all. To say no.'

Was the floor bowed beneath his feet? It felt so. Bowed and sinking, like marshy land. But still he tried to reach for something solid. Something to hang on to so he could yet pull himself out.

'Is this because of what you told me? About your parents' attempt to wed you off against your will? I am not trying to force you, Phoebe. I am offering—' he drew another deep breath; it was definitely becoming difficult to breathe '—a partnership. In mind and body. We…we work well together.'

Her hands rose, fists touching, knuckles to knuckles.

'Why can you not accept that I do not wish to wed? We should leave now. Milly will be expecting me. We can speak again…tomorrow.'

'Devil take tomorrow. Goddamn it, *look* at me.'

Her shoulders hunched and she turned away from him, but her scent, soft and warm, reached out to him, drawing out the need that was gritting its teeth inside him. His body, primed and ready, was swept over by a wave of scalding, clenching heat. He slipped his arms around her waist, pulling her back towards him, his eyes closing without thought as his body pressed against the length of hers.

When the devil had she become quite so necessary? It had crept up on him, confidence by confidence, look by look, touch by touch. They might not have known each other long, but it was there—recognition—and it ran deep. How could she not feel it? It felt so damn *right*. To hold her, to feel her warmth, the pressure of her bones, the pliant flesh of her waist… Phoebe.

'Tell me you don't feel this.' His voice was a growl against her hair, scraping so harshly against his throat it ached. 'Tell me you don't want me to taste every inch of you. Kiss the soft skin right here…' He brushed his palm over her stomach and downwards, feeling the shudder course through her with an almost vicious satisfaction. 'And here…' His hand shifted lower, pressing the fabric between her legs and, with a sound that was half whimper, half gasp, her thighs tightened, trapping him there.

'This…this has nothing to do with matrimony,' she said through clenched teeth.

He withdrew his hand and took a step back. And another. 'I see.'

'No, Dominic…' Her voice wobbled a bit, either with regret or remorse. 'You don't understand…'

'Oh, I understand. You don't mind bedding me, but that's the sum of it. Don't worry. I'm well used to that. God forbid you find yourself saddled with a penniless wastrel whose only use is in the sack.'

'Don't! That *isn't* what I mean.' There was that fierceness in her eyes she rarely showed. And something else. Despair. 'Please, Dominic. Please let's not argue now. *Please.*'

Dominic could understand Samson. The wish to howl to the heavens and bring the temple down about his ears from hurt and disappointment. But he was still sensible enough to know howling would get him precisely nowhere. It was foolish to expect Phoebe to share his feelings simply because he willed it. Phoebe was a survivor—wary and slow to trust. Hurrying her would only drive her away. If she came to him at all she would come out of choice, not because she was over-whelmed with feelings she couldn't recognise or understand.

Very well, he still had more than half a week according to her terms. He would stop trying to seduce his future wife and set himself to woo-ing her.

Chapter Twenty-Four

Dominic presented himself at the Gioconda at noon with the full intention of engaging in some gentle wooing.

He was fully prepared for resistance. He was not prepared to be told Phoebe and Milly had left the hotel at dawn.

'What do you mean, they left? Left where?' Dominic demanded in Italian of the Gioconda's parlour maid, who had hurried up the stairs when he rang the bell in Milly's empty room. She bobbed another curtsey, her hands twisting her apron into knots.

'I do not know. They left with all their baggage.'

Shock, fury, and pain chased each other in swirling circles, but he was still enough an agent for a portion of his mind to stay on the right track. He showed her a coin and her eyes widened.

'To the mainland?'

'Oh, no, *signor*. It was my cousin Giuseppe who took them and he told me they hired a ship to sail to Pescara.'

Dominic gritted his teeth and took another coin from his pocket. 'You're a bright girl. What else did you hear?'

The maid screwed up her face in concentration. 'They were upset with each other. Those two, as close as mother and child, but the lady, she was shaking her head and the quiet one, she was sad. Oh, very sad. She is always polite and nice, but she did not look at me once, not even when she thanked me. I think something happened. Some bad news, perhaps? It is a pity. I liked them and now we are a very few here at the hotel. My uncle shall not pay us well until there are more guests.'

Dominic took the hint and pulled out a third coin. The maid took them happily and darted off, as if he might demand their return. When she was gone he stared at the faded wallpaper and a crooked candle sconce.

Phoebe had warned him, hadn't she? *I cannot give you more than that.* But he'd kept pressing and so she'd bolted.

At least she was being honest. Why couldn't he accept that she didn't want him? Not in any way that mattered. Why should she? Even if he hadn't played the drunk, the fool, the wastrel... What could he offer her but a damaged soul, an untrustworthy libido that might yet seize up again like rusted cogs in a clock, and perhaps a few hundred pounds of his depleted inheritance? Clearly her comfortable, familiar life with her indulgent aunt outweighed anything he had to offer.

Dominic left the palazzo and walked blindly towards Palazzo di Benedetti. He passed Signora Cavalli's shop, remembering how he had stubbornly waited for Phoebe outside. She'd wanted none of him then, too. Fool. He could see her turn the corner with Martelli's book tucked under her arm. She might be gone but now he was doomed to see her in his mind every time he turned a corner in this damned city.

Venice should be a comfort to him. A second home.

She'd ruined that, too.

He couldn't even blame her. It was his stupidity for falling in love with her. All she'd wanted was a passing dalliance to add some flavour to her life before she returned to her safe little arrangement.

He'd been useful, indeed.

Anger, piercing and hot, flared. He hoped it bubbled over into hatred. Something, anything that would eradicate these feelings.

He walked faster. As soon as Marcus arrived he would tell him to send him somewhere else… Anywhere else. His idyll with Venice was over.

A rush of wind made the roses dance as he walked up the path to the palazzo. The blooms were already fading, rusting at the edges. Soon it would be full autumn and all the politicians would make their way to Verona for the Congress. Marcus would probably want him there to keep an eye on the Continental powers as they conspired to bring Spain and Italy more firmly under their control. The divide between them and England would only grow. That meant more work for spies like him, but he found no satisfaction in that. It felt empty and dull.

He felt empty and dull. Miserable. Pathetic.

Was this what Marcus had felt when he realised he was betrothed to the wrong woman? When he realised he would have to spend his life married to one woman and in love with another? But Marcus had managed to extricate himself from that impending disaster. Or rather Lily had extricated him, and Lily had been in love with Marcus. That wasn't the case here. There was no one to rescue him from this pit.

The pain cleaved through him again; an axe's blow through his chest. He drew a deep, shaky breath and rubbed at the slicing pain.

Pathetic.

Since when had he depended on anyone to rescue him from pits?

He'd blundered and driven her off, but that didn't mean he had to admit defeat. Phoebe's defences were ten times thicker than his, yet she'd told him of her childhood, come to watch him play *calcio*, her face alight with a joy and tenderness he'd not seen her show anyone, and she'd trusted him with her body… Made love with him.

Made love.

Careful, Dom. Don't presume.

It was true that *he'd* made love to her that night. Perhaps he was only capable of setting his body free when his mind was as well.

He wished he knew that that was true of her as well, at least with respect to what had happened between them at the di Benedetti Palazzo, but he couldn't be certain. Most people weren't like him and there was no reason for Phoebe to be. She might be attracted to him—well, he knew she was—but he doubted he had become as necessary to her as she had become to him. He could have built something on that foundation of attraction and affection. Instead he'd tried to seduce her in a church and blabbered about finding a priest and… God, he was an idiot. A colossal idiot.

What had the maid said? Pescara? That probably meant they would head overland for Rome. Good. Once he had a word with Marcus he would make his way there and see if he couldn't repair the damage he'd wrought.

This time he would play by her rules. No more cornering her in abandoned churches. He would be calm and respectful and trustworthy, and he would keep his hands off her if it killed him, which it probably would.

Chapter Twenty-Five

Phoebe leaned over the ship's railing, watching the last miles between them and land slip by as dawn rose. An elderly sailor watched her worriedly as he went about his business of preparing to dock. Perhaps he thought she was feeling ill. Or considering jumping into the murky sea.

It wasn't the rocking of the boat that was making her ill. She was accomplishing that all on her own.

All night long she'd stood here, watching the changing shades of the Adriatic, the glimpses of light from towns and the dark, hulking blackness of the hills. And now the grey of an overcast dawn that seemed to depress even the waves, for the sea was flat and sullen.

It was a fitting exit from the most momentous event of her life. Only yesterday she'd been torn between agony and bliss, and today... She hunched over as another wave of misery washed over her.

'Coward!'

Phoebe straightened in alarm and turned to face the craggy-faced sailor behind her. Had he truly called her a coward? It was the truth, but…

'Pescara,' he intoned more slowly, pointing towards a town sitting at the foot of scrubby green hills. *'Ancora un'ora.'*

Phoebe managed a smile and thanked him. It had been nothing but her own mind playing tricks on her.

No—speaking the truth.

She glanced over at Milly, who was half asleep on a cloth and reed chair in the middle of the deck. Phoebe should have rested as well. The road from Pescara that went through the mountains was far rougher than this pleasant sailing. Once in Rome they would make contact and await their new assignment. And that would be that.

Once again panic and bile rose inside her.

That would be that. What a lie.

With every mile and moment passed her misery grew like a monstrous pustule, pressing against her insides, alive with pain and anger. Fury. She hadn't felt such fury since she'd resolved to turn her back on God's Flock.

She'd told herself then—she would go her own way no matter the cost. She'd even been willing for them to catch her and punish her, but she'd known absolutely that eventually she *would* escape. Somehow, no matter what they did, she would escape. She'd been fuelled by determination and fury and she'd *known*.

This time the fury wasn't against her parents or the Flock, but against herself. For the second time in her life she wanted something wholly for herself. Not freedom *from* this time, but freedom to choose to be herself with a person she loved. Really be with him.

Dominic had woken this part of her she hadn't even realised had gone to sleep after she'd remade herself as one of Sir Oswald's elusive Zephyrs. And now it was awake, it was roaring. Wanting. Demanding.

I was *happy* with him. He saw me. He saw *me*. I saw *myself* beyond the little world you built and I liked what I saw.

All well and good, replied the voice of reason, unfurling its list of objections. *But are you willing to make the sacrifices to be with him? You love what you do. It gives you purpose and excitement and challenges you... And even without that, being with him, you would be risking too much—pain, loss, heartbreak, disappointment. Eventually he will tire of you or get himself killed...*

A sob carved its way upwards through her icy interior. Fury curled in on itself like a wounded animal.

Even the thought of something happening to him was unbearable.

All the more reason to get away before it became worse…

Coward. That's what you are in the end. You excel at running away. Perfected that skill, didn't you? The Zephyr melting away, keeping yourself going so you don't stop and think. Did you even mourn Jack? No. You carried on the assignment and then straight into another. Milly mourned and you comforted her and waited for her to move on so you could concentrate on what you thought mattered. Yes, it hurt, but you didn't allow it to settle, did you? You were sensible.

You were dead.

Still are.

Because you are a coward.

That's why you ran. You didn't even have the courage to face him. You packed your few belongings in the dark and forced poor Milly onto a rickety ship at midnight. Without even a note.

Coward.

Dominic was right. If you truly wished for something, your twisty mind would find a way to make it work. At least for now. But you never gave it a chance. Never gave him a chance. Because you're afraid of yourself. Not of him. Afraid of this fury and feeling and need and…

Phoebe covered her mouth but the word burst out of her anyway.

'Stop.'

The ship sailed on, unimpressed. The hills slid

by, low and scrubby, waiting for her. She dropped her hand, turned her back on them.

'Stop! *Fermi! Dobbiamo tornare indietro!*' Her voice cut above the sound of the water and the chatter of the sailors, and jerked Milly out of her half-slumber. Her instincts were still stellar, for she was on her feet in a jolt, her hand inside her reticule.

'Wha…? What happened?'

'Nothing. But we cannot go to Rome, Milly. We must turn back.'

Milly blinked at her, but withdrew her hand from her reticule, glancing at the approaching coastline.

'Back?'

'To Venice. This is a mistake. Leaving. We must return.'

'Return. What did I miss, Phoebe? I'm completely adrift here.'

Phoebe tried to smile at her aunt's pun. 'You were right, Milly. I can't run away. I know I probably have no future with Dominic, but at least we could have a little more of the present. And if he *is* involved in something dangerous, I could try and help. I can't leave. I just can't. I mean, I know I *can*, we could just keep sailing and then in Rome we can take another assignment and keep doing what we do… I know that soon enough we shall have to return to that life, but not yet. This is mine. For the first time I have something that is just mine and I don't want to lose it before I even have it. You said I should make something I can take with me and I thought I had and that it would be enough, but it isn't. I can't bear the thought of leaving now. I'll work my way around Sherbourne. Ask him to keep quiet. Maybe in a few weeks I—'

'Phoebe.' Milly grasped Phoebe's hands and gave them a shake, interrupting her tumble of words. 'You don't have to convince me. I knew this was a mistake. Didn't I tell you that you would regret running away? Though I do wish you'd had this revelation before we sailed all this way. Now, stop blabbering and go and tell the captain we are turning about. No, better yet, I'll tell him. He'll likely need some charming to convince him to sail all the way back to Venice and you aren't at your best at the moment.'

'I'm so, so sorry, Milly.'

'Hush, love. I'm not. There is nothing in this world I want more than your happiness. Not a thing. And that damned fool makes you happy. We shall find a way to make this work. We are Zephyrs after all. There is nothing we cannot manage if we put our minds to it.'

Chapter Twenty-Six

'About bloody time! Where the devil were you, Marcus?'

Marcus Endicott, Earl of Sherbourne and director of the Foreign Office's agents, set down his hat and cane and raised one dark brow.

'This is not quite the welcome I was expecting, Dom. Foolish of me, but I actually thought you might be a tad happy to see me.'

'I'm ecstatic to see you, but I expected you yesterday!'

'Ah. That was Mina's fault. Colic. I wanted to see Lily and the children—*your* godchildren—settled comfortably with my family in Ravenna before I came to offer you my congratulations on your upcoming nuptials.'

Dominic flushed a little, but he was in no mood to be rebuked. Still, he went and poured Marcus a glass of wine as he answered.

'Since I've been jilted I don't need your damned congratulations.'

'Ah. Then your pressing need to see me was not to impart the news?'

'I knew you would hear of it the moment you docked in Ravenna. My pressing need was to get your approval to leave Venice.'

That caught Marcus's attention. He eyed Dominic over the rim of his wine glass.

'Trouble?'

'Not that kind. I need to go after Phoebe, but I had to speak with you first. I was expecting you yesterday.'

'Phoebe.'

'Playing coy doesn't suit you, Marcus. If you heard the news, I doubt you've forgotten the name of the woman I am engaged to.'

'I was informed you were engaged to a Miss Brimford, lady's companion.'

'Phoebe Brimford, companion and niece of Lady Grafton.'

'Indeed. In fact, you should count yourself lucky that I did hear the gossip. Otherwise I would not have been convinced to leave Lily and the children so precipitously. In all the years we have known each other and worked together, there have been occasions where you surprised me, Dominic. Never quite as much as when I disembarked and was met with the information of your engagement.'

'Thank you. Before you lecture me, I should tell you that I intend to do my best to convince her to marry me. That may take a while. Until then I am on indefinite leave. Sebastian can manage here.'

'And in Verona next month? A great deal is at stake there.'

'A great deal is at stake right here. If she will have none of me...' He paused and drew breath before continuing. 'If I can't even convince her to try, then I shall be there and do my best to keep an eye on the rats that will be gathering. But once you lot disperse back home I'm afraid I shall have to be off again.'

'Where?'

'Back to doing my best to convince her I'm worthy. Given my history, that might take a while.'

'Yet you are confident you will succeed?'

'Not in the least. But... Damn it, Marcus. I have to try. I can't... It matters. *She* matters.' The pain was rising again, choking him.

Damn. He didn't want to make a fool of himself. Not yet at least. He went to pour himself a glass of wine as well. Marcus didn't speak and Dominic was grateful for the chance to gather his slipping reins. When he could breathe again he turned to his friend and tried to smile, and instead of saying what he'd meant to, he said, '*I* matter.'

Marcus's lids lowered, shielding the yellow-amber eyes, but he still didn't speak, so Dominic continued.

'You know me better than anyone, Marcus. You might very well be the only person who *does* know me. You know I don't trust, I don't want, and I damn well never love.' He couldn't stop the faint snarl of derision as he spat out that word. He wished it was all still true, but it wasn't. 'I am good at other things entirely. I act. I manage. I create what needs to be created to get the job done. That's always been enough—*more* than enough for me.'

'Not any more?'

'I'm afraid not. I don't know how it happened but she blew down my defences like Joshua's trumpets. Something in me trusts her as much as I trust you, which is nothing short of insanity. And needs her. Not just that. I've never been happier making anyone happy. I would live to make her smile, to see her light up, to make her feel safe. Oh, hell. I sound like a besotted fool, but that's the truth, Marc. I *need* to go after her.'

Marcus nodded slowly.

'May I ask why she…ah…jilted you? Perhaps she had a wealthier heir to a dukedom in mind? Or perhaps she had objections on moral grounds?'

Dominic could not help smiling. 'Neither. If it was merely moral rectitude and wealth she was after I rather think she could have snagged our old friend von Haas.'

'Dear God. What a span of choice. So what *was* her objection, then?'

'Aside from the fact that she probably does not care for me in the same way as I care for her, Phoebe has a problem…trusting people. With good reason. Her parents aren't worthy of the name and all she has is her aunt and I cannot blame her for not wanting to risk herself on… on who I am, let alone who I present myself to be. She knows I'm not the drunkard I've convinced the world I am, but only because she's convinced I'm either a thief or a rebel hiding under that mask. I need your approval to convince her I'm neither.'

'Ah. Hence your impatience with my colicky delay. You plan to go after her and tell her what? The truth? Do you imagine a woman with trust issues will be assuaged by being told you are a spy? That you put your life at risk on a regular basis?'

Dominic winced. 'I wasn't thinking of telling her the spy part, at least not quite yet. I was thinking of beginning by telling her the nice part of the truth—that I work for the Foreign Office. It is slightly better than being a gambler or a thief, no?'

Marcus cleared his throat. 'It is indeed. Did you mention she is intelligent?'

'Smart as a whip. With a damned twisty mind.'

'I see. So you plan to tell her that you work for the British Foreign Office, though no one in this gossip-ridden city knows that you are thus respectably employed. And she will have to weigh your claim against your behaviour and activities, which she has witnessed over all these weeks. Correct me if I am wrong, but I am merely trying to imagine the response of a suspicious, twisty-minded woman when you lay out that tale for her.'

'But it's the truth!'

'In this particular case the truth shall mostly likely bite you on your arse and you know it, Dom. You wanted me here not merely because you wanted my permission to tell her half-truths, but because you need my advice.'

Dominic sank into an armchair, shoving his hands through his hair.

'You're right. But I can't go after her unless I can tell her the truth, or at least some of it. I don't want to lie to her, but I can't endanger you and any other agent, either. I don't even know if it will make it better or worse. Who the devil would want to marry a spy? I could tell her I will leave all that behind me if she wants, but in truth I don't know if she will… Want me, that is. Not beyond—' he drew a deep breath '—not beyond the bedroom, that is.'

'You think it is merely an attraction on her be-half? An infatuation?'

'I don't know. Not an infatuation, precisely. I *know* she likes me. There is something…natural between us. If anything, I was attracted to her first.'

Marcus's brows rose in real surprise this time.

'You are attracted to her? As in *physically* attracted?'

Dominic squirmed. He'd almost forgotten Marcus was the only one to know the truth about his aberration.

'Yes, devil take her. She's stripped me of that shield as well.'

Marcus grinned. 'Well, well, well.'

'Don't sound so delighted. I'll admit it's a…a revelation. I finally understand what you idiots have been going on about. But it only makes everything a thousand times worse. Right now I damn well wish I'd stayed in my state of comfortable numbness.'

'Well, I don't. It just proves my theory.'

'Heaven help me. Is there anything I can do to prevent you from sharing that theory?'

'Not a thing. To be fair, it is more Lily's theory. Apparently you really do trust Miss Phoebe Brimford.'

'I told you I do.'

'Hmm…' Marcus sat down in the armchair opposite, twisting the stem of his wine glass between his fingers.

A surge of affection managed to make its way through the maelstrom of conflicting and confusing emotions roiling inside Dominic and he smiled and said impulsively, 'I'm so damn glad you're here, Marc. Whatever happens. I feel like

I've been going a little mad trying to decide what to do.'

Marcus smiled back, his eyes crinkling at the corners, accentuating the silver at his temples.

'Have you ever considered she might have left because she was the one not telling the truth?'

Dominic straightened. 'What? Why would you say that? Do you know something about...?' He broke off at a faint tinkling sound. Marcus turned his head as well.

'Expecting visitors?'

'No. Perhaps it's Sebastian. He might have heard you'd arrived.'

The door opened and Emilio entered.

'A lady to see you, Signor Domenico.'

'A lady?'

'She wears a veil like a widow. I tell her you are not at home. She says she will wait. She says it is important. She is English, but her Italian is most excellent. Simple clothes, but expensive cloth.'

Dominic's heartbeat bounded ahead with each of Emilio's disclosures. But it was Marcus who spoke.

'Do show in this mystery woman, Emilio. We should not keep a lady waiting at this late hour.'

'It's not her. It can't be. Why would it be her?' Dominic said, trying to beat back hope.

'Well, we shall soon know. Would you mind pouring me some more wine, Dominic? Keep yourself busy,' Marcus added as Dominic glared at him. But he clenched his teeth and did as he was told, his mind working feverishly as he re-filled Marcus's glass.

Most likely it wasn't her. He'd been accosted by enough women over the years; there was no need to start believing it was the one woman he wished to be accosted by.

When the door opened again he was as tense as a topsail. For a moment he stood there, facing the slim figure clad all in black, with a widow's veil completely obscuring her face and hair. Something between a sigh and a cry echoed deep in his chest, nothing that either Marcus or Phoebe could hear. He saw her head turn from him to Marcus. And stop.

'Good evening, Miss Brimford,' Marcus said softly.

Phoebe seemed to waver and Dominic finally broke out of his stupor, heat flooding through him as he moved towards her.

'Phoebe.'

She jerked her head back towards him, her hands rising and then falling back.

'I'm sorry. I didn't know you had guests.'

She sounded absurdly formal, but all Dominic cared about was that she was here. But now that his first shock of joy had swept over him, suspicion was surfacing.

'I thought you'd sailed.'

'I... We did. We had to turn back.'

'Turn back… Phoebe, has something happened? To Milly?' He caught her hand in his and raised her veil with the other. He might resent her dependence on her aunt, but the last thing he wanted was for her to lose the one person she truly loved. Her face was as pale as alabaster, her eyes marked by dark smudges. She looked lovely and miserable and his heart all but broke at the sight of her. 'Phoebe, sweetheart, what is it?'

Her eyes glistened with moisture and she shut them and shook her head. 'Nothing has happened to Milly. She has gone to a hotel. I came here. I shouldn't have. You have guests. I should leave.'

'Like hell you will. Don't mind Marcus. Why did you come…? Hell, I don't care why you came. You're here. Let's go somewhere—'

'Just a moment, Dominic,' Marcus interrupted softly. 'Before you throw her over your shoulder and stalk off we should offer Miss Brimford a glass of wine.'

'I will, Marc. But not here. Phoebe and I need to speak alone. I'll talk with you later.'

'No. I think it is best the three of us have a little chat and clear the air first. Don't you, Miss Brimford?'

Phoebe gave a slight shake of her head, and in an instant all the emotion was stripped from her eyes and face. Marcus didn't appear to notice.

'Perhaps it might help if I mention I happened to encounter a mutual acquaintance of ours in

Ravenna? He was on his way to Verona to meet with some people ahead of the Congress. We had an interesting *tête-à-tête*.'

'What mutual acquaintance?' Dominic demanded, but Marcus's gaze was fixed on Phoebe. Dominic tightened his hold on Phoebe's cold hand. 'What is he talking about, Phoebe?'

'I have no idea what he is referring to,' she said coldly, and there was a new tone in her voice, a warning. 'I think your friend must be mistaken. Perhaps he has confused me with someone else.'

Marcus smiled. 'Oh, I think not. My memory for faces has always been exemplary. Even when I only see them for a few short moments in the office of the, ah, said acquaintance, six years ago.'

'Exemplary is not infallible,' Phoebe replied.

'What acquaintance?' Dominic demanded again. He knew Marcus would not make that claim unless he was certain. A whole new flavour of tension had joined the party inside him. He couldn't stop himself from inspecting Phoebe, the cool, hard look that had replaced the tears and confusion. Adamant. This was the Phoebe he had seen all along underneath the different shades of her. The one who had survived God's Flock.

He took her other hand and held them both in his. 'It doesn't matter.'

Her gaze turned to him, a flicker of surprise in the depths of her golden eyes. He glanced over his shoulder at Marcus.

'Whatever you're playing at, Marc, it will have to wait. I want to speak with Phoebe now.'

'Aren't you at all curious to know the truth about the woman you say you wish to marry?' Marcus challenged.

'Right now I'm just happy she is back in Venice. All your grand revelations will have to wait for later. Come, Phoebe...'

He tried to guide her towards the door and to his surprise this time it was she who stopped him, her tone as defiant as she looked.

'Don't you want to know what your friend thinks he knows? He might know something terrible about me.'

He sighed. 'There isn't a damn thing he can say that will change my mind about wanting to marry you. You and Milly could be the carnival thief or assassins for all I care... Well, that's not true. Both sound like rather risky occupations... What is so amusing?' he asked as her eyes crinkled in sudden amusement.

'I thought *you* were the thief.'

'Well, I'm not. I gather you're not either?'

She shook her head and then canted it. It felt as if she was actually looking at him for the first time since she'd entered. Her gaze moved over his face, softening, and the glaze of tears returned.

It had the same devastating effect on him as before, melting him inside into a hot, gooey mess even as it shot like quicksilver through his veins, raising the hair on his arms and nape as if he was being stalked by a rabid wolf, or being seduced by a siren. He pulled her hands to his chest, closing the distance between them.

'I don't care what you are, Phoebe, because I know you. Whatever the truth of it, I know you.'

'Here, have some wine, Miss Brimford,' Marcus interceded in a far lighter tone, approaching them with a glass in his hand. 'I know you want to whisk her off, Dom, but first I really must insist on that chat.'

Phoebe took the glass, her confusion mirroring Dominic's at Marcus's change in tone.

'Devil take you, Marcus. What are you playing at?'

But Marcus ignored him, smiling at Phoebe. 'Did you really think Dominic was the carnival thief? Why?'

Phoebe moved away from both of them, cradling her wine glass. She cast a glance at Dominic and looked away almost guiltily. He smiled.

'Yes, Phoebe, do tell Marcus why.'

'Why? No reason other than that you are a consummate liar and actor who has all of Venice believing he is a drunkard and half the city believing you slept with the other half. Or perhaps because you have an annoying tendency to appear where and when you are least wanted and then leave by anything but the door. Oh, and because you lose far more money to Montillio's than you could ever repay and…' Her words petered out as her gaze switched from Dominic to Marcus. For the space of two breaths she just stared at him before she continued in a very different tone. 'And your closest friend is Lord Sherbourne.'

'That does rather put an interesting spin on matters, doesn't it?' Marcus said.

'What has that to say to anything?' Dominic asked. 'As for the rest, Phoebe, it isn't what it seems…' He stopped, realising he had no right to disclose anything. But Phoebe didn't even appear to have heard him. Her gaze had gone inwards, her face blank and pale. She drew a deep breath, let it out. Took another. He moved towards her, but she stepped back, wine sloshing out of the glass and onto the carpet as her gaze moved over him.

Marcus tutted. 'Let her be for a moment, Dom. This was rather inevitable the moment she entered this room. *You* might be a trifle slow, but she was bound to work it out eventually.'

'Work what out? Stop toying with me and tell me what you know, Marcus. Have you two met before?'

'Only in passing. But more importantly I've heard of her before and so have you.'

Dominic shook his head, confused. 'Ladies' companions don't precisely come my way often.'

'No. Wrong profession, if you can call it a profession.'

Dominic found himself doing precisely what

Phoebe had done to him. His gaze moved over her, his mind trying to resist the thought from settling.

Phoebe. A spy.

His Phoebe was a *spy*.

That thought was immediately followed by another. *Whose?*

'You wouldn't have sent someone to Venice without telling me, so she's not yours,' Dominic said slowly, preparing himself for the worst. It wouldn't matter, not in the end, but it could make his life very, very complicated.

'No, pity, that,' Sherbourne said mournfully. 'This is the first time I've heard of her cocking up, though. Oswald was very surprised.'

Phoebe bared her pretty little teeth at Marcus. Under other circumstances Dominic might have found that amusing, but right now he was shaken to his core with surprise and shock. And relief.

'Christ. She's Sir Oswald's?'

Lord Sherbourne answered for her. 'Yes. Allow me to introduce one of Oswald's Zephyrs. Passing through like a breeze and leaving no trace. Until now. Oswald was inclined to blame you for this mess, Dom.'

Dominic laughed, several tonnes of ballast slipping from his shoulders.

'He was completely correct. I made a hash of things, didn't I, sweetheart?'

Phoebe turned to him and he watched as the

fight leeched out of her eyes. She looked tired and…lost. Dominic glanced over his shoulder at Marcus.

'I'm quite certain Emilio has your usual room ready by now, Marcus. You can take your wine with you.'

'Are you telling me I am *de trop*?'

'Absolutely.'

Marcus laughed. When he reached the door he turned.

'Lily tells me my timing is often impeccable. I think she would agree I've outdone myself today. Oh, and Miss Brimford…?'

Phoebe turned, the same half-feral look returning to her gaze. Marcus's cheek twitched.

'Oswald sends his regards. He expects you in Verona next week. And wishes to inform you that following the unfortunate demise of Lord Castlereagh and the imminent dissolution of the Congress system, we have decided that England would benefit from closer cooperation between the agents of the Foreign Office and the War Office. So the two of you had best learn to play nicely together. Good night.'

The door closed behind him with the lightest of clicks. For a long while the only sound in the room was the muted ticking of the clock. And the pumping of blood in his veins.

'I'm feeling rather a fool at the moment,' he said, trying for lightness.

She straightened, shoulders back.

'No more than I. I had every reason to suspect you, while you had very little reason to suspect me.'

'I beg to differ. I had many good reasons to suspect you and, to give me some credit, I did suspect you a little, but I was rather…distracted and never followed those suspicions through even in my own mind.' He frowned, finally beginning to fit the pieces into place. 'Razumov. That was you, yes?'

'Milly and I.'

'Bloody hell. What a fool I was. So all that with von Haas…'

She nodded. 'I needed to learn enough about him to ensure Razumov's transgression would be taken personally. I also needed to find a way into the Procuratie.'

'The Giardini Reali. You little madwoman. If he'd discovered your involvement…'

She sighed. 'This is what I do, Dominic. Though in this particular case it was Milly who went in. I was at the Imperial ball, remember? That was how this whole imbroglio between us began.'

He flushed a little at her snide comment. 'No, our so-called imbroglio began well before that. How long have you worked for Oswald?'

'Ten years or so. My uncle worked for him.'

'The one who rescued you?'

'Yes. He posed as a merchant and it served his purpose to have a family as part of his façade, but after a couple years Milly and I realised he was rather more than that. With time we became useful. Especially the more he drank after his lover died. We tried to protect him by ensuring he completed his missions, but in the end we failed. When Oswald discovered what we were doing, he was furious.'

'But he kept you on.'

'Yes. We had learned quite a bit by then. And we were useful.'

'Bloody hell.'

'It was sometimes.' She drew a deep breath. 'I'm sorry, Dominic.'

'About which part of it?'

'All of it. We both got in each other's way. I knew something about your façade was deeply wrong, but I made some horrid assumptions about you.'

His nerves buzzed suddenly, fear pushing its way back onto the stage. He hadn't considered that possibility. He tried to keep his tone offhand. 'So getting close to me was all in aid of solving your puzzle?'

'No.'

They faced each other in silence for a moment. He could imagine she was doing as much re-calculating as he was.

'Ten years. You've been at this almost as long as I have,' he said abruptly.

'Yes.'

'Why? Are you doing it for the money?'

'No. Not for the glory either, even if there was any. It is simply what I do. I cannot imagine not doing this. I am good at it. At least I was. I also learn from my mistakes.'

'I see. I'm a mistake.'

'No, not at all. My mistake was to be surprised by my own weakness. If I had been better prepared I would have managed it better. I don't regret what happened between us in the least. I only regret how poorly I dealt with it. And with you.'

He planted his hands on his hips. 'Are you planning on claiming *all* the moral high ground, Phoebe?'

A painful knot in his chest unravelled as her mouth finally curved into the smile that had the power to transform his day.

'Not *all* of it, Lord Wrexham. I think I left you a few patches over by the swamps.'

'Considerate of you.'

'I try to be. I'm not even going to ask you what you were looking for in von Haas's office, and before that at Sir Henry's. Or whether you were successful.'

'Considerate *and* restrained. I think you've managed to annex most of the swamplands as well. And yes, I was successful. But all this doesn't answer one very basic question, though.'

'What question?'

'Why did you run away?'

Once again she straightened and adopted her soldier's drill posture.

'I did not run away; I left. You said you suspected me. When was that? That first time you followed me from Martelli's bookshop?'

He knew a diversion when he saw one. He shoved his hands in his pockets so he wouldn't reach for her. Not yet.

'Do you really expect honesty from us bog dwellers, sweetheart?'

She shrugged. 'It would explain why you were so…insistent.'

'Ah. I see. I followed you about, letting you pluck my feathers and lash me with your sharp little tongue merely as a matter of expediency.'

'Why not? You risked your neck on enough window ledges—spying on me was easy by comparison.'

'Easy is one word I would never apply to you, darling. Swimming to Turkey with my arms tied behind my back would have been easier.'

'I apologise for making your life so difficult.'

'I'm not. I suspect this is only the beginning. I suspect marriage with you will be anything but easy.'

She drew a deep breath. 'Dominic, while I am

very, *very* relieved there are no more lies between us, you must realise there is no question of us going through with that ridiculous idea of marriage. I am a spy. I was a spy and I shall remain a spy. I enjoy being a spy. I am good at—'

'Being a spy. Yes. I *can* conjugate, you know.'

'Excellent. I was beginning to have doubts. And while there is no question of marriage, I returned merely because I wished to tell you that I am more than willing to pursue other forms of… of relations for the, uh, foreseeable future, should you find that agreeable. Now we know the truth about each other, this option is even more sensible.' She raised her chin and met his gaze. 'You may inform me of your decision. Now I had best return to the hotel—'

Before she could close the distance to the door, Dominic slipped into the gap.

'I don't think so, love. I shall send word to your aunt that you are the guest of the Contessa di Benedetti tonight. But at the moment you're staying where I can keep an eye on you. Amongst other things.'

'You cannot force me to stay.'

'Of course I can. I won't, though. I'm merely complying with your terms.'

'My what?'

'Your willingness to… How did you put it? Pursue other forms of relations?'

'Oh.'

He backed her against the door. 'Your *"oh"*s are deadly, Phoebe. You are staying here tonight. After the last few days I'm not risking having you melt into the night again. I've heard of the Zephyrs. They have no footprint. Gone with the morning mist. And all along they're in plain sight.'

She didn't reply, but the anger had faded from her eyes. Even with her cheeks flushed, she looked as she had when she had first entered—tired and lost. His heart lurched and cracked like an egg. He wanted so badly to make her happy, to soothe away the weariness and the worry. To fill her with love and joy. He touched his palm to her cheek.

'I don't know what the hell to think about all this, Phoebe, but there's a certain justice that of all the people in the world to upend my life it would be another spy.'

She swallowed, her lashes flickering as he traced a line down the side of her throat, resting his hand against her pulse.

'I could say the same.'

Another sharp wave of heat coursed through his veins, but he kept his tone light, coaxing. They would get to that later.

'Perhaps we have a tell, like a gambler's bluff. Something that doesn't fit. Perhaps despite your abysmal opinion of me, that twisty part of your mind noticed something you didn't. As for me, I just knew you were special.'

* * *

Phoebe wished he wouldn't say such things. No, she loved it when he did, but it kept wringing her insides like a wet rag and making a soggy mess of her. She rested her hand on his chest, carefully. There was something very strange about being able to lay any claim to him at all.

She drew a deep breath to counter the heat bubbling through her body, but it merely brought with it his scent and with it that shivering of need, and, even worse, that promise of warmth and comfort and acceptance…

'You're exhausted, sweetheart,' he murmured. 'Let's leave all the big thinking for tomorrow and just *be* tonight, yes?' He slipped an arm around her waist, pulling her against him, raising her on tiptoes. 'Tonight you stay here in this little nest of spies and fill my very empty bed.'

'I can't… Not with Lord Sherbourne…'

He laughed and bent to brush a kiss over her lips. 'What a prude you are. Marcus is safely in the other end of the palazzo. That excuse won't work. Try another.'

There were probably others. She just couldn't think of any while his mouth teased that absurdly sensitive point on her neck that made her body tingle with alternating shards of ice and heat. She couldn't breathe normally, and he was already untangling the laces of her dress. She felt both heavy and soft, and she let her head lean back against the door to give him better access.

'This is a lovely dress, sweetheart, and I'm very much looking forward to unwrapping you. But slowly. I have you all night this time. I mean to make you pay for breaking my heart.'

Breaking his heart?

Her mind stumbled over the words and let them slip away. A figure of speech, surely?

Leave all the big thinking for tomorrow, he'd said. And just be. Tonight she would just *be*. Just do what she wanted without thought or fear.

And right now she wanted to take his hand and press it against the heat gathering in her loins. One didn't do that, did one? What *did* one do? Why hadn't she paid more attention to Milly's tales and to the detailed descriptions in all those books instead of guiltily skimming over those parts? What a waste.

She knotted her fingers in his shirt, pulling it from his waistband, spreading her palms up his back. His muscles flexed and he made that sound she loved so much, between a growl and a moan. He took one of her hands and pressed it to the hard heat of his crotch. Apparently one *did* do that. Her jaw tightened with a pleasure she'd not felt before. Possession, power. *She* could do this to him.

She'd never exulted in making a man hard for her before, but that was what it felt like—an exultant victory. She curved her hand, cupping him, tightening. It was so good. So right. His heat against her hand. Hers.

He groaned, dragging her hard against him.

'Upstairs.'

'I want you to touch me like that, too,' she whispered, still half embarrassed.

'Oh, I will, and more. But not here. Did I mention I have a bed that has felt damnably empty since you left?'

A shudder ran through her as he traced her earlobe with his tongue and nuzzled the sensitive skin below it.

'Now, upstairs before I decide to do something about it right here, guests and servants notwithstanding.'

They made it, barely, to his bedroom.

'Too many damned laces,' he grunted. 'I like your companion dresses better. Turn around.'

Phoebe did as she was told and with a sharp tug the dress crumpled about her ankles. She leaned one arm on the wall and laughed with excitement and abandon. 'Can I tear your clothes off as well?'

'With pleasure, darling. But let me enjoy this first. God, you're beautiful from behind as well. No, don't move. Lean both hands on the wall.'

Phoebe did as she was told, and when his hands settled gently on her shoulders she let her eyes drift shut. His hands moved lightly down her back, sloping into her waist, tightening for a moment on her hips as he drew a deep breath, as if steadying himself. Then they continued, moving over her abdomen and sending almost unbearable shooting sparks of need into her loins.

She had no notion why his touch could transform somewhere utterly mundane in her body into a trigger and a fuse that weakened her knees and made every muscle in her body clench. When he removed his hands she sagged forward, leaning her forearms against the rough plaster. She hadn't done anything, but she already felt exhausted and elated and unravelled. But before she could recover her mind, he pulled her back against him and the heat of his naked skin was like a brand of fire. His thighs were hard against the softer skin of her behind, his erection pulsing hotly against her, his arms hard and heavy around her midriff.

It felt so good, to lean back against the heat of his body, to feel his hands cup her breasts, raising them gently, his thumbs just teasing the skin around her tightening nipples. When they flicked the tight peaks she moaned and her head fell back against his shoulder, as if she could be absorbed into him.

His voice, low and raw, was doing as much damage as his touch. His low, urgent words kept washing over her, driving the heat deeper and darker with each movement.

'God, if I wasn't coming apart I could do this all night, Phoebe. I want to take you to heaven and back, but I don't want to stop touching you. Just feeling you against me like this is beautiful agony. I never knew there was such pleasure in just being close.'

She shook her head because she couldn't think clearly enough to speak. She was one pulsing mass of need and when his hand moved down, his fingers slipping into the curls between her thighs to find the core of her current torment, her own hand caught his, pressing it there, hard. He curved his body tighter about her, his mouth pressing into the slope of her neck, his teeth scraping her skin as his hand moved gently between her legs, seeking and finding a rhythm with her tortured breathing.

Her tense silence broke on a long, shuddering moan. 'I need you.' The words burst out of her, half a command but mostly a plea, and his body bucked a little against her, as if prodded, but his fingers kept stroking, swirling agony into a tight ball inside her. He turned his head to kiss the lobe of her ear, catching it between his teeth as he spoke.

'How much, sweetheart? How much do you need me?'

'Too much.' Her voice was as raw as she felt.

'It can't be too much for me, love. Do you like this?'

'I love it… It's unbearable. Please, please don't stop…'

'Hell, Phoebe, I want you so damn badly. I want to make you happy… That's right, come for me, don't fight it, love, let go… I have you…'

A great, wrenching shudder racked her body and she fell apart, her knees buckling, her hand pressing hard against his torturing fingers, holding him there against the waves of pleasure that radiated out from his touch. She felt…beautiful, heavenly, happy… Complete…

He held her, half supporting her back against him as he murmured her name again and again, brushing little kisses against her hair and temple as if she'd done something brilliant. It felt as if she had. She smiled at the colours dancing on her closed eyelids—sunset colours, gold and purple and orange. Like the Schiavantis' wine.

When her breathing calmed he moved her towards the bed and laid her out as if she were made of spun moonlight, as if she might drift away. She felt just as light and magical.

She finally found the strength to open her eyes and look up at him. He was so beautiful. And for now he was hers and she had never been happier in her life. She smiled. He smiled back, shaking his head a little, as if in wonder.

'The eighth wonder of the world, sweetheart. Watching you come.'

'That's silly. And I'm so selfish. I should have waited for you but suddenly I was already there.'

'How can you be selfish when you've given me

the most precious gift I could dream of? It only makes me want you more.'

She traced his cheek with her fingers, words bubbling inside her. She wondered if the next time they would escape her. She seemed to lose herself so much in those moments. She *wanted* to lose herself...find herself... And him.

She let her fingers roam downwards. Now that the ache of need that had been chasing her for days had calmed there was a different kind of pleasure in exploring him. In feeling the way his muscles tensed at her touch, his breathing becoming shallow, his eyelids lowering. She touched her tongue to her lips and his gaze followed, turning darker, his own lips parting. It felt so marvellous to control him like this, to feel her pull on him. She looked down to his erection.

'How much do you need *me*, Dominic?' she murmured, returning his question to him even as she remembered how desperate she'd felt when those words coursed through her. He shook his head as if to fight that pull.

'Far, far too much for my peace of mind, Phoebe. What the hell am I saying? I haven't had any peace of mind or body for weeks now...' He sucked in his breath as her hand closed around his erection. 'Christ, that feels so damn good. Tighter.'

She obliged, then softened her hold, caressing the length of his shaft with her palm as she watched him struggle against the current of his needs. She closed her hand around him again. Tight. His eyes closed and he surged against her hand.

'Damn you, Phoebe. Don't you disappear on me again.'

She pulled him down against her, feeling the shiver of his unravelling control everywhere their bodies touched. This was a different kind of pleasure—possessive, powerful, a strength in giving something she hadn't realised she possessed. She revelled in it as much as in her own pleasure.

'I love your weight on me, Dominic. Your heat. I love watching your eyes turn dark with need.'

'Phoebe…' Her name was a long groan, which turned into a hissed breath as he settled between her legs, his erection pressing against her damp heat. 'Hell, I… I need to protect you.'

It took her a moment to realise what he was referring to and for a moment she was so tempted to take that risk. He raised himself a little, his chest heaving, his voice tight, almost accusing.

'No. I want you to choose to be with me, not be trapped into it.'

She nodded, a little frightened by a shadow behind those words. She did not want to think beyond tonight. Not yet. But she let him bring the box and when he was ready he stroked her face and kissed her fear away and replaced it with a whole new form of tension.

When he entered her, vivid pleasure filled her as well. That he was hers, that he wanted her, that he cared... That he... She pushed those half-formed thoughts away and moved with him, her hands caressing and scraping at his back, pulling his head to hers to kiss him with all the love and fear that felt as if it would explode inside her. When he climaxed he called out her name with a long, hoarse groan and she took his weight with fierce joy as he sank down on her.

As she slid with him into exhaustion her last thought was—this is *right*.

For the first time in her life she knew absolutely that something was *right*.

It was the coolest, most silent hour of the night when she felt him shift and she woke as he raised himself above her, his eyes dilated and dark. The moon was already sinking, now directly outside the ornate window. It cast silvery shadows along the taut muscles of his arms, making him shimmer like a mystical being.

A shiver of fear coursed through her. These dark hours of the night were dangerous, especially when she couldn't hide behind the fog of lust and heat that had completely enveloped her earlier. She wasn't afraid of him, but of *this*. This strange power that seemed only to grow between them. Of the look on his face that she'd never seen except when he looked at her. She was afraid because she wanted it so badly to mean this man was now part of her… The thought of him slipping away, her little universe shrinking back to her carefully set perimeters… It was unthinkable.

He touched his palm to her cheek, brushing the pad of his thumb under her eye. She hadn't even realised a treacherous tear had sneaked out. She closed her eyes to shut him out. She could cope with disasters; she didn't know how to cope with dreams.

'Look at me, Phoebe.' His words were tight, accusing. She swallowed and opened her eyes.

He gave a brief nod and continued.

'I know the smart thing is to wait for morning and good counsel so we can work through this like sensible adults, but I don't want to. Especially not now you finally know the truth about me and vice versa. This is utterly new territory for me, but if there is one thing I know it's that I'm not letting you go. I *can't* let you go. If I have to follow you about like a damn lackey, that is what I will do. You do know that, don't you?'

'I said I was willing to…to continue like this.'

He shook his head. 'This isn't enough. I want more than an affair where we share a bed when our paths happen to cross. I want our paths woven together, Phoebe. I want to be with you and discover everything about your brilliant mind and your addictive body. I want to marry you and live with you…' He broke off as if alarmed by his own words.

Phoebe could almost hear the crumbling of her defences, but they were still powerful. She wanted everything to stop right there before they ruined it.

'Why can't you be happy with what we have, Dominic?'

'I *am* happy with what we have, Phoebe. So goddamned delighted that I go to bed plotting when I can next corner you and have you scold me into bliss. This whole month has been a damned revelation, like one of those saints waking up being able to talk to the birds or bounce arrows off his arse. I may not understand how this happened, but it has, and whether you are comfortable with it or not, you have become the most important thing in my life.' He drew a sharp breath and shook his head. 'Don't you understand? I don't want to be with you because I want to bed you, I want to bed you because I want to be with you. This is love. I *love* you. *And* I'm in love with you. Those two seem to be two different things, but they're both true in my case. Look at me and tell me you don't know I love you.'

Phoebe shook her head, fear caught like a fist in her throat. 'No one has ever been in love with me before, Dominic.'

His voice softened and some of the serious harshness in his expression fled. 'I'd wager you never gave them half a chance. You certainly did your best to get rid of me, too, but I'm a persistent fellow. And no one has never been in love with me, either.'

'That is patently untrue. I've seen—'

He interrupted her. 'No one has been in love with *me*. Are…are you trying to tell me you are or that you aren't? Or can't? Or won't?'

She was terrified, but even more, she couldn't bear him hurting. And there was only one answer, after all. Everything else would have to follow.

'I am trying to tell you I don't want to lose what I am, but I cannot bear losing you, either. I don't know how to bring those two together. I love you so much that I am terrified, and I *hate* being terrified. It isn't *me*.'

The coldness evaporated from Dominic's eyes like the sun breaking through a cloud, but his voice was taut when he spoke. 'Say that again. The good part only. We'll deal with the rest in a moment.'

'Oh, damn you, Dominic. I *love* you.' The words were part strangled sob, part accusation. 'You must know I do. I've never made such a fool of myself in all my life. Never. I love being with you and I love the way you make me do things and tell you things I think I don't wish to, but I actually do wish to…and it would break my heart to walk away. It *did* break my heart… I can't do it. I don't want to. I need to be myself, but I need you too and I don't know how to do both.'

His hand shook a little as he brushed her cheek with his palm.

'Phoebe. My brilliant, brave darling… I'm willing to find whatever compromise you feel you can bear. But a compromise means you must give ground, too. All I want is to be part of your life. That isn't so horrible, is it?'

Phoebe's heart ached, her chest ached, her throat was burning. It was horrid that being in love felt like an apoplexy. She pressed one hand to her heart, the other to her mouth, but it didn't help. The tears welled out and a muted cry pushed past her barrier.

'It *is* horrible. It is horribly wonderful,' she sobbed, covering her face. 'I don't *do* wonderful.'

She didn't stop crying when he pulled her into his arms, wrapping her in warmth, stroking her hair. 'I think you do wonderful wonderfully, love.'

She sobbed harder. 'Stop being so *good* to me.'

'Can't. I love being good to you. It's become an object of mine to make you happy. If it makes you feel any better, it is purely selfish on my part. Making you happy is a potent aphrodisiac. Even making you cry is making me hard—that's how bad an influence you are on me, Phoebe.'

Her laugh was watery and she hauled the sheet to her and wiped her cheeks with it. For a moment they sat in silence, her head against his shoulder, just breathing him, trying to find strength to step off the head of the needle she was teetering on.

'Why don't we try?' he said at last as he stroked her hair, her back, his hands just as soothing as his voice. 'We have a few weeks to practise in Verona while all those idiot politicians and diplomats make another mess of the world. All I'm asking is that you try. What is the worst that could happen?'

'The worse that could happen is that I will fall even more in love with you. And then I might lose you. Or lose myself. Or both.'

His arms closed about her, tight, just like his breathing. When her own breathing calmed a little, he unlocked his arms and dried her face, brushing her hair back from her damp cheeks.

'Nothing could be more awful than not having you in my life, Phoebe. Not a damn thing. I'm as out of my depth as you are, which is a damned awkward way to begin something I fully intend to last us a lifetime, but whatever it takes to work through this, that is what we will do. We will go at your pace, we will find a way to make this work with you and Milly and Oswald and Marcus. I am willing to compromise on quite a few fronts to make this work, but there is one thing I absolutely will not concede an inch on.'

She needed his touch, so she took his hand and pressed it to her cheek. The firm warmth of his skin against hers felt so right it made her want to cry again.

'What is that thing?'

'This is one mission we undertake together. We work through the details, the problems, the pitfalls together. No running away when we're frightened, which we probably will be. When you want to run you tell me to my face and we both try and work our way through it. And even if you decide you want none of me, you tell me so.'

She tightened her hold on his hand and flung herself off the cliff. 'Yes.'

'Yes, as in you want none of me?'

She buried her face against his neck. 'Yes, I want all of you. As soon as possible.'

He laughed and his hand curved over her behind, bringing her even closer, but he shook his head. 'Not good enough, Phoebe, my love. The correct answer is: yes, I agree to your terms, Dominic. I will stand and fight with you for what I want.'

'I would rather lie down and make love to you until you beg for mercy.'

'I'm very, very happy to hear that because I'm all but bursting at the seams here, but I need to hear you say it, love. That you want to do this with me.'

She loved that he didn't try to hide his uncertainty, his need. It made her feel…safe.

'I want to do this with you more than I have ever wanted anything in my life, Dominic. I love you so much I ache with it all the time, right here.'

She took his hand and pressed it to the ache in below her breasts. 'I never knew heartache was something real, but it actually hurts when I force myself to think of leaving you.'

His hand softened on her ribs, rubbing gently. 'There's a remedy for that, you know. Stop thinking about leaving me and start putting that clever mind of yours to work figuring out how to make this work. I have more faith in you than you do yourself, sweetheart. If there is something you want, you can achieve it.'

'The only thing I want is for you to love me back.'

'Done. That was too easy, try something harder.'

'Don't be flippant.'

'One of us has to be—you are far too serious. Now, move over and let me lie down so you can have your evil way with me again.'

Epilogue

Ten years later, Sherbourne Hall, Hampshire

'It was a good kick. Right into the corner. At least it would have been if Ginnie hadn't shoved me.'

The words were defiant, but Dominic could hear the waver of worry beneath his son's voice and there was a sheen of tears in his gold-flecked eyes.

He went down on his haunches and brushed a smudge of dirt from Sebastian's soft cheek. At eight years old he was beginning to show all the signs of being a beautiful boy and Dominic's heart twisted inside him even as he reminded himself that, despite his and Phoebe's peculiar occupation, their children were being raised in a house full of love and laughter and friends. That they were being raised as children, not as objects.

He smiled at his son. 'It was a damn good kick.

I saw it from the window. You curved it like the best of *calcio* players.'

Sebastian's face broke into a smile and he rubbed away the threatening tears. 'I'm sorry about the greenhouse. Will Uncle Marcus be angry?'

'You know full well that Uncle Marcus is almost never angry. He's very annoying that way. But try not to break the rest of the hall while Mama and I are away, yes?'

Sebastian's smile flickered and fled as they faced the real issue at hand. 'I wish I could go with you, Papa. I like it when we travel together and see places.'

'I know, Sebastian, and we shall continue to travel together often, but not this time. Mama and I are celebrating ten years together and you and Ginnie will have a grand time with Milly and Lily and Marcus and the children and the rest of the Sherbourne madhouse.'

'I know. I *do* love being here. It is only…' He shrugged. 'I shall miss you and Mama.'

'We'll miss you more. Mama will likely write to you every day and worry every night. Have you and Ginnie practised your code?'

Sebastian's eyes lit up. Dominic was both proud and alarmed by his children's skill with numbers. What he and Phoebe had learned through years of practice was a game for them. It was early days yet for five-year-old Ginnie, but it was clear that

Sebastian already had all the makings of an excellent code-breaker. And *calcio*-player. Neither was an occupation Dominic wished for his son and the future Duke of Rutherford, but he knew better than to interfere with what gave his children pleasure.

'We have,' Sebastian replied happily, his worry receding. 'Uncle Marcus found me a book written by Cardano. I think I shall add imaginary numbers to the code, though Ginnie doesn't know square roots yet, so I shall have to explain…'

Dominic listened to his son's excited chatter as he led him up to the nursery to wash. Lily and Marcus's brood of four were already there and making a great deal of noise as usual. Both the Sherbourne and Wrexham clans showed definite evidence of Italian roots in both their looks and exuberant behaviour. Ginnie caught sight of them and dashed over, tossing herself into her father's arms, only to bestow a wet kiss on his cheek and wiggle out of his embrace, inserting herself back into the happy fray. Dominic stood watching them all for a moment, his heart thumping with that ineffable sensation people called love, and then went to find his wife.

Phoebe looked up from her book when he entered their bedroom.

'Crisis averted?'

Dominic plucked the book from her hands and

tossed it aside, settling himself on the side of the bed next to her, his thigh against hers. The need to be close hadn't changed in the decade since their unusual courtship. He smiled at his wife and tucked her long, silky hair behind her ear.

'Poor fellow was feeling guilty. That's why he hid. I wish he was less scrupulous. It was a damned good kick, though. He's better than I am.'

'Both our children are an improvement on us, thank goodness.' Phoebe laughed lightly and raised his hand to brush a kiss across his knuckles, sending tingling warmth up his arm. He shifted closer.

'He's worried about us leaving. It will be our first time on a mission without them and Milly.'

The warmth in her eyes faltered and the line between her eyes appeared. 'Maybe we should…'

'No. We discussed this. You know they will be absolutely fine here. We spend as much time here as at home anyway. And with Milly here and even Oswald as honorary uncle… How the devil Milly managed to snare that dry stick, I'll never know.'

Phoebe laughed, the worry melting away as he had hoped. 'She's been in love with him for ages. I'm glad she finally turned her considerable powers into making him realise what a treasure he'd been ignoring all these years.'

She sighed, brushing her palm up his forearm so lightly the hair rose in search of her touch.

It still amazed him how easily she could wake

his body. During the first couple of years after their marriage in Venice he'd waited anxiously for his body to revert to its cold shell or to manifest some other unbidden form of rebellion. But it appeared to be well pleased with its new state of devotion at the altar of Phoebe's body. Pleased and comfortable and vividly alive. Because of the woman who had changed his life.

He wrapped his hand about her elbow, stilling her touch.

'Do you know how much I love you, my amazing, brilliant, delectable Phoebe?'

Her eyes, wide and golden like their son's, darkened, and her voice was hoarse when she answered.

'You never let me forget. It's very annoying.'

'I know. I'm insufferable.' He eased the sleeve of her gown off her shoulder and bent to brush his lips over the warm curve. 'We have an hour before dinner. A whole hour. Or rather…*only* an hour.'

She let him press her back, her face taking on that glow of love and warmth that rocked his insides no matter how often he saw it.

'That will be one definite benefit of going on a mission alone.' She sighed with pleasure as her body took his weight. 'No children opening our locked bedroom door in the middle of a mutual ravishing… I told you it was a bad idea to teach them how to spring a lock before they can even spell.'

'Thank goodness we were so randy we hadn't even bothered to undress. But Ginnie is a marvel, isn't she? Magical hands. And speaking of magical hands…' He sucked in his breath as Phoebe slipped her hands up under his shirt.

'Mmm… Your own magical hands shall be needed soon. I'm very randy right now, but I want that shirt off or I might have to tear it off like your *calcio* admirers.'

'You're more than welcome to tear anything you want off me, sweetheart.'

She shook her head, wrapping her arms around his nape. 'You said that once, remember?'

He thought back and smiled, touching the lobe of his ear. 'God, yes. That day at the Gioconda with that ridiculous ruby earring. I can still feel your fingers right here. I was hot and bothered before I even knew what that meant.'

'So was I.' She rose to brush her lips over his earlobe as lightly as a butterfly flitting by a flower. 'I love you so much, Dominic. So much. Some days I think of those hours on the ship to Pescara, running away from you. I was so close to losing you, us. I never thought I could be *happy*. Content, satisfied, yes, but not joyful and so full of love for you and our children that I feel ten times more real than I ever did. When I think I might have walked away… It frightens me.'

Dominic rested his palm to her cheek, his heart echoing the rapid tattoo of her pulse against his body. He could feel the fear still there, the yearning—set free but still wary. Phoebe. His love.

'I'm very, very glad you turned that ship around. But I wouldn't have let you walk away, love. Not without a protracted and highly annoying pursuit, and probably not even then. I adore you with every fibre of my being. You know that, don't you?'

Her eyes filled with tears, her lips pressing together hard. She swallowed and answered.

'I do now.'

'It took me a while to believe you loved me, too, my heart. Trust was not our strong suit. But even old dogs like us can learn new tricks. And once we are alone and not at risk of having our budding little thieves find a way to defeat even our chair-shoved-under-the-doorknob method, we shall learn a few new tricks together.'

'New tricks?'

'Signor Martelli very kindly sent a gift for our tenth anniversary. An Italian translation of a book of erotic lovemaking from India...'

Phoebe's eyes widened. 'What? Where is it...? Why didn't you...?'

Dominic pressed a laughing kiss to her lips. 'Such enthusiasm. I knew I should have kept it a secret until we were in Vienna. I'll need all the weapons at my disposal for when you encounter your old admirer. I don't trust that damned icicle von Haas. He'll be showing you all those enticingly manicured Viennese gardens and seducing you with tales of thick, spiked fences.'

'Were you truly jealous of von Haas?'

'I would have happily shoved *him* off a bridge. Pity there aren't any canals in Vienna. There's always the Danube, though.'

Phoebe smiled and shook her head.

'You have no cause to be jealous, Dominic. You're the only man I've ever wanted to ravish or be ravished by. That hasn't changed one iota. We shall have a grand time in Vienna rooting out our traitor, with or without books about lovemaking. In fact, we can always write our own book.'

'Excellent idea. I can already see it gracing Martelli's shelves: *Lovemaking Manual for the Late-Blooming Lover* by Her Grace, the Duchess of Rutherford.'

'No, no. I shan't take credit. And we need a shorter title. What do you think of *How to Bed your Bemused Betrothed*? Referring to myself, of course.'

'In that case, I think *How to Catch and Keep your Reluctant Betrothed* is more accurate. I was definitely better at the catching than the keeping.'

Phoebe huffed in disdain even as she slipped her hands under his shirt, sending shivers of anticipation through him. 'As I recall, I all but threw myself into your net before you even left port, Dominic.'

'Perhaps that was my plan all along, Rosie

mine? Imagine if all along I knew precisely what I was doing, reeling you in, inch by devious inch.'

He demonstrated by tracing ever-tightening circles on the swell of her breast above her shift, delighting in watching her breath turn shallow and a flush rise over her cheeks.

'Perhaps this was *my* plan all along,' she said, her hands tightening on his back, nails pressing into his skin. 'Perhaps we should call our book *The Proper Way to Catch a Reluctant Rake*.'

He kissed the swell of her breast, slipping his hand under the covers to find the hem of her shift. 'Oh, no, love, I wasn't in the least reluctant, and there certainly was nothing proper about the way we caught each other. Everything we did was highly improper, often wrong, and…absolutely perfect.'

'Mmm…' Phoebe let her eyes drift shut, concentrating on his magical hands. 'All those titles are too unwieldy. I think we should call it simply *And They Loved Happily Ever After…*'

* * * * *

COMING SOON!

We really hope you enjoyed reading this book. If you're looking for more romance, be sure to head to the shops when new books are available on

Thursday 19th January

MILLS & BOON®

Coming next month

A SEASON OF FLIRTATION
Julia Justiss

Maggie gave her a shrewd look. 'What do you think of him? You've met, I trust?'

'He's an impressive young man,' Laura said carefully, trying to keep her tone neutral.

"Is he handsome?" Eliza prodded with a grin.

"Quite." Laura laughed. "Also quite dismissive of Society ladies. He thinks we are all empty-headed and frivolous."

"You'd be the lady to convince him otherwise," Maggie said. "Laura the mathematician. Not that you need to win his favor, of course. A banker's rich daughter may find an aristocratic husband, but a banker's son would be entirely ineligible as a match for you."

"How fortunate I am not angling for a husband," Laura retorted. No matter how appealing she might find the admittedly unsuitable Mr. Rochdale.

Continue reading
A SEASON OF FLIRTATION
Julia Justiss

Available next month
www.millsandboon.co.uk

MILLS & BOON

THE HEART OF ROMANCE

A ROMANCE FOR EVERY READER

MODERN

Prepare to be swept off your feet by sophisticated, sexy and seductive heroes, in some of the world's most glamourous and romantic locations, where power and passion collide.

HISTORICAL

Escape with historical heroes from time gone by. Whether your passion is for wicked Regency Rakes, muscled Vikings or rugged Highlanders, awaken the romance of the past.

MEDICAL

Set your pulse racing with dedicated, delectable doctors in the high-pressure world of medicine, where emotions run high and passion, comfort and love are the best medicine.

True Love

Celebrate true love with tender stories of heartfelt romance, from the rush of falling in love to the joy a new baby can bring, and a focus on the emotional heart of a relationship.

Desire

Indulge in secrets and scandal, intense drama and plenty of sizzling hot action with powerful and passionate heroes who have it all: wealth, status, good looks…everything but the right woman.

HEROES

Experience all the excitement of a gripping thriller, with an intense romance at its heart. Resourceful, true-to-life women and strong, fearless men face danger and desire - a killer combination!

To see which titles are coming soon, please visit

millsandboon.co.uk/nextmonth